Hannah W. Smith, Alice B. Whitall

On the Rock

a memoir of Alice B. Whitall

Hannah W. Smith, Alice B. Whitall

On the Rock
a memoir of Alice B. Whitall

ISBN/EAN: 9783337230531

Printed in Europe, USA, Canada, Australia, Japan

Cover: Foto ©Andreas Hilbeck / pixelio.de

More available books at **www.hansebooks.com**

A Memoir

OF

ALICE B. WHITALL.

" My hope is built on nothing less
  Than Jesus' blood and righteousness;
  I dare not trust the sweetest frame,
  But wholly lean on Jesus' name:
  On Christ the solid rock I stand;
  All other ground is sinking sand."
  —*Bonar.*

" Whose faith follow, considering the end of their conversation; Jesus Christ the same yesterday, and to-day, and for ever."—*Heb.* xiii. 7, 8.

PHILADELPHIA AND BOSTON:
GEORGE MACLEAN.

NEW YORK: MACLEAN, GIBSON, & CO.

TO "AUNT ALICE'S"

LITTLE NEPHEWS AND NIECES.

———◆———

IT has pleased our Heavenly Father to take home to Himself your dear "Aunt Alice" before you are old enough to understand all that you have lost in her; but may you never forget her sweet spiritual face, and the calm, heavenly look in her deep blue eyes as she bade you a loving farewell on that last Sabbath afternoon of her life on earth; and may the Holy Spirit ever keep fresh in your memory her last charges to you to trust in Jesus as your Saviour, and to meet her in heaven. You little know what you have lost in losing her prayers, her love, her tender sympathy, and gentle care and teaching. She took each of you into her heart, which had a mother's capacity for loving, and earnestly longed that you might all be safely sheltered in the peaceful fold of the Good Shepherd.

May the record of her devotion to the cause of her dear Saviour stir in your hearts a desire to follow her, as she followed Christ!

MEMOIR

OF

ALICE B. WHITALL.

CHAPTER I.

ALICE B. WHITALL was the youngest of three children—all daughters—and was born in Philadelphia on the 11th of 6th mo., 1839. When she was six years of age, her parents removed to Millville, New Jersey, where her father was managing partner of the glass-works. Here we can imagine the little blue-eyed and flaxen-haired Alice, her wee hand clasped tightly in that of her father, watching the making and packing of the many-sized glass bottles, or playing on the portico with her little dog Carlo or favourite pussy, and now and then employing her busy little fingers in dressing her canary's cage with green and chickweed.

Alice was about ten years of age when her parents removed to reside again in Philadelphia, where they lived, spending several summers at a country residence near Norristown, until she was fourteen years

old, when her father's business required their removal
to New York.

From her earliest infancy Alice had always been
delicate, and could never be kept at school for more
than a few months at a time, on account of distressing
headaches, which often entirely unfitted her for study.
In after years she spoke of her childhood as being far
from the happiest period of her life. Of a highly
nervous temperament, she was continually haunted
by thoughts of death, and at night fearful dreams
would often be followed by long seasons of wakeful-
ness. She said years after, in reference to this time,
"No one can know what I suffered during those long
nights, nor how I dreaded going to bed. I don't
think I ever felt entirely safe or comfortable unless
mother would let me curl up myself to sleep in her
arms. My first ideas of the joys of heaven were connected with 'There shall be no night there.'"

On reading the life of Charlotte Bronte, she remarked that the account of her childhood was the
only thing she had ever read which at all corres-
ponded with her own. She said, "At night I was
troubled by bad dreams, and even in the daytime the
thought of death followed me like a spectre. How
often have I stopped in a game of blind man's buff,
or some other childish sport, saying to myself, 'Well
it is of no use, we shall all have to die and be buried
in the ground.'"

She was very sensitive and loving, and very ima-
ginative. Many years afterward she confessed that
dreaming day-dreams was one of her chief occupa-
tions when a child.

Naturally conscientious, she early acquired a habit

of self-examination by taking her little rocking-chair and sitting down by her mother before bedtime, to think over her words and actions of the past day. Even when in her teens, and almost ashamed of anything so childish, she could not compose herself to sleep until she had received an answer to the question, "Have I been a good girl to-day?" She thus refers to this habit in a letter to her mother, written when on a visit to Millville, in 1857 :—

"It is getting near bedtime, and I seem to need some one to kiss, and ask, 'Have I been a good girl to-day?' How those old times come back to me, when thou and I used to sit here in this very room together, just at twilight, and 'think over.' I am afraid I am not half as dutiful a daughter now, though if all the stories I hear about myself are true, I could not have been anything very wonderful then."

On the first page of her journal, begun when she was fifteen years old, she thus states her reason for keeping it :—

"New York, 2d mo. 2d, 1855. My purpose in commencing a journal is to put down every day, or as often as I can, all my little sins as soon as committed, so that at the end of the week I can look back, and, by the aid of this little book, remember more distinctly how I have spent the time.

"It seems so hard for me to bridle my tongue, and still harder to control my feelings. Oh, that I might be worthy of myself; the longing is intense within me. But I can do nothing of myself; I am very weak, not worthy even to creep upon the dust; yet how conceited I am; how I rest in my own strength! Oh, to be able to do something, to make some sacri-

fice ! But this is vain ; I ought to be contented in
performing those little everyday duties, which are so
difficult because they are so small."

The following extracts are from the pages of this
journal :—

" 2d mo. 4th. At times I have felt an humbling
sense of my own unworthiness, and seen very clearly
how wrong I am in many of my feelings and desires.
That I may some day be enabled to serve God better,
and love Him more, is my humble prayer. To-morrow is meeting-day, and I am so glad, for to go to
meeting is, I think, my greatest pleasure ; but I fear
I do not always make the best use of my time there.
I am too fond of just sitting still and feeling that quiet
happiness, without thinking of my sins and transgressions."

After mentioning some impatient words spoken to
one of the family on the previous day, she says :—

" 2d mo. 6th. . . . After tea H—— came with
C. T——, and we spent quite a pleasant evening ; but
I secretly felt very unhappy, for I had been doing
wrong, and I knew it. . . .

" This morning, when I arose, the sun was shining
brightly ;' all nature seemed to praise God, but I
could not ; so I went about in that hardened indifference that is so terrible, not feeling exactly comfortable, still not feeling sorry. About ten o'clock I
went with Carrie to Gurney's to get her picture, and
when we returned I lay down, not feeling very well.
After dinner I went about feeling very unhappy, not
actually sinning in word or action, still sinning greatly
in my heart all the time.

" Since tea I have been looking out the window.

It is clear moonlight, and the stars are shining brightly; they seem to speak right to my heart, and make me feel worse than ever. So now I have finished !

"Oh, dear ! Oh, dear ! I cannot pray. What shall I do ? It seems wrong for me even to write that little word, *pray.*"

Thus was her young heart groping in darkness for that rest and peace which came not until four years after, when she found the Lord Jesus Christ, who satisfied the desire of her soul.

At this time the happy trio of sisters was broken in upon by the marriage of the eldest, and her removal to Salem, Mass. Alice thus refers to it in her journal :—

" 4th mo. 12th, 1855. The wedding is over. Dear Annie is married and gone. How many thoughts and feelings, both painful and pleasant, crowd upon me as I write these words ! They tell me that one dear sister has gone far from us, leaving an empty seat by our fireside, and a desolate feeling in our hearts. But I must not complain ; it is all for the best, I do not doubt. I would not have my sisters remain single, yet it is hard to part.

" The world is full of sadness, and I cannot expect to escape from some portion of sorrow. Heretofore my life has been very tranquil—too much so, I sometimes think, to last ; I cannot expect to pass through this world and meet nothing but sunshine." . . .

" Oct. 8th. It has been a long time since I last took up my pen to write in this little book. . . . Yes, I am now sixteen, I am forced to confess it, and I am afraid not much better, if any; but I still continue to hope that, through our blessed Redeemer, I may take courage. . . .

"Jan. 1856. Again a whole month has passed since I have written in this journal, and yet I am still alive, and what the world would call happy; but I feel that I never can be happy until this hard and sinful heart is changed, and I can feel that I am regenerated, and that I am living for God alone.

"Oh, it is the earnest prayer of my heart at times, that I may learn to give up my will to Him in all things, and have no other desire than to follow Him in the narrow path that leadeth unto life eternal. But, oh, the wickedness of the human heart! How it clings to the world, and how impossible it would be, if it were not for the never-failing mercy of our Lord and Master, for us ever to rise above earthly things!"

.   .   .   .   .   .

"Aug. 31st, 1856. . . . I can scarcely believe that I am really seventeen; no longer a child, but standing, as it were, on the threshold of womanhood, with the future stretching out before me, overshadowed with so much mystery, and, in my hours of despondency, with so much dread; but I feel sure that it is wrong to despond, for if we constantly seek strength where no poor repentant sinner ever looked in vain, we shall be able to rise above the tempestuous billows that everywhere beset us, and at the end of life's stormy day rest in the assurance of acceptance in that happy land where perfect rest and peace and joy abound."

"Dec. 28th, 1856. . . . May God be pleased to take the whole of this wicked heart to Himself! It is, indeed, very unworthy of acceptance, and oh, I

do so fear that I shall stray entirely away, and become
worldly, and that God will be angry, and never strive
with me any more.

"Oh, I am altogether so wicked, I don't know
what will ever become of me? God, I know, *is* good,
and if I would only strive with all my strength, and
pray with all my heart, He would give me more
strength, and a warmer heart; but I don't, and it
seems to me as though I cannot, I am so utterly vile.
When I think of all the innumerable blessings and
mercies which my Heavenly Father has showered
upon me ever since I was born, I look in wonder
at my stony heart, that it does not overflow with
thankfulness."

.   .   .   .   .   .

Dear Alice's desires after salvation were much
stimulated by her intercourse with her eldest sister,
who, after many weary months of deep conviction
for sin, was led, shortly after her marriage, to see
that in Christ was her only hope of redemption. It
was not until years after that she came out into the
full light of the Redeemer's love; but, though clinging to Christ with a trembling faith, she still felt that
her trust in her Saviour was worth all the wealth of
all the worlds, for it was her only hope of eternal
life; and she longed that her sisters might relinquish
what she could not but see were their vain efforts to
build up a righteousness of their own, and trust in
that Saviour, who was daily becoming more precious
to her. Her prayers for them were unceasing, and
she often spoke to them of Christ as the Saviour of
sinners.

Alice was much moved by the entreaties of this

dear sister, and confessed some years after that the first glimpse she had of the truth as it is in Jesus came to her through some words spoken by Annie in the Lord's strength. She said that during her visits to this sister, when Annie would read to her from the Bible, and pray for and with her, she would be almost persuaded to trust simply to Christ for salvation, but that on her return home the combined influence of some very dear friends of Unitarian tendencies was too much for her feeble, fluctuating faith; and although calling Christ her Saviour, she came to look upon Him in the light of a "helper" and great "exemplar," and, in the effort to make her life like His, forgot and practically ignored the blood of cleansing.

The following letter, which shows the depth and earnestness of her feeling, was written in the spring of this year, and is in reply to one from this sister, who ceased not her efforts until Alice became a decided Christian :—

"NEW YORK, 3d mo., 1857.

" MY DEAREST SISTER, —

"Thy letter came to me to-day, thou cannot tell how acceptably. It made me cry so that I did not finish it for at least fifteen minutes after I commenced to read it; and now I can scarcely write, my tears fall so fast; for, O Annie! I have been so unfaithful, so miserable!

"I have gradually this winter become more interested in dress, and the opinion of others, until my devotional duties have become—how can I say it?—a task, my prayers hurried, and sometimes almost omitted, and yet, canst thou believe it, I was scarcely aware of it until I read thy letter. Yes; I must have known it, but I was not willing to think about it, and now I am so afraid this is but a fleeting knowledge of my sin. . . .

" Oh, how I wish that my whole life had been spent in earnestly trying to glorify Him. I know we can do nothing of ourselves; but God loves us when we try to please Him. Oh, to think of His anger! May He have mercy upon me, or soon it will be too late. I have been so sinful! but by God's grace I will look for redemption through Christ; although it seems scarcely possible that He will give such a sinful wretch as I His Spirit to comfort and guide me. .Oh, that God would change my heart, and make me love Him. I do want to do right, but it seems as if I cannot even want to do right long at a time.

" I intend to write to thee always and tell thee just how I get along, and how hard I find it. Do' write me letters of advice, and keep me in mind of all I ought to do. . . .

"If my blessings could do thee any good, they would not cease to fall upon thee day and night; but God will bless thee for all thy help to me. Good night. ALICE."

While dear Alice's inner life was thus full of conflict, and she was wearily seeking strength to fight the battle of life, and failing, because she sought it not through the blood of the Atonement, her outward life was also full of interest, and called forth much feeling.

Her only remaining sister was married in the 4th

mo. of this year—1857—and Alice, while giving out her sympathies to their fullest extent, in the prospect of happiness opening to her sister, and bearing her own burden of loneliness at the separation, was, through all, learning more and more of the sinfulness of her own heart, and longing more anxiously to find peace to her soul.

She was also at this time much occupied in arrangements for the removal of the family to a country residence, near Norristown. Though anticipating much enjoyment in her new home, it was still a trial for Alice to leave New York. She had made warm friends there, and was, beside, much attached to the house itself, particularly to a little sitting-room in the third story, with its open-grate fire, and deep window-seats filled with her own choice plants. She used sometimes to say laughingly that she was like a cat in her attachment to localities, and she thought no room, however elegant, could ever be like this little sitting-room, where she had spent so many delightful hours with her sister, sewing and reading, or sitting before their bright fire conversing, often until a late hour at night.

Shortly after the marriage of this sister, Alice bade a last farewell to her New York home, and went with the bride and groom to visit their sister Annie, who some time before had removed to reside in St John, N. B. Alice's letters speak of her joy at again embracing this dear sister, and for the first time seeing her new nephew, Charley, "who," she adds, "is as fine a little fellow as ever owned an Aunt Alice."

After a short but delightful visit, the party returned, leaving Alice at her new country home, near Philadelphia, where her parents had already preceded her.

This home was, for the remainder of Alice's life, the one spot on earth where her interests and affections centred. Natural beauty had always a great charm for her, and this place, commanding a fine view of the Schuylkill valley, and the blue hills rising in the distance, was well calculated to satisfy her love for the beautiful. The prospect from the room which her father had built especially for Alice was truly lovely. It gave her great enjoyment to sit in the recess of her large bay window, and, while engaged in reading or writing, to view the varied landscape—sometimes watching the mists roll off the opposite hills, or the shadows of the clouds as they chased each other over the sunny slopes.

This place in Alice's room might also be called her Bethel. Here she resorted for reading and prayer, and sometimes, after all the family had retired for the night, she would sit for hours in the calm moonlight, enjoying these seasons of meditation and communion much more than she could those taken from the hurry and bustle of the day.

She was much interested in the naming of this place, and "Tswedelle," which was finally settled upon by her father, recalled many pleasant associations to Alice's mind. It was the sound of the note of a favourite bird, which, during her childhood at Millville, came regularly every day in winter, and perched himself upon a certain woodpile near the house, and sang his morning song "Tswedelle, tswedelle, tswedelle, tswee," to the great delight of his little friend, who would often try to imitate his clear melodious note.

To the many friends who were entertained by her here, the name "Tswedelle" instantly recalls Alice, as, in health and happiness, she graced this beautiful home, as well as when during her lingering illness, by her cheerful faith and resignation, she shed a hallowed lustre upon all the scene.

In the planning and laying out of the grounds her taste was much consulted, and one walk leading to the woods which skirted the south corner of the lawn was entirely of her own devising, and was always called Alice's walk. It was her delight to search here early in the spring for the first delicate wild-flowers.

She selected the spot and chose the design for a lovely rustic summer-house, which also bears her name, from which is a beautiful view down the hill-side to the hollow, named by her father "The Dimple," and off through the vista of trees to the valley below, and the blue hills beyond. The groups of flowering shrubs which conceal it from view, and the vines which twine over its rustic sides, all speak of her taste and energy. Indeed there is not a spot about the place which is not associated with memories of Alice, for a tree or shrub could not be planted without her judgment, and the designing and arrangement of the beds of flowers were left entirely to her.

Her conservatory was also a source of much enjoyment, and in these pure and simple pleasures she maintained her interest throughout her life, although after her conversion they became subservient to her work for her Master.

She was truly the sunshine of the whole place. Her "bright way," as one of her sisters termed it, was peculiarly her own. Her light step and sweet voice, as she went round the house singing like a bird, gladdened every heart, and although, at the time of their removal to Tswedelle—as has been manifested in her letters—feeling the innate corruption of her nature, and realising the necessity of a change of heart, she was to the observer the thoughtful, affectionate daughter, the unselfish sister, and the true and sympathising friend.

From this time it does not appear that Alice wrote anything in her journal, and her letters during the first year of their residence at Tswedelle seldom refer to her inner life; something of it, however, is revealed in the following extract from a letter written to an intimate friend, in the latter part of 1858, and is full of interest, as expressing her earnest desires after righteousness and her increasing dissatisfaction with her own vain efforts at self-improvement.

She was in the habit, in writing as well as in speaking, of using the pronouns "thee" and "thou" to her own family, and to those of her correspondents who belonged to the Society of Friends, of which she was a member, and it has been thought that it would seem more natural and like herself to give the letters just as they were written.

To A. U. C.

"TSWEDELLE, *Sept.* 1858.

. . . "Allow me to tell thee, dear A——,that thy last letter just suits me. I would not give a fig for a letter that tells me about everybody else and nothing of the dear one who writes it; so do please be egotistical, if the only effect is to make thee speak of thyself and thy own feelings. To speak of myself, I do not know what is to become of me. When I look back and remember the dawn of my fifteenth birthday, how very bright it was, and as I watched the sun rise in the east, how full my soul was of hopes and aspirations; how determined I felt then, on the very threshold of youth, to take a stand for the right, to live from that time for duty and not for pleasure,— yes, when I look back I am almost disheartened, for in the four years which have passed since then I have nothing to look upon but resolutions forgotten, intentions unfulfilled, and at best but a weak groping after light that came not. . . . But in this time when the grace of God seems so bountifully poured out upon our land, I dare to hope that He will extend His mercy unto me and take my heart, for I am utterly unable even to give it to Him. I don't know how I came to write this to thee, darling; I had no intention of doing so when I commenced, but it seemed impossible to help it; in fact, for months past this subject has been much in my mind."

The following letter was written from Millville, the home of her childhood, where her sister "Carrie" resided for some years after her marriage. It is in reply to one from her eldest sister, begging her to write more freely of spiritual things :—

"MILLVILLE, *Dec.* 1858.

"MY DEAREST SISTER ANNIE,—

"As Carrie is occupied, I embrace this opportunity to tell thee how much obliged I am for thy dear little note. It is very nice to have thee take such' a deep interest in me.

"I feel, indeed, that I have no merit of my own, and I have no hope but in a redeeming Saviour, who has promised to aid all that come to Him, however weak or wicked. I do, indeed, desire to have no other wish than to serve Him, no other aim than to perform the work He requires at my hand, no other love to compare with my love for Him, and no other hope but the hope of receiving mercy at His hand. I am, indeed, very far from this ; but He never requires anything that He will not give us the strength to perform ; all we have to do is to live as near as we can to what we see to be right, and to trust all the rest to the working of His Holy Spirit in our hearts."

Such was the state of her soul in the latter part of the year 1858. The great foundation truth that we must be born again in order to enter into the kingdom of God, and that this new birth must take place before the soul can know the *indwelling* and *guidance* of the Holy Spirit, which is the gift of God to those who believe in Jesus, was not yet comprehended by her. The sentiment expressed in the last letter, that we must do the best we can and leave the rest to the Holy Spirit, is the natural feeling of many unconverted hearts, and very often, as was the case with Alice, lulls the awakened sinner for a time into a false peace.

CHAPTER II.

BUT God had better things in store for Alice; and in the early part of the year 1859 she was brought to realise her soul's true needs, and her eyes were opened to see in the Lord Jesus Christ a Saviour just suited to meet these needs.

The three or four letters which follow tell the story of this blessed change :—

"TSWEDELLE, First day morning,
2d mo. 6th, 1859.

"MY DARLING CARRIE,—

"I cannot go to meeting this morning, on account of neuralgia in my face, so I am going to write a letter to thee instead.

"There is one subject on which we have never used sufficient freedom in speaking, and that is the all-important one of religion; and I feel all the more strongly inclined to speak of it this morning, as I am convinced that we have been very much mistaken in our views. We have—thou and I, dear—been always building up for ourselves a religion of *works*. I never thought so, but now I feel sure of it. I am now sure that nothing but *faith* in the Lord Jesus Christ will save us. Faith is the first thing: it is all we can do for ourselves, and, indeed, we can't do that unless we have help; but we can believe as far as we are able, and He will assuredly perfect that faith and make us able to perform works that are acceptable to Him, because we believe in Him. We must believe that Christ came into the world to save sinners, and that all that *look* to Him for salvation will surely be saved. It seems to me that there is so much in the Bible that cannot mean anything else. In the third chapter of the Gospel of St John, there is ample proof in the words of Christ himself. He there alludes to the serpent which Moses lifted up in the wilderness : and says, verse 15th, 'Even so must the Son of man be lifted up ; that whosoever believeth in Him should not perish, but have eternal life.' Of course this belief must be a spiritual one ; but we know that God never requires more than we can give, and if we believe as far as we are able, and say, 'I believe, Lord, help Thou mine unbelief,' He will do it, and we have no right to doubt it; and if we continue steadfast in that faith, we shall 'work the works of God ;' but if we fail in this thing, how can we? For in John vi. 29, when they asked Him, 'What shall we do that we may work the works of God?' Jesus answered, 'This is the work of God, that ye *believe* on Him whom He hath sent.'

"In many places Christ says such things as, 'Whosoever doth not bear his cross, and come after me, cannot be my disciple ;' but how can we do so unless we have a full belief in His power to save us entirely by His mercy? For unless we follow Him as our *Saviour* and our Lord, we do not fulfil this commandment. We must believe first, and then all the

B

Scripture promises apply to us as disciples of the Lord Jesus; we have entered into the strait and narrow way, which the Friends so often tell us leadeth unto life. But let us remember that Christ is the gate, and that we must enter in through that gate, 'for there is none other name under heaven given among men whereby we must be saved.' . . .

We ought to come to Him, offering all that we possess the power of giving, and promise to believe in Him as fully as our poor, weak, sinful hearts will let us, asking Him to give us a 'new heart,' and a full belief in Him, and we will as surely get it as we ask. This I believe to be all He requires us to do, and when we have done it we ought to feel perfectly sure that He will give us salvation, because He has said so, and we dare not doubt His word. Although we see no good in ourselves, we may be confident that 'He is able to save to the uttermost all those who come unto God by Him.' If we feel nothing, it only proves what we knew before, that we are wicked and need a Saviour. If we accept Him, we must say, with the old man—

'I am a poor sinner, and nothing at all,
But Jesus Christ is my all and in all.'

"My own darling Carrie, all this I write to thee because I love thee so much, and want thee to be as happy in believing and casting all doubt and care and trouble on 'the Lamb of God, who taketh away the sin of the world,' as I am. Although I am only a weak infant in the faith, yet would I call upon thee to see the light and rejoice.

"Look in the Bible, dear, and see what it says there to *sinners ;* do not mistake what is meant for *believers* as applicable for others.

. . . "I have been looking out all the texts bearing on the question, 'What shall I do to be saved?' At first I did not feel quite willing to give up doing a little something for myself, but while copying out the texts above mentioned, I became convinced that this is the true gospel plan of salvation, and made up my mind to accept it as nearly like a little child as I could ; and although I know that I am thoroughly wicked, yet I have a hope in Christ ; and oh, it is such an inexpressible comfort ! It is even possible that I may fall from this belief into the old doctrine of works, but it will be because I fall, not because the gospel truths are not just as clear in the Bible as day.

"It was hard for me to sit down and write this letter, but I hope I have been able to make thee understand a little what I believe. I know thee too well to think thou wilt attribute this to a desire to teach ; no indeed, only I do so long for thee to see and accept this wonderful gospel plan of salvation. It is all through the Bible ; every chapter, if we did but understand it aright, testifies to the truth.

"That our Father in heaven may make thee to see it clearly, is the earnest prayer of

"Thy loving sister,

"ALICE."

This letter was Alice's first confession of Christ. She had learned to know Him as her Saviour in the privacy of her own chamber, and for some days her newly-found faith and joy in Him were kept to herself. She was suffering at the time from a severe attack of neuralgia, but as soon as she was able she wrote to her sister as given above.

She said afterward, " I cannot describe the feeling of peaceful rest with which I lay down to sleep after I had written that letter. I felt so light-hearted and happy, for now I had confessed my Saviour, and I thought if I should die suddenly in the night they would know that I was trusting only in Christ, and not in any efforts of my own, for salvation."

Her faith was also much strengthened by this confession, and she found daily more "peace and joy in believing." At first she could not wait to dress in the morning before opening her Bible at the third chapter of John, to assure herself that those precious promises were still there; and the more she examined the foundation of her faith and hope in the Scriptures, the more was the conviction brought home to her heart by the Spirit, that she was building on the Rock that can never be moved.

The letters which Alice soon after wrote to her eldest sister on this subject have been omitted, to avoid repetition, as she did not explain herself so fully in them, knowing that Annie would immediately understand her change of views, and rejoice with her that she had found the Saviour.

In the latter part of the third month Alice returned with her sister Carrie to Millville, her heart full of prayer that they who had always been so united in all other things might also be made one in Christ Jesus. During this visit her prayers were wonderfully answered, and dear Alice had the unspeakable joy of seeing her beloved sister brought into the exercise of like precious faith with herself.

The latter some time afterward wrote concerning it :. "It was but a month or two after Alice's conversion that I too became a child of God; then, indeed, we were doubly united. Alice said that her one desire and prayer was, that I also might realise the glorious truth which had made her so inexpressibly happy. And when the light did burst in upon my soul, as we were sitting together reading Malan's 'True Cross,' she could hardly believe that the Lord had answered her prayers so soon. The remaining few weeks of her visit were indeed a source of strengthening and establishing to me. We had but one subject of conversation—Jesus and His work for sinners, and of this we never tired. There was but one book that we cared to read, and that was our constant companion, whether riding or boating. How much we found to talk about in its inspired pages, and how confirming was every verse to our new faith!"

Not only to her sisters did she write of the great change she had experienced. She wished all her friends to know that she had received the forgiveness of her sins through her Saviour, and to those to whom she had no opportunity of speaking she wrote letters, hoping that the story of her experience might incline their hearts to "come, taste, and see that the Lord is good."

The two or three next letters, though of later date than those which follow, are inserted here, as they speak more particularly of her conversion.

"My Dear A——,

"It has been a long time since I have heard from thee; I wonder why? . . .

"Dost thou know, dear, to-day is my birthday? And in coming to the close of this, my twentieth year, I have been thinking that I have wronged thee, and, therefore, come now to ask pardon, and to do all I can to make up for it.

"I have often heard thee say that when intimate friends are separated, their letters are supposed to put each in possession of all the principal interests, changes, and events in the life of the other; and it is because I have left thee ignorant so long of the greatest change and most important event of my life that I feel condemned.

"Dost thou remember, last September, getting a letter from me, in which I told thee I was feeling great dissatisfaction with my past life, and that I did not know what I should do to make it better, and finished by hoping that, in a time when God seemed in an especial manner to be pouring out His Spirit upon our land, He would look down in mercy upon me?

"And indeed He has been most merciful in bringing me in by the only true door to the sheepfold, Jesus Christ our Lord. The fact was, that I had always been and was then striving to walk in the 'narrow way' before going in at the 'strait gate.' I sadly mixed the law and the gospel; I thought we had at least to prove our earnest desire to become the children of God before we could be accepted as such; and as I did not see in myself this earnest striving, I did not think I could be accepted.

"I did not see, as M—— beautifully expresses it, that it is the law that says, 'This do, and thou shalt live,' and the gospel that says, 'Live, and then thou shalt do.' It is so glorious to think that He first makes us His children, and then gives us the will and the strength to serve Him; to think that He accepts us freely just as sinners; that He will wash us clean in His blood, and that He will be made unto us 'wisdom and righteousness, sanctification and redemption,' if we will only give up the idea of saving ourselves, and honour God by believing what He says, and be willing to receive as such 'the gift of God, which is eternal life.' This certainly would not be man's way of saving sinners, but I am convinced that it is God's way.

"Even as short a time ago as the first of last January, I was in darkness as to the truths of the Bible. I had silenced all my feelings of dissatisfaction by making up my mind to be more earnest in prayer and good works, and trust more to the guidance of the Holy Spirit to lead me into the paths of righteousness. About this time I went to spend the night with H. W. S. While there she explained the simple gospel of Christ to me; and I came home the next day with a list in my pocket of the texts in the Bible answering the question, 'What shall I do to be saved?' and with a doubt in my heart whether my answer was the true one, which was, 'Work the works of righteousness, by the aid of the Holy Spirit, which aid thou never couldst have had if Christ had not died; therefore, Christ is the Saviour, inasmuch as without His aid thou never couldst work them and enter heaven.'

"I took the Bible and looked for the texts; I went as far as the third chapter of John, 14th, 15th, and 16th verses, and I stopped. I thought of the scene in the wilderness, when the brazen serpent was raised in the camp of the Israelites, and God declared, by the mouth of His servant, that notwithstanding the people were receiving the just reward of their wickedness, if they would but look at the serpent which He had set up, they should be healed. The act of looking I knew was simply an act of faith, for if they had not believed that He could do what He said He would, they would not have looked; for how utterly unreasonable it must have seemed to them to be told that just casting their eyes upon one object more than another would heal their deadly wounds. And yet we know that as many as looked lived; and the Scriptures say, 'Even so must the Son of man be lifted up, that whosoever believeth on Him should not perish, but have eternal life.'

"I had found the answer to the question, 'Believe on the Lord Jesus Christ;' and the way to believe, even as the Israelites believed God when they looked at the serpent; and I thought, Cannot I now take God at His word, and believe that Christ died for *me*, and that, therefore, I shall not perish, but have everlasting life, as He says so? The words, 'I believe, Lord, help Thou mine unbelief,' sprang from my heart. Could any really believe that Christ died for them, Himself bore the penalty for their sins, and, therefore, they should be saved, without experiencing a love and gratitude toward that Saviour to spring up in their heart, which would give a far stronger and deeper motive for working in His service than any other?

"I have many times since then been tempted to doubt, but I always go to the Bible, and come away surer than ever that the atonement of Christ is a finished work, perfect and entire, and that He is able to save me without my doing a single thing to merit it. Oh! the peace of this resting like a little child upon such a glorious Saviour; to know that He will be our sanctification as well as our redemption; will not only take us into His service, but will make us fit for that service; will not only give us work to do, but strength to do it!

"How beautifully He has shown us the position of the Christian, in the parable of the vine and the branches. How utterly impossible it would be for a branch to bring forth fruit of itself is evident to all; and it is just as unreasonable to expect a man to bring forth works which would be acceptable in the sight of God until he is joined by faith to Christ, who is the only true vine, and can alone give the power.

"It is such a very common thing for persons to impress the necessity of a holy life, and a greater willingness to walk in the narrow way, upon young people who are not yet within the fold, instead of pointing them to Christ, 'the Way, the Truth, and the Life.' I have received a great deal of advice which would do for the Christian, but little that was calculated to make me think whether I was one or not.

"I have, dear A——, spoken very freely to thee, as I felt I could do no less; and, indeed, my heart prompted me to do so some time ago, but I hoped to see thee so soon, and it is so much easier to make one's self understood by talking than writing when one's heart is full.

"Do not hesitate, darling, to sit down and write all thou hast in thy heart to say to me. Do let me know how thou feels and thinks. I love thee so much, I long for thy sympathy and encouragement. But if it be that I have startled thee, if thou art an unbeliever in what some people call sudden conversions, or if thou art yet inclined to think that we are justified equally by works and by faith, as some one says, and, therefore, we must not rejoice in the light of a Redeemer's love until we have both; under any circumstances do not, pray do not, let my frankness make thee feel reserved; and do not, darling, expect to find me entirely changed in outward action, as thou must remember I am only a 'babe in Christ,' and all unused to the ways of godliness. I should, indeed, despair of ever living a life acceptable in the sight of God, but that I trust that Christ will subdue this heart entirely unto Himself, for He is able to do all things. Oh, it is true that the weakest believer could say, if he would, with the Apostle, 'I can do all things through Christ, which strengtheneth me.'

"Carrie told me, I think, that she wrote thee explaining the change in her views. O A——! I cannot begin to express the happiness I felt at seeing her come, with simple, childlike faith, to the feet of Jesus, some two months after I laid my weary load of sin there. And oh, may the habitual attitude of our souls be to lie at the foot of the cross, utterly helpless in ourselves, but trusting in Him for everything. May we always continue in the spirit of the little hymn that says—

> "I am a poor sinner, and nothing at all,
> But Jesus Christ is my all and in all.'"

To M. M. J.

A FRIEND AT BOARDING-SCHOOL.

"June 29, 1859.

. . . "I sympathise very much with your dread of the examination; but, dear M——, there is one thought that comes to me very often, that if we are doing or have done our duty as God would have us do it, if we can feel that we have done it to please Him, and that He is pleased with us, what difference, comparatively, does it make what people think of us? I know it is very pleasant to have our undertakings succeed in the eyes of the world; but I am convinced that we ought to have but *one* motive for everything we do, even our smallest everyday duties, that of serving our Lord and Master; and then you know if we succeed in that great object, the approbation of the world will be as nothing. If the Lord is our friend, all our disappointments and sorrows will work together for our good, for He will take care of His children.

"Oh, the great privilege of knowing that you are a child of God! And, indeed, I think it is the duty of all to know whether they are or not. How could a man fight, if placed in a battlefield, without knowing to which army he belonged? . . .

"Dear M——, I have spoken more at length on this

subject, because it is one which is very near my heart. You will doubtless be surprised when I tell you that I have come to see the great truths of the Bible very differently within the last year.

" The difference is this ; before I looked at them with my mind, now I look at them with my heart. Now I know that Jesus died for *me*. I know it because I believe what the Bible says, and it says He died for all sinners, paid the full price, took our sins upon Himself, and that He will give the gift of eternal life to any who will come to Him, and honour Him by believing that He is able and willing to do what He has said He will.

" Oh, the gospel of Jesus Christ is indeed 'good news' to sinners. It is strange how many years I listened to these truths, and never understood them ; for while I acknowledged Jesus Christ as the Saviour, in my heart I only looked upon Him as a helper. I thought that by His death on the cross He had removed the natural curse which rested upon all the seed of Adam, and had thus opened and procured the means of obtaining a salvation to which otherwise I should never have had access. I thought thus that my salvation would be my own work, one which, however, I did not expect to do without help from on high.

" I often felt sad ; for I had many misgivings as to whether the work was progressing, and whether I had done enough, should I be suddenly called away. If I ever saw something of the truth when reading such passages as, ' Believe on the Lord Jesus Christ, and thou shalt be saved,' and began to put my trust in Him, I would surely meet such a passage as ' Faith without works is dead,' and in my blindness I did not see that it was my faith that was weak, therefore the works were not visible in me, and instead of striving after more faith, I went about to establish myself in my own righteousness, supposing that if I saw in myself the good works, I should be sure I had the faith, and so came round to the same old point in darkness.

"Imagine, then, my feelings when my eyes were opened to see that the Saviour's atonement is a finished work. . . . It really seems almost too good news to be true, that Christ does all, and that we have only to honour Him by believing that He is able to save to the uttermost all those who come unto God by Him. He even gives us a reason, which we can understand, for this, 'It is not of works, lest any man should boast.' What a very different motive for working does it give to one who has accepted this perfect salvation, even that of glorifying the God who so loved us, that He gave His only-begotten Son, that whosoever believeth in Him should not perish, but have everlasting life.

"Oh, the wonderful riches of the goodness and mercy of God! Is it any wonder, dear friend, that I should be quite overwhelmed that one, so altogether sinful as I know myself to be, should be allowed to see, even dimly, these glorious truths of the gospel? . . .

"Dear M——, I have been trying to be a Christian, as you know, for these many years; but I wanted to do it partly myself, and I would not submit myself wholly to Christ as a little child, just to be saved out of pure mercy, and consequently was not happy; but since I have been brought to see Jesus as 'the Way, the Truth, and the Life,' and have rested entirely on Him, I have indeed been happy. I have spoken thus frankly to you, as I feel that I must tell all those I love how mistaken I have always been, and what a glorious Saviour I have found."

To N. O.

"TSWEDELLE, 1859.

" MY DEAR N——,

"I received your letter this morning, and I cannot tell you how I thank you for your kind interest, and warm invitation to visit you. I should enjoy doing so extremely, particularly as I should so appreciate your sympathy and counsel; we should have nice times quietly reading and talking about our dear Lord Jesus, and how to live so as to glorify Him. Indeed I would love to come, but I have not thought of leaving home at all this summer, excepting for a short visit to Carrie.   .   .   .

"You ask me to tell you all about myself, dear N——; the Lord has promised to carry the lambs in His bosom, and indeed I have only a story of the mercy of the Lord to tell. He has brought another poor sinner out of the drear wilderness darkness into the glorious light of the Redeemer's love. A poor little weak babe in Christ am I, but I can do nothing but rejoice—rejoice that I have found so glorious a Saviour. Even the fear that I shall dishonour Him by not living a life to His glory, is swallowed up in the thought that He will not only 'save from wrath, but make me pure.'

"It is indeed perfect rest to trust Him for everything ; and yet it is a struggle, a fight of faith—a fight to keep our faith, and not begin trusting in our own strength again."

"MILLVILLE, *April* 14, 1859.

" MY DARLING SISTER ANNIE,—

. . . "My heart overflows with love and gratitude to our Heavenly Father when I think of the 'good news' in which we all three now rejoice. What a wonderful blessing it is that we can sympathise in this the greatest joy one can know, the knowledge of Jesus Christ and Him crucified. O Annie ! I long unspeakably to talk all these things over with thee.

"To think that I have so long resisted the truth and dishonoured my Saviour, by not being willing to give up the idea of helping to save myself, and that now I should be allowed to feel such comfort in believing, really seems wonderful. I feel as though I ought to be overwhelmed with my own sinfulness ; but when I look at my glorious Redeemer it is impossible, for if my sins are so great, it only makes it more wonderful that He is able and willing to save me. He is all things, and I am nothing— nothing but an empty shell, which if filled with Christ will be accepted. How blessed to be such a shell ! Oh, for more entire submission and more grace, that we may so live as to honour Him and glorify His name !

"It seems so strange that I could have listened so often to the truth, and never understood it. I look back now to some of those conversations we—thou and I used to have, and see so clearly that many things thou used to say are the very same that come over me now with such force. And it is just so in reading the Bible: chapters that I was perfectly familiar with, now burst on me with such new meaning, and are so glorious !

"I used to wonder how any one could really want to talk to people—that is, people who cared nothing about it—on the subject of religion; but now it seems as if I long to make known the 'glad tidings to every one, as I feel so sure that it would make them very happy if they only would listen to it. . .

"I do hope I shall not bring dishonour on the cause, I am so very weak and sinful, and sometimes so cold; but I stand upon the Rock of Ages. . . .

"Thou asks us to pray for thee, and I can assure thee it is a great pleasure to do so, for what a blessing it is to be able to go to God, really as our Father, to ask good things for a sister in Christ. Only a few months ago this sentence would have appeared without meaning, but now I thank God for it—it is different.

"This is the first time I have been here since little Alice's birth; she is now three months old, and I can assure thee is a great pet with her auntie. I am writing now in the nursery, and have had to stop every two minutes to talk to the baby, who has been sitting in her nurse's arms saying, 'Goo, goo,' and laughing so cunningly that she was really irresistible. I do not know that she is very pretty, but if she were a little fairy we could not make more fuss over her, for we think her about perfect."

A memoir of dear Alice would be incomplete without mentioning what joy it gave her that three

very dear cousins came to the experimental knowledge of the Saviour about the same time with herself. There were then, with Alice's two sisters, a
little band of six cousins, to all of whom, except her
eldest sister, who, as has been mentioned, had been a
Christian four years, the life of faith in Christ was a
new joy. The first time these cousins met together
after the separation caused by the marriage and
removal of some, it was to rejoice in the stronger
bond in which they were now united. This meeting
took place at Alice's uncle's, the family home of her
three cousins. Here they sought a little room in a
retired part of the house, and sitting down together
they communed upon their newly-found joy.

To the eldest of these cousins, Alice, though herself the youngest, was united by an uncommon love.
She had been the recipient of all her doubts and
conflicts before she found the Saviour, and to her, so
far as human instrumentalities were concerned, Alice
owed the knowledge of the truth which had set her
free, as will be seen by reference to a letter dated
"June 11, 1859." The tie which had before bound
them was thus made doubly strong by their union in
Christ, and Alice ever after gave her the sweet name
of "sister cousin."

"TSWEDELLE, 4th mo. 22, 1859.

"MY DEAR CARRIE,—

. . . "The way seems to open for me to go
to New York yearly meeting, and I do not know but
it may be best; I only want to do my duty, and in
this, as well as every other action of my life, I must, as
Paul says, 'do all to the glory of God.'

"I have been reading the third, fourth, and fifth chapters of Romans, and they never seemed half so beautiful, and clear, and so comforting. I felt so cold this morning, and after breakfast spoke impatiently to ——, and was almost upset for the whole day; but I thought of the little hymn :—

> 'I am a poor sinner, and nothing at all,
>   But Jesus Christ is my all and in all ;'

and then I prayed and read some in that precious Bible, and now I *feel* that I am one of Christ's children, though a very weak one ; however, we know that feeling, though a great blessing, is not the one essential thing. . . .

"Do not, darling, let thy coldness make thee feel discouraged, but struggle against temptations, and never forget that it is the Lord who must make thee fit for His own service ; so be more earnest in prayer for a fervent spirit to be always zealous in His cause. Remember where James says, 'Count it all joy when ye fall into divers temptations ; knowing this, that the trying of your faith worketh patience. But let patience have her perfect work, that ye may be perfect and entire, wanting nothing. If any of you lack wisdom, let him ask of God, that giveth to all men liberally, and upbraideth not, and it shall be given him.'"

Reference is made in the above letter to an impatient word spoken. After dear Alice's conversion, as well as before, she found impatience to be her greatest temptation. Naturally very quick in taking in an idea as well as putting it into execution, and being also exceedingly thoughtful of the comfort of others,

she often felt tried at those who were slower or less
thoughtful than herself. This was somewhat owing
to physical causes. She was frequently a great sufferer from neuralgic headaches, and would sometimes
make the exertion to go down to breakfast, when a
heavy step, or loud tone of voice, or the hasty shut-
ting of a door, grated so harshly on her nerves, as to
make it seem almost impossible to withhold some
expression of impatience or irritability of feeling.
She knew that as a Christian, having the power of a
new life, she should be lifted above these things. She
felt it her privilege to have such a well of quiet within
as would enable her to say, "None of these things
move me." This temptation was made an especial
subject of prayer, and she gained so complete a victory over any outward expression of it, that few
imagined she had such feelings to contend with.

The little piece entitled "The Quiet Mind,"
which will be found at the end of this volume, in
connection with a few of Alice's favourite hymns, was
so expressive of her thoughts and desires that she
learned it by heart, and so often repeated it, that to
some of her intimate friends it is very closely connected with their recollections of her. Adelaide
Newton's hymn, "All, all is known to Thee," was
also often the language of her heart. Upon one occasion she repeated the following verse to her sister:—

> "When in the morning unrefreshed I wake,
> Or in the night but little sleep I take,
> This brief appeal submissively I make —
> All, all is known to Thee;"

remarking, "No one but an invalid could have
written that;" and then, referring to the preceding

verse, "The little everyday noises, discussions, &c., which are scarcely noticed by one in health, become to the invalid nothing less than 'turmoil and din.'"

But although dear Alice was always delicate and often a great sufferer, yet when she was in her usual health she was so full of spirits and energy, always so ready to exert all the strength she had for others, and her manner was so entirely free from that languor which is common to invalids, that her friends could scarcely help forgetting that she was less strong than themselves.

EXTRACTS FROM LETTERS TO HER SISTER CARRIE.

"*April* 23, 1859.

. . . "There are several things I want to say to thee, dear; one is not to feel any fear about your little meetings: just leave it all to the Lord, and pray for His strength to enable thee to do thy duty concerning them. Is it not written, 'Casting all your care upon Him, for He careth for you?' Just think, after such an invitation, that we should be tempted to carry our own load of care instead of trusting it to One who we know is worthy of trust, and able to do all things. How far we are from realising what it would be to render our whole body, soul, and spirit to the service of Christ, whose we are; this is what we ought to aim at—entire consecration; and how very much that means! . . .

Dear, dear Carrie, do not be discouraged; the Lord is so merciful, He will not let His own children go wrong if they only have faith in Him, that when they have asked Him to keep them from falling, that

He will. May our Lord bless us both, darling, and make us do right;

> 'Lord, I am blind, be thou my sight;
> Lord, I am weak, be thou my might!'"

"*April* 1859, Third day afternoon.

. . . "Yesterday I was very busy all the morning, excepting my own precious hour for devotion. In the afternoon I drove to see J. M. She is coming to spend to-night with me. Oh, how I do pray the Lord to bless this visit, and teach me just what to say! I feel very weak, but 'the Lord is my Shepherd, I shall not want.' He has been wonderfully good to me."

"*May* 2, 1859.

"We went to meeting yesterday morning as usual. . . . I had a most delightful meeting, realising what a glorious thing it is to be a disciple of such a great and merciful Saviour. I could not help saying over to myself the prophecy concerning Him in Isaiah xlii., 'A bruised reed shall He not break, and the smoking flax shall He not quench.'"

CHAPTER III.

IN the fifth month Alice paid a visit to her "sister cousin" who resided in Philadelphia. These visits were always seasons of great enjoyment to her, and at this time the cousins were particularly interested in the subject of the Christian's growth and advancement in the divine life. They felt that although conscious of pardon and peace with God through our Lord Jesus Christ, they still did not realise that continual victory over sin and deadness to it which they saw in the Scriptures to be the Christian's birthright. During this visit they earnestly sought to find out the secret of the life of victory and triumph realised by the apostles and early Christians. The blessed truth of a present practical sanctification by faith—Christ made unto us wisdom, righteousness, sanctification, and redemption—was much opened to their understanding. Alice especially seemed to receive this truth into her heart, and very largely in her after experience realised the joy and peace of taking Christ to be to her, not only her justification from all the guilt of sin, but also her sanctification from its present dominion and power. Her letters for some years dwell much upon this subject, and all who knew her felt the quiet influence of a life that had become to a great degree " hid with Christ in God." Still her experience in this respect was not an unwavering one, owing to many adverse influences, and chiefly to the reasonings of some very dear friends, through which her intellectual under-standing of this subject became clouded ; and this, reacting on her experience, caused her somewhat to decline from her early power and joy, and her letters make less and less mention of it. But she seems never to have lost the experience entirely, and always found far more rest and strength in a simple trusting to Christ for the supply of all her needs, than many of the believers with whom she associated.

In the latter part of her life the Lord graciously restored to her a knowledge of His perfect salvation, as will be noticed in the course of this narrative.

"May 19, 1859.

" My Darling Carrie,—

. . . "I did have such a nice time in the city last week, it refreshed my spirits so much. I brought 'The Higher Christian Life' home with me, but I have not yet finished ' Adelaide Newton.'

"I long to tell thee all about my visit, but I don't know how to begin. I was at M——'s Bible-class twice, and enjoyed it exceedingly ; beautiful thoughts dropped from his lips like a shower of diamonds, and the only trouble was, you could not gather them all, they fell so fast. The sanctification of the Christian was the subject which occupied almost all of our private conversation, and, as it is the one which has engaged my thoughts much of late, I was intensely interested, and I do hope I have been profited.

"I saw Mrs K——, the Methodist lady, who is so entirely dedicated to the service of Christ. We went to a prayer-meeting at her house, where she spoke beautifully. The subject was giving ourselves up entirely to do the will of our Father, without even asking why we, instead of another, are called to do that work, just as if He would require us to do anything for which He would not give us the needed strength; we ought not to linger, but jump quickly and gladly, never doubting Him, but considering it a privilege to be a tool in the hands of one so mighty. I can, of course, give thee no idea of what she said, it was so comforting and encouraging, and still showing very plainly what a mean thing it is to doubt. She made me despise myself more than ever.

"I had a class of boys out at the Refuge last first day morning, and found great comfort in speaking of Christ to them; although my words were imperfect, the truth I felt to be mighty.

"And now, dear, that He may 'sanctify *us* wholly' is the earnest prayer of thy loving　　　ALICE."

Frequent mention is made in the letters which follow of visits to "I——'s" and other families living in the neighbourhood. On the side of the hill just below Tswedelle were several little cottages which Alice often used to visit, and where her presence was welcomed with delight. In one of these families particularly, she took a great interest. It consisted of a man, "I——," and his wife and child. They were much interested in hearing her read and explain the Scriptures, and her earnest pleadings with them to attend without delay to their soul's best interests seemed to awaken them to a sense of its paramount importance. Previous to Alice's visits they were not in the habit of going to any place of worship, but afterwards they became constant attenders. At one time Alice had strong hopes that the wife had experienced a change of heart, but subsequently had reason to fear that in both the man and his wife the word of life was like the good seed sown on stony ground and among thorns.

All the neighbours and poor families living near Tswedelle speak of Alice with great affection. One said to her sister, who was visiting her in her cottage a short time after Alice's death, at the same time turning away her face to hide the falling tears, " Her death was one of those mysterious providences for which we cannot account. She was a great loss to the neighbourhood." Many such remarks have been made by those who now miss her bright face and affectionate interest in both their temporal and spiritual welfare. In the following letter to her sister Carrie, " I——" is first mentioned :—

"TSWEDELLE, *June* 19, 1859.

. . . " I felt very drowsy in meeting this morning. I do think I tried with all my human strength to resist it, but all of no avail; then I made up my mind that there was some way for me to get rid of it, as it certainly was not the Lord's will for me to sleep, and, as I had found it utterly impossible to do it myself, He would certainly take it away if I asked with faith. So I asked not only to be kept from drowsi-

ness, but to be made to think just what He would have
me to think; and, indeed, dear Carrie, I never had a
meeting when I seemed so near to Christ; I could
not feel sleepy any more, my heart was so busy praising Him.   I seemed to come to the conclusion, without any effort of thought on my part, that it was my
duty to present the truth to I——'s family; I do not
know what made me even think of them, but I could
not feel a doubt as to my duty.   .   .   .

"After tea I went, and found his wife washing up
the tea things.   I sat down and commenced to talk,
and was in the midst of reading the third chapter of
John when I—— came in, and then I presented the
Gospel.   They seemed to like to hear; said they
knew they were doing wrong in putting off religion
until they should have more time.   I told them they
were neglecting the only thing that could ever make
them happy.   I tried to show them Jesus Christ as
the Way, the Truth, and the Life.   I think I set forth
Christ and nothing else, and urged them to accept
Him now while they had the time and opportunity.
The beautiful plan of salvation never seemed so dear
to me as when I was telling them about it.   They invited me to come again next Sabbath, and I intend
going if nothing happens to prevent.   I gave them
my little 'Come to Jesus,' and I hope they will read
it.

"Pray for me, dear, that I may be enabled not
only to see my duty, but to do it with a real *love*
for it.

"I feel that there is one person before whom I
must lay the truth more fully than I have ever done.
Oh, may the Lord enable me to do it just as He

would have me to do it, with great humbleness, meekness, and gentleness, that I may not injure the cause by any appearance of setting myself up above others ! "

"June 15, 1859.

"Did I tell thee, dear, that father brought me an invitation from Miss —— to meet a few friends there to tea on third day. I felt uncertain as to how large a company it would be, and fortunately met Miss —— at Mrs B——'s that afternoon. I found it was to be quite a large dancing party, and so declined, on the plea that I never intend to go to any more dancing parties or even large companies of any kind. They evidently thought it very strange, but I am glad that I got off on the *true* ground.

. . . "I do hope, my precious sister, that thou mayest be enabled to see thy duty clearly with regard to the work at M——, and that thou mayest have strength given thee from the only true Source to labour faithfully in His cause. Remember that 'His strength is made perfect in our weakness,' and if He has anything for us to do, He will certainly fit us for it ; we ought not to doubt it for a moment.

"I cannot write more now ; but do write to me and strengthen me. With an earnest prayer that we may both be kept in the full light of the Sun of Righteousness, I remain, very lovingly, thy sister,

"ALICE."

To H. W. S.

" TSWEDELLE, *July* 1, 1859.

. . . "I have thought of thee much, dear H——; I know thou hast a very responsible position to fill, and if thou wast alone I should indeed tremble for thee; but I know that He who has all power is simply using thee as an instrument to accomplish His own work, and oh, it is such a comfort to think that as a carpenter does not send his chisel or hammer to do a piece of work, and stand at a distance to watch it, but carefully guides it with his own hand, and it is his skill and power that accomplishes the work, so our great Master does not send His tools to work away from Him, but comes and is Himself the power and skill needed. Surely we should not think it modesty in the poorest tool in the sculptor's studio, should he choose to use it on his finest marble, to refuse on the ground that the end could not be accomplished with it; would it not rather be doubting its master's skill and judgment? The more we realise this, the more our minds will be at rest regarding any labour we may be called to perform." . . .

"*July* 3, 1859.

"My own Dear Carrie,—

. . . "I am sitting in my bay window; it is just after sunset, and the wind, which blows very cool and strong from the west, is bending and tossing about the soft green tree-tops in the woods in the most fascinating and graceful manner, making a delightful, wavy, rustling sound, that really reminds one of the ocean. How lovely our Lord has made everything.

"I have been thinking about holiness, dear Carrie, and I have trembled at the thought of expecting to be kept from sin; but we know that our Master never tells us to do what we cannot do, and He will Himself give us strength to do all things. He says, 'There hath no temptation taken you but such as is common to man; but God *is faithful*, who will not suffer you to be tempted above that ye are able, but will with the temptation also make a way of escape that ye may be able to bear it.' I do believe, Carrie, that we may fail through unbelief and forgetfulness; but then we must always come right back to the blood of cleansing, and promise, through Christ strengthening us, never to do so again. I do not know how to explain myself, but at first I thought that if I should once fall I would never be able to try again, but now I see that it would simply be because I did not have faith enough; so all we must do is to seek for more faith, and keep nearer to Jesus, our strength. . . .

"I have been talking with M—— (the coachman) about Jesus; he says he never prays but in church, but he said he would pray Jesus to give him a new heart, that he might love and serve Him. I wish he really would do it, but I am afraid he will forget it. . . .

"I have a whole heartful to say to thee, darling, but I will only enclose a little piece of poetry I have been enjoying very much. I alter the last two lines of the first verse :—

> 'Father, I know that all my life
>   Is portioned out for me,
> And the changes that are sure to come
>   I do not fear to see;
> For every one will only bring
>   Me nearer home to Thee;

"instead of

> 'But I ask Thee for a present mind
>   Intent on pleasing Thee.'

" I only change it because it gives me more comfort my way.   I enjoy saying it over to myself so much.

" Carrie, dear, there is one thing which I must tell thee, and that is, if thou wants to receive much grace, thou must pray much.   There are many promises in the Bible that we shall receive what we ask for, but He does not promise to give them to us unless we ask for them.   Mrs K—— gave me an idea which I have indeed proved to be true, and one which I confess I was too forgetful of before.   It is the necessity of having frequent stated times during the day when we can stop doing everything else, and pray to and commune with our Lord alone. She said she believed the idea that many had, that if they kept in a spirit of prayer all the time there was no necessity for withdrawing alone for a season of prayer, was the cause of their not growing more in grace. 'We must remember,' said she, 'that our souls must be fed, or we cannot do anything aright, and when we are not in the spirit of prayer, that is just the time when we need the more to go and ask Him who is able to do all things to give us the spirit of prayer.' "

" TSWEDELLE, *July* 19, 1859.

.   .   .   " Thou need not look for us, dear Carrie, until the last of next week, for there are many things I must do first; .   .   .   and what is of far more importance, I have I—— and his wife particularly on my mind just now. .   .   .   I feel such a deep interest in them, and I do pray the Lord to bless them, and make them really His own ; and oh ! I hope He will keep Satan from making me feel for an instant that I have had anything to do in this matter, more than to

deliver the message of the Lord. Indeed I do realise
how perfectly powerless *I* am, and I hope He will
make me realise it more fully still."

To A. U. C.

"TSWEDELLE, *Aug.* 10, 1859.

" MY DEAR FRIEND,—

" I suppose before this reaches thee you will have
heard of the death of our darling little ' baby Alice ; '
but I feel that I must take this first opportunity to tell
you a little more particularly about it, and in what an
especial manner this blow has been softened to her
mother, by the same hand that dealt it. Indeed it
has filled me with wonder to see how He took every
rebellious feeling out of her heart ; and even the sel-
fish sorrow which we by our nature must feel for our
loss seems almost swallowed up in the thought that it
is His will, who doeth all things well ; and then what
is there left for her to mourn for?

" We all know that there is, and must be for a long,
long time, a void, an aching void, in that mother's
heart, which we can little understand, as we cannot
even imagine what the love of a mother towards her
child is ; but when we remember how entirely that
little life was interwoven with her own, how for nearly
eight months that little being was her constant care,
our hearts must ache for her ; but if He fills the
vacancy with Himself, as I know He will, we must
rejoice.

" I must tell thee a little about our darling. Nearly
two weeks ago she was taken with summer complaint,
but was so much better when I arrived at Millville,
just a week ago yesterday, that she came out to the

gate to meet me in her little carriage, looking bright and fat and well. Oh, I should so have loved to have had you see her as she looked that day, in her short clothes, her dainty little feet in such a tiny pair of patent leather slippers, and her whole person so perfectly cunning; but her little face leaning so shyly against the side of her carriage, I do not know how to describe. She never was, before her sickness, what one would call a beautiful child, but that day her great dark violet eyes, so deep and full of meaning, had a peculiar look in them that did not belong to a child of her age, which made me feel anxious about her from that moment. Her complexion was very fair, so pure and transparent that the delicate colouring on her little cheeks was more exquisite than I ever imagined human flesh could be ; and then the sweet rosebud mouth, with the lips just parted in astonishment at her old auntie's big face thrust in her little carriage so unceremoniously. But we have had to watch that darling face grow thinner and paler, and those bright eyes grow dim, until the expression of patient suffering was changed for the peaceful smile of death. She grew worse again the night I got there, although we had no idea that she was dangerously ill until seventh day, when, at the doctor's suggestion, we brought her home to Tswedelle, for change of air, and that night our doctor said she was very sick, that he feared her brain was affected, which indeed proved to be the truth. She rapidly sank, growing weaker and weaker, until second day morning at a quarter to eight o'clock she quietly ceased to breathe, and we knew that her spirit had fled.

" We took her little body to Laurel Hill yesterday,

where they have bought a small piece of ground under the overspreading branches of a great old tulip poplar, in a very retired spot, where the birds sing, and the sun shines through the leaves all day long, on the soft green grass—a fit spot to lay the casket that held our little treasure." . . .

After the funeral of her baby niece, Alice accompanied her sister and brother-in-law on a short journey to Saratoga and the Catskill Mountains; and soon after their return, with her usual disinterested thoughtfulness, went to visit and cheer her sister during her many lonely hours at Millville. The following letters give some account of the journey, and of her visit to Millville :—

"CATSKILL MOUNTAINS, 8th mo. 21, 1859.

"MY OWN DEAREST MOTHER,—

"We received thy note and M——'s this morning : they were forwarded from Saratoga, which place we left yesterday morning. We seemed to get through our visit there, so thought it would be pleasant to just step up here, and take a look off the top; and I am delighted that we did. I think the falls are perfectly lovely; I could spend a day there, for indeed I felt as if I could not help sketching every tree and rock I came to.

"Uncle W—— and Aunt P—— arrived last evening to meet us, and this morning we went to the top of North Mountain, where we sat down on the rocks under the shade of some trees, and read and talked about Jesus.

. . . "Thee don't know, my own sweet little

D -

mother, how it rejoiced my old heart to get thy little bit of a note ; but one thing I missed, and that was a message from father.   Why didn't that dear man send his love ? "

"TSWEDELLE, *Sept.* 6, 1859.

" MY OWN ANNIE,—

.   .   . " Thou art in my mind continually, my darling sister.   It does not seem as if we are so far separated now as we used to be, for we meet every day, and many times a day, at the mercy-seat, and that brings us in reality very near.

" I am so glad thou likes ' The Assurance of Faith;' I think it sets forth the truth in a very clear light; but then, after all, it depends entirely upon the Holy Spirit to bring it home to the heart.   I see more and more clearly that it is not in the power of any one to make another understand the truth ; we can present it, but that is all, and when their eyes are opened then they will see.   .   .   .

" M. M. J—— goes home next week.   I shall be sorry to have her go, for she is so much company, and makes the house so cheerful with her pretty German face always so bright and happy, and her broken English, so quaint it often makes me laugh; and her voice ! I wish thou could hear her sing. She is very lovely and lovable, and, what is better, I do believe, a real Christian, and our mutual love for the Saviour has brought us nearer together than anything else could.   It is so nice to be able to read the Scriptures together, and talk of our glorious hope as we read.   How I long, darling, to enjoy this sweet communion with thee ; but we must not think of what we cannot have; and, indeed, when we have Christ, and the Bible to tell us about Him, and the Holy Spirit to make us understand its teachings, we have enough spiritual blessings to make us wonder how He could be so good to us, in whom, we know, there is no good thing.

. . . "How I do long to see Charley and dear little baby Anna, my only little niece on earth now. I can scarcely bear her to grow so old without my seeing anything of her, and all the sweet little baby ways I love to watch. It seems to me I feel my loss in our little Alice's removal more now than I have at all. While I was with Carrie I was thinking of her loss, but now I am beginning to realise how much I loved her."

CHAPTER IV.

ONE of the first fruits of Alice's labour for the salvation of others was her young friend M. M. J——, who had been spending her summer vacation at Tswedelle. She had enjoyed very few outward religious privileges, but the Lord had prepared her heart, and during this visit she was enabled to receive with remarkable fulness the glorious salvation of Jesus, which it was Alice's privilege to set before her. To her the following letter was addressed :—

"MILLVILLE, *Sept.* 18, 1859.

"MY DEAR M——,

. . . "Tuesday we spent all day, until three o'clock, shopping. I then went up to G——'s, very warm and very tired, and she petted me up, and made me lie down and take a good nap, from which I got up refreshed about tea-time. In the evening we went to see R——'s musical friend. She sang for us, but her voice (don't let it make you vain, little pussy) was not half so sweet to *my* ears as a little robin's I know, so I did not care much for it.

"The next morning I started for Millville, and had

a long and tiresome ride, but as the people in the stage were very quiet, I had a nice time thinking over all that R—— told us the day before. He dwelt on such precious truths, none of which is more necessary to be kept in mind than that of Christ's love. The more we realise this, the more will our poor hearts be filled with peace and joy, and an overwhelming love in return. If we find our hearts growing cold, or doubting, or desponding ; if we see in ourselves a tendency to dislike the work He has given us to do ; or if we feel sad and lonely, or uncharitable to those around us, we will find that it is because we are not looking at Christ's love to us, that wondrous love, which, as we realise it, will fill every want in man's nature. If we dwell on anything short of Christ and His unchanging love, which first awoke us, while we were yet dead in trespasses and sins, to a knowledge of Himself, and which will not surely now forsake us, we find ourselves in darkness. . . .

" It seemed inexpressibly sad to come here and find no baby ; but now it is like a dream that we ever had one at all, it seems so long ago.

" Carrie and I have had two delightful rides on horseback together, but all day yesterday and the day before it rained very hard, so that we did not go out, but I sewed and Carrie read to me in D' Aubigné." . . .

It had been the custom of these sisters during Alice's frequent visits to Millville, before her conversion, to spend much time in boating. Alice was very fond of sketching, and the Maurice River, which ran directly along the foot of the hill upon which the residence of her brother-in-law was situated, the banks of which are very woody and picturesque, afforded her an opportunity of gratifying her taste. Early in the morning, Alice and her sister used to get into their little boat, and row themselves about three-quarters of a mile up the river, where they entered a region so wild and entirely uncultivated that it seemed as if there human beings had never before found their way. The water coming from the cedar swamps was of a dark amber colour, and so clear that the pebbly bottom was plainly visible. In some places the trees nearly met overhead, and here, before some grand old giant of the forest, would they moor their little boat, and while Alice, with sketch-book and pencil, transferred its gnarled and knotty branches to paper, her sister read to her from some favourite author.

In her subsequent visits to Millville, Alice preferred spending the time in visiting the labourers on the place, endeavouring in her weakness to sow precious seed, by bearing the "glad tidings" from house to house. They often, however, spent moonlight evenings on the river, and at such times, while their little bark floated noiselessly on the water, Alice's sweet voice might be heard singing her favourite hymns. Among those most fresh in the recollection of her companions are :—

> " Nearer, my God, to Thee,
> Nearer to Thee,"

and

> "We rest in Christ, the Son of God ;"

also,

> " Guide me, oh, Thou great Jehovah."

One of her especial favourites was " The Lord will

provide." This she committed to memory, and would sometimes repeat for her own and others' comfort. The metrical version of the 23d Psalm was also a great favourite, and was frequently sung by her on these occasions. Her sister, in writing about it after her death, says, "How those times come back to me as I write about them! Precious Alice! I can almost hear her sweet voice floating gently over the water, and feel myself now, as then, drawn nearer to God and our heavenly home."

Alice also very much enjoyed horseback excursions. She was a fearless and daring rider, managing with perfect ease a horse which most ladies would fear to mount, always taking the poorest saddle, and acting as escort to her more timid companion.

Thus would these sisters scour the country for miles around, exploring all the narrow and unfrequented wood roads they came upon. Sometimes they would lose their way, and ride for miles before coming to a log cabin to inquire the direction homeward. These excursions were often turned into work for the Lord, whom they both now delighted to serve. At the lonely cabin of some woodcutter they would stop, and there tell of the gospel of Jesus Christ, which was to these poor ignorant ones good news indeed. Alice generally carried some tracts or leaflets, which she would hand, with a few pleasant words, to the teamsters whom they met, and often as they rode along, her little Testament would be drawn from her pocket, and she would dwell with delight on some comforting promise or sweet assurance of love and support in every time of need.

Her sister relates that on one occasion as they were

returning from a visit to an old hermit, who for fifteen
years had lived by himself in the woods, and though
now dying of consumption, and scarcely able to
gather a few sticks together for a fire, still preferred
his solitary cabin, Alice remarked, "How precious a
thing it is that we have a *free* salvation to offer to the
poor and the ignorant. If they had to do one thing
to earn it, or to make themselves ready to receive it,
I should not be half so happy as I go among them.
Now I go full of joy, knowing that nothing but their
unwillingness to receive the forgiveness of all their
sins through Jesus Christ stands between them and
eternal life. It seems to me it is such an honour to
be allowed the privilege of proclaiming this glorious
gospel of the free mercy and grace of God. I have
been thinking all the morning of that text in Isaiah :
'How beautiful upon the mountains are the feet of
Him that bringeth good tidings, that publisheth salvation,'" adding, "I wonder if it is wrong to apply
it to one's self?"

To A. U. C.

"MILLVILLE, *Sept.* 21, 1859.

"MY OWN DEAR FRIEND,—

  . . . "Carrie and I have been enjoying D'Aubigné's 'History of the Reformation' so much. I do
not see how any one can read it without becoming
convinced that justification by faith in Jesus Christ is
not simply a doctrine of particular sects, but is at the
root of *all* Christianity. 'The Church has fallen,
says D' Aubigné, 'because the great doctrine of justification by faith in the Saviour had been taken away
from her. It was necessary, therefore, before she

could rise again, that this fundamental truth should
be restored to her.' It was this doctrine that was the
stronghold of Luther, and gave him, a poor monk,
with nothing but the truth of God to lean upon, the
power to overthrow the mighty Church of Rome.
'This article of justification,' says Luther, 'is what
creates the Church, nourishes it, edifies it, preserves
and defends it. No one can teach worthily in the
Church, or oppose an adversary with success, if he
does not adhere to this truth.' Let me give thee one
more quotation, but first"—— . . .

The other sheet of this letter has been lost; instead
thereof some of her favourite passages are given as
they were marked and underscored by her, in the
volume of the Reformation which she was then reading.

"I see," says Luther, "that the devil is continually
attacking this fundamental article." . . . "Well,
then, I, Dr Martin Luther, unworthy herald of the
gospel of our Lord Jesus Christ, confess this article,
that *faith alone without works justifies before God.*"
. . . "There is no one," continues he, "who has
died for our sins, if not Jesus Christ the Son of God.
. . . And if it is He alone that taketh away our
sins, it cannot be ourselves and our works. But
good works *follow* redemption, as the fruit grows on
the tree." And of himself he says, "Although I
was a holy and blameless monk, my conscience was
nevertheless full of trouble and anguish. I could not
endure those words—' The righteousness of God.'
. . . But when by the Spirit of God I understood
these words, when I learned how the justification of
the sinner proceeds from the free mercy of our God

through faith, then I felt born again like a new man;
I entered through the open doors into the very para-
dise of God. Henceforward, also, I saw the beloved
and Holy Scriptures with other eyes. . . . And
as previously I had detested with all my heart those
words, 'the righteousness of God,' I began from that
hour to value them and to love them as the sweetest
and most consoling words in the Bible."

Although the subject is too sacred to be fully dwelt
upon, a word must be said in reference to Alice's devotion to her beloved parents. Realising that, as the
only child remaining at home, she was the object of
their tenderest love, it was the natural result of this
feeling to manifest, by every word and action, the
affectionate solicitude of her heart. When absent
from them, she took refuge from undue anxiety on
their account by casting her care upon the Lord, as
will be seen in the following letter :—

"MILLVILLE, *Sept.* 19, 1859.

"MY OWN DARLING MOTHER,—

"Not a word from thee since third day! I try not to
feel anxious, as I know that you are in the hands of
our dear Master, who can and does take a great deal
better care of you than I could were I at home. It
is indeed an inexpressible comfort to leave you with
implicit confidence in His hand, and to know that it
is with a love far surpassing mine that He watches
over my own darling parents, who seem to grow so
much dearer to me every day. . . .

"I often think when we are having a nice cosy
time, one sewing and the other reading aloud in

D'Aubigné, how splendid it would be if we could only have our precious mother sitting with us; but nevertheless truth compels me to say that we have very nice times as it is, and I hope that it is not pleasure alone that we derive from each other's constant companionship. Indeed we ought, with all the privileges that are so mercifully granted us, to grow daily in grace, and learn constantly how best to serve that Master who has done so much for us; and I think nothing will fill the soul so full of a steadfast, resolute endeavour to serve Him, as contemplating the wondrous love and perfect work of our Saviour. The fear of our Creator as a righteous and just Judge may force us into outward obedience, but nothing except looking unto Him, as David did, as ' our *strength* and our *Redeemer*,' can melt our hearts into love and submission to His will and His commandments.

"We rode on horseback out to old Mrs Loder's the other day. Her husband, who, thou knowest, has been feeble for years, is much worse. I do not suppose he can live a great while; but he says he does not dread to go, for although he has never done anything good enough for his Heavenly Father to forgive him his many sins for, yet he feels sure that they will be forgiven and washed away in the blood of ' the Lamb of God, which taketh away the sin of the world.'

" Is it not a noticeable fact that both the great Dr Johnson, who for so many years was diligent in his efforts to win heaven by his own works, and this poor old man, on their deathbeds found their only comfort in abandoning their own righteousness for the righteousness of Christ? "

The old man above referred to, when first visited by the sisters, and questioned as to his hopes of heaven, replied, " That he thought he had as good a right to go happy as anybody ; he hadn't been like other folks, he had always kept the Sabbath, and, when he was well, been to church regular, and he was sure he hadn't never done no harm to nobody." At first it seemed hopeless to find a lodgment for the truth that " *all* have sinned and come short of the glory of God," for " whosoever shall keep the whole law, and yet offend in *one* point, he is guilty of all," and that though " the *wages* of sin " must be " death," " the *gift* of God is eternal life, through Jesus Christ our Lord." It was only after many months visiting that the Holy Spirit opened his understanding to see and his heart to believe that salvation is not of works, but a *free gift* of grace, through faith in Christ Jesus.

He lived some years after this, and it was really delightful to witness his simple childlike faith in his Saviour. Alice's visits were among his chief pleasures ; he particularly delighted in the sweet hymns she loved so much to sing to him. At such times the radiant expression of his face, and the clasping of his hands, while he sat in rapt attention, occasionally breaking in with such exclamations as " That's true ! " or " Precious Jesus ! " would have formed a study for a painter. Though sometimes questioned pretty closely as to the ground of his hope and confidence, the answer was always the same—" *Jesus*," " Jesus has forgiven," or " Jesus is on my side." His past inoffensive life was not now, as formerly, his hope and dependence, but he felt that his feet were firmly planted upon "the Rock of Ages," which could never be moved.

"Tswedelle, *Nov.* 12, 1859.

"My own Carrie,—

"I went to the city on fifth day, and stayed all night with H——. In the evening we had a good talk all by ourselves, but it can't be retailed. One thing H—— talked about that did me good. It was the necessity of making the work which we do especially for Christ the main object, not only of our life, but of every day, and hour, and minute of it. That we should make all our household and social duties subservient to it, instead of it to them, as she clearly showed me that we do. She says we ought every moment, no matter what we are doing, to be watching and waiting for an opportunity of doing or saying something in His cause. If we are not thus waiting, we are making something else the object of our lives, at least for that moment. If we were always thus holding other things subservient to our Master's work, how much more we would find to do ; and even if we did not find anything for a whole day, we should have glorified Him all the same.

"In the morning we spent an hour with Mrs K——. H—— asked her to explain more about 'the gift of holiness,' which the Methodists talk so much about, and which she professes. I wish I could give thee even an idea of what she said. I believe it is simply an entire consecration of the *will*, and an acceptance of Christ as our *strength*. She said it presented itself to her thus : 'Hitherto I have considered that I was free to choose my will or the Lord's

will, to follow Him where He leads or not; but now
I will give up that power and bind myself to choose
the Lord's will always.' And it is from *this* that she
has never fallen; that is, she has never voluntarily
chosen her own way instead of the Lord's. She says
she would not say she has not sinned, for she has
been overcome suddenly, and may sin unconsciously,
but she trusts the Lord for that, and, indeed, for
everything. Personally, she is charming in conversation; but, better than that, I hope I have learned from
her. How I wished for thee! Darling, is thy will con-
secrated? I think mine *is*. It is a fearfully solemn
thing to say, but it is a solemn thing to live."

"Nov. 23d, 1859. I have been walking very
quietly the past week, dear Carrie, doing little
apparently for the Lord. I have been held by the
iron fingers of surrounding circumstances; but I
know that it is for some good purpose, or the Lord
would not have allowed it. . I hope and pray that it
may teach me the lesson intended.

"I have been made to think very seriously about
those passages: 'If any man will confess me before
men, him will I confess before my Father' (Matt. x.
32). 'If thou shalt confess with thy *mouth* the Lord
Jesus, and shalt believe in thine heart that God hath
raised Him from the dead, thou shalt be saved'
(Rom. x. 9). . . .

"I was very glad to hear about thy talks with J.
M—— and B——; how strange it is that it takes us
so long to learn that these things are privileges! I
wonder when we shall begin to think how much we can
do, and not how little. The trouble is, that we think

we do want to do much, but it must be just what
suits our tastes. What hearts we have!"

To M. M. J.

"Tswedelle, *Dec.* 3, 1859.

"My Dear M——,

"I took tea with R—— the other evening, and we
had a good talk about the things of the kingdom, and
our dear Saviour's love to us. Just think, dear
M——, of our all singing praises together some day,
before the throne of the Lamb! How very trivial
are all the cares and troubles that look to us now so
very grievous, when compared with the great joy
that will fill our hearts then; and to think that it will
last *for ever!* The thought of its all being a free gift,
just given to us out of mercy, makes me so happy.
Sometimes I think Christians are very apt, in directing
all their attention to living a Christian life, to forget
about this great salvation which we have so freely received, and the love that gave it, which always remains the same, however we may change. They
really forget the gift, in their anxiety to show their
gratitude for it; in fact, they get to looking at themselves instead of at Christ. My heart's desire and
prayer for us both is, that we may be filled with the
love of Christ, until all *self* is lost in Him.

"In thinking, darling, about the prayers of other
Christians being more likely to be answered than our
own, I think we should take into consideration what
it is that makes a prayer effectual. Let us use an
illustration. Suppose a prisoner is entreating a judge
for pardon; the first thing urged is the great need for
the favour asked, and the next and all-important thing

is a righteous plea, or ground on which it can be granted without offending stern justice. Now, if such a plea be wanting, however eloquently the case is urged, if the judge is righteous, the favour is not granted; but if the plea be good, no matter how feebly the thing is stated, it will be granted.

"And is it not the same with our petitions to our Heavenly Father? Have we not all great need? and oh, happy thought! have not all who believe in Jesus a righteous plea to bring? And if so, have they not all the same reason why their prayers should be answered? If it depended upon our own righteousness, or the eloquence of our appeals, whether our prayers would be heard, then, indeed, would our humility force us to feel that others' prayers were more acceptable than our own. But when we remember that our requests are not granted for *our* sakes but for *Christ's* sake, we must be convinced that it makes no difference by whom the prayer is offered, if it be but asked believing that it will be answered for Christ's sake. Do not misunderstand me, dear, and think that I do not value the prayers of others. I think it a great comfort to be able to pray for our friends, and also to feel that they pray for us. . . .

"It is very nice, dear M——, to think of you as taking the same comfort that I do in feeling that our Lord knows and permits every little occurrence in our lives, and that nothing could happen to us without His will; when we realise that He is constantly watching over and loving us, it is much easier to get along.

"You speak of your Sabbath-school. I am very

glad you have a class. Do not be discouraged, even if your scholars seem unpromising; remember it is the Lord's work, and He will take care of it and fit you for it. It is a great comfort to me whenever I think of speaking to any one about Christ, to realise that if the Lord has anything for me to say to them, He will show me what it is, and will give me both the opportunity and the strength to say it. I really am astonished more and more every day at the great goodness of the Lord. O M——! we need never fear: He will take care of us. Sometimes when, as you say, a cloud seems to cover us, and we cannot see Him, or realise that He really does love and pity us, it is very hard to hold fast to our faith. But do not let us doubt Him. Surely it was out of pure mercy that ' He spared not His own Son, but delivered Him up for us all; how shall He not with Him also freely give us all things?' . . .

"With an earnest prayer to our Lord Jesus Christ, that He will perfect His will both in you and through you to those around you, I am your affectionate friend."

"PHILA., *Dec.* 28, 1859.

"MY OWN PRECIOUS MAMMA,—

"Thy letter, written yesterday, came to hand at dinner-time, much to my satisfaction. If thee isn't the sweetest little mother that ever lived to say so kindly that thee is not lonely, and that I had better stay a few days longer, if I wish to! But I would not encroach upon thy kindness, if there were not some reasons why it seems evidently best. , . .
I hope by staying to get a chance of presenting the

E

gospel to L——, and letting her see at least what the Christian faith *is*. She is in such a net of Unitarianism that she has probably seldom heard much of anything else. I am also very glad of another chance of hearing Guinness, as I feel I am learning from him. The more I see of him, the more surprised I am to find how much he preaches many of the truths held by Friends, the guidance of the Holy Spirit, &c.

. . . "I expect you are enjoying D'Aubigné very much. I think I never read anything, the Bible, of course, excepted, that proves so clearly that 'justification by faith in Christ is, as he says, at the root of *all* Christianity. How clearly he shows that when the Church lost this fundamental truth, it sank into heathenish darkness, until our kind Heavenly Father sent Luther to preach the glorious truth that salvation is the ·gift of God,' and cannot be bought by 'indulgences,' fastings, or *any other* good works of our own."

To a friend about to be married, she writes :—

"TSWEDELLE, *Jan.* 4, 1860.

. . . "Dear ——, I long to see thee wedded to another, a *heavenly* Bridegroom, one from whom death could not separate thee, nor time estrange. I should then, indeed, be sure that thou would be happier than any earthly circumstances, however propitious, could possibly make thee. O dear friend! to know and be sure that death to thee will be but the Bridegroom taking the bride home to Himself, is inexpressibly sweet. But, dear, thou never can know this until thou hast cast thyself as a helpless,

sinful child, upon the Lord Jesus Christ, to be and
do everything for thee, to cleanse thee from thy sins,
to save thee from the consequences of them, to sanctify thy soul, and to give thee of His strength that
thou may glorify Him. Until thou trusts Him entirely and *alone*, and ceases to trust in thyself for
salvation, and hast become, like Abraham, fully
persuaded that ' what He hath promised He is able
also to perform,' thou never can know this rest. I
am confident that in the bottom of thy heart thou
feels that trusting in a general way to the mercy of
God is very unsatisfactory. I know that there is a
fascination in dwelling upon what we conceive to be
the nobleness, greatness, and goodness of humanity,
until in our own wisdom we exclaim, ' God has said
He is a God of *love ;* surely if He is so, He cannot
refuse to pardon man, at least while he has this *germ*
of good in him so fit to be ripened in heaven.'
But, ah, God's ways are not as our ways, neither
are His thoughts as our thoughts ; and is it not just
possible that God, in the light of His own perfect
righteousness, may pronounce as ' filthy rags ' what
our poor sin-defiled eyes can only behold as the most
precious cloth of gold? I have become satisfied that
it is poorly worth while for us, with our finite minds,
to judge what the infinite Being has declared, by what
seems right to our reason. If God had not spoken
to man, then man would have been left to use his own
imagination ; but God *has* spoken, and requires that
man should believe what He says, even if it does
seem like foolishness to him, for ' the foolishness of
God is wiser than men.' Is not this what earthly
parents require of their children ? and has not the

Creator a vastly superior right to act thus towards us?

"Excuse me, dear, for speaking thus freely; but I do so long that thou should be convinced that there are not *many* ways of salvation, but only *one;* that 'there is none other name under heaven given among men whereby we must be saved but that of Jesus Christ.' . . . All are under condemnation until they are washed and made clean in the blood of Jesus; and until a person is convinced of this, there is no use in speaking of that great Saviour who died that all who put their trust in Him might live; for behold, they make this wondrous sacrifice for sin of none effect, for if it is not needed by man, then, indeed, has Christ died in vain. And it amounts to the same thing to say that one can be accepted of God without a real vital union with Christ. . .

"I suppose you have heard of H. Grattan Guin. ness, the Irish preacher, who is doing such a wonderful work in Philadelphia. I did not expect to like him, as popular men so seldom preach only 'Christ, and Him crucified,' as St Paul said he did; but Guinness really does, and with wonderful power."

"TSWEDELLE, *Jan.* 4, 1860.

" MY DEAR CARRIE,—

. . . "It has been so very long since I have written thee, at least I have lived such a lifetime since then, that I hardly know what to say. I have so much, so very much, that I long to make thee understand; but even if I were with thee, I do not think I could put it all in words, much less on paper.

"In the first place, I have not written thee since I

stood by E——'s bed, a short time before she breathed her last. I cannot express all it made me realise. I am sure I never realised before the greatness of the gift of eternal life, and what a Saviour Christ is. Oh, what should we do without Him? How could we live, and how could we meet death? We are, indeed, but as an atom of dust, utterly helpless. If His hand should cease to hold us up, where should we be? I could have said all this before, but I never knew what it meant; but, oh! what inexpressible comfort to hear Christ say, 'Whosoever believeth in me, though he were dead, yet shall he live, and whosoever liveth and believeth in me shall never die.'

"I spent Christmas week with H—— in the city; we heard Guinness almost every day, and I felt very thankful for the privilege, for he has taught me a great deal, particularly with regard to the love of God. I thought I knew it, but I find that I am only beginning to learn a part of it. I enjoyed my visit thoroughly, but have been tempted by Satan to sink under the weight of responsibility, yet hope I am learning that 'faith is without anxiety.'"

January 6, 1860.

"I want to tell thee, darling Carrie, how my heart has been drawn out in prayer for ——, I have such strong faith that it really surprises myself. I think it has come in answer to prayer that I might have the faith; and while outwardly there is no apparent hope, I believe the Lord *will do it*, although I have often to fight to keep this faith. And now I do so wish thou could let thy whole heart out in prayer that the Lord will glorify Himself in this instance. Do beseech Him to give thee faith, and pray *daily* and *hourly ;* for the promise is clear, 'If two of you shall agree on earth as touching anything that they shall ask, it shall be done for them of my Father which is in heaven.'"

"TSWEDELLE, *Jan.* 13, 1860.

" DEAREST CARRIE,—

" It is just a week to-day since I have been in the house with this cold, and I really can say that I am thankful for it—this week of quiet I mean—for I have realised that the Lord knew all about it, and that He had not a thing for me to do out of the house, or He would not have shut me up so completely. Being, therefore, at ease concerning the whole world, I turned my attention to trying to fulfil His will in retirement, and I think He has been teaching me.

" In the first place, I have found that it is harder to keep one's own spirit right one hour, lying on the bed doing nothing, than to do a great many outwardly hard things; and I have had such a realisation that Christ is as really and actually our strength for this as for other things. I don't know exactly how to express what I mean, but without a single good feeling to look up and say—

'Lord, I am Thine, be Thou my might,'

and know that He is keeping us that moment. This is the kind of faith that I believe we must exercise if we would be kept from sin; and it is this I have been learning practically. But as I know that with every accession of faith there must come, also, the trial of that faith, so I can hardly call this my own or fairly in my possession until it has passed through trials which I know are to come. . . .

" I understand what thou means by speaking to, and praying for, people ; I am convinced it is a great truth, so let us be encouraged ; we can pray always when we have no opening for outward service. Do not be discouraged, dear ; the Lord has thy life laid out as an outline map ; He knows all about it, and is portioning out every day as it comes. All thy part is to look up and say, ' Let Thy will be done this day ;' and so, giving thy hand to Him, let Him lead thee. This is very simple, but hard to practice.

" This quiet the Lord gives thee is not for naught ; He is preparing thee for His own work in some way known only to Himself. . . .

" One thing more, dear ; do let us make it an especial subject of prayer that, during our expected visit to New York, we may both be enabled to live every moment to the glory of God, doing everything as unto the Lord, and never forgetting for an instant whose we are. I feel this particularly important, as I know that polite conversation on general topics is a great snare to me, as I am very apt not to take my religion into it ; and I know that if the Lord does not keep me I shall dishonour Him. Thou knows our old way of looking at things is entirely opposed to the religion of Jesus, and I think our enemy will strive to entice us, at least in a degree, to return to things which are behind, instead of pressing forward to those which are before. Ah ! to walk in the spirit of Christ, that is what we are to do ; and He alone can keep *me*."

In the early part of second month Alice went, in

company with her sister Carrie, to New York, to
attend the wedding of a friend, to whom she was to
act as bridesmaid. As might be expected from the
prayerful spirit in which this visit was undertaken,
which is manifested in the foregoing letter, while she
went through with all the duties of her position, she
was very much preserved from a worldly spirit, as
will be seen by the following letters to her sister,
who returned to her home shortly after the wedding :—

"NEW YORK, *February* 9, 1860.

" MY OWN DARLING CARRIE,—

" Thou cannot tell how alone I felt yesterday morning after seeing you off; but I concluded it was a good
chance riding up in the omnibus to have a quiet time,
so shut my eyes to keep the world out, and though
the enemy tried his best to put worldly thoughts under
the eyelids, I appealed to One who is greater than he,
and I realised Him as my strength.

" Thou knows we were engaged to —— for that
evening. In the afternoon there were many little
things to do, and then came the weary dressing ; it
was more tiresome even than the evening before, but
finally the bride and three bridesmaids descended to
the parlours at exactly nine o'clock, ready to go. It
was almost as great a crowd as the night before, and
such dressing ! This is the outside; as for the inside,
it was more satisfactory than some of the parties have
been. I could say, ' Jesus, lover of my soul,' and
feel that He was hiding me in His bosom. I had a
chance to confess Christ to —— . . .

" I have just had a little talk with ——. She has cut me to the heart; she thinks that the Unitarians do not dishonour Christ at all, and that there is no harm in their doctrine; they say there is something divine in every heart which only needs developing, and she says this is Christ appearing in their hearts, and if they honour and obey it they honour Him, and are all right. Oh, do pray for us; my heart aches in its very depths! . . .

" I have said little of my inner life; but, oh! there is such a fight all the time going on there to keep the faith, and finish the work He has given me to do, that I am so tired." . . .

"NEW YORK, *Feb.* 18, 1860.

" I have much to tell thee, dear C——, but I don't know where to begin. I do not know when I shall go home: I seem to have a concern on my mind not yet fulfilled; but I hope by the last of the week to feel at liberty to return to the quiet of my peaceful home. My visit here has been much more satisfactory since the parties were over.

" I had a very nice visit to ——. I spent two hours, I should think, with them; it was intensely interesting, and very satisfactory. I had a great concern on my mind about ——'s preaching that we have the *guidance* of the Holy Spirit before we are Christians. I could not bear that with so much truth he should preach this error which undermines the whole, so I concluded he should be made to think about it any way, if the Lord should give me opportunity, which He did that afternoon. —— seemed to agree very nearly with me, and said she had been thinking

much on the subject, and felt it to be a very important one.   .   .   .

"I wish I knew what the Lord's will really is about
my going home. I don't feel as if my mission is
accomplished, so I am afraid to set the time, and yet
I cannot leave it unset. I have not yet found a private
opportunity to speak to ——, although I think he has
heard considerable truth; but he is not aware that he
needs Jesus. I have left it with the Lord; I know He
will take care of it.   .   .   .

"The other day I went with N. S. to see Bella
Cooke, a woman who enjoys what the Methodists
call 'the gift of holiness.' She has been confined
to her bed for years, and yet seems to do nothing but
praise the Lord all the time. It was perfectly refreshing to see her, and hear her talk. She gave us a little
history of her life, which made me cry. How I wish
thou could see her. My darling, I am in the same
loving and protecting arms,   THY SISTER."

"TSWEDELLE, *Feb.* 28, 1860.

"MY DEAR CARRIE,—

"I am by the Lord's will safely home once more,
and am determined to spend a part of this first evening talking to thee, while dear mother sits by me
talking to me. Well it is all over, and I don't know
how to thank the dear Lord for His goodness to me
during this season of so much temptation and such great
responsibilities. I doubtless have erred in judgment
many times, but I feel sure that He will overrule even this
to His own glory. There is such a great work going
on among our friends in New York, or, perhaps, I
should say the beginning of a great work. —— came

with me this morning as far as Elizabethtown. He evidently has and approves of the assurance of faith, as he said that no one could serve God until he had received pardon. He says he is free to confess that he has come to much clearer views on this subject lately, much to the comfort of his own soul; and he thinks the Bible is so very clear all through in setting forth that we must be justified before we can be sanctified, that he can scarcely see how we could have remained so long in darkness on this most important subject.

"I also had several very interesting talks with ———. He declared he never had heard of this gospel before. He thought it beautiful, and meant to go to the Bible to see if it were true. May the Lord take the truth home to his heart!"

"TSWEDELLE, *March* 2, 1860.

"DEAR CARRIE,—

"It is a glorious morning! The sun shines down upon the earth, and the earth seems to smile back upon the sun. I really seem to hear nature's hymn of praise to the Lord, and my heart sings too. I am convinced that we don't praise Him enough practically. We surely ought to look more at His mercy and power, and not so much at the temptation around us. For myself, I know that I often gaze and gaze at the snares and pitfalls around me, until I sigh, thinking, 'How shall I ever get by them?' when I ought to rejoice in that His powerful arm is my aid, and there is no fear while resting entirely on Him; but I do not realise enough the personality of Jesus, and His power and glory."

To M. M. J.

"Does my dear little M—— think that her old friend has forsaken her or forgotten her? Oh, no, no: she knows better than that; for even if my old affection should grow cold—which it never will—there is—oh happy thought!—a new bond of sympathy between us, which all eternity can never change; for have we not the same precious Saviour, and does He not watch over us both with the same unchanging love? and when we raise our hearts in love and adoration to Him, do we not meet there? It is very sweet to think of this; and it draws us very close together, does it not? . . . I will try to give you a glimpse of my doings since New Year's, when we were together.

"I had a bad attack of neuralgia after I returned from the city, which, with a severe cold, kept me in the house and bed about two weeks; and, will you believe it, I really enjoyed it, I had such a splendid time to think over all Guinness had taught me of the wondrous love of God. It is enough to occupy our thoughts for all our lives, and even then we shall not know it all. Truly, as he said, there is no rest but in the love of Christ. O M—— ! I have had such a treat in reading A. Newton on the Songs of Solomon. I feel now that I never read any poetry before I read these songs. They develop 'the idea of Christ as the Bridegroom of the Church,' which is one of great comfort and joy to me. I do nothing but dream Solomon's Songs now; but I cannot stop to try even to tell you what deeper depths of Christ's love I have been allowed to contemplate lately.

"You know I was to go to N. Y., to be bridesmaid for a friend, in February. C—— and I spent a week first in Brooklyn, and had a very nice time ; then came the wedding and all the gaieties. I did not know that I should have to go to so many parties, or I would have hesitated about accepting the honour of bridesmaid ; but as it was, they did me no harm, and on several occasions I had a chance to speak a word for Jesus at them, so I did not mind it much.

. . . "May you indeed grow in the knowledge of the love of God, for the more we know of His love, the more we shall love, and serve, and glorify Him. With this prayer, I am, as ever, your loving

"ALICE."

CHAPTER V.

ALICE was deeply concerned for the salvation of her unconverted friends, and many letters written to such are remarkable for their clear and simple statements of gospel truth. It has, however, been found impossible to insert them all, and only some of those written in the earlier part of her Christian life have been retained. While much of the fruit of her labours has been manifested, eternity alone will reveal all the blessings which are the result of these letters, written in faith and with many prayers.

"TSWEDELLE, *April* 19, 1860.

"MY DEAR FRIEND,—

"I am as much surprised at finding myself writing to you again as you probably are at receiving another letter from me. I should not have thought of doing so, but I believe the Lord has given me a concern to write to you, for I cannot shake it off. It certainly is not the Lord's will that you should continue thus doubting His mercy toward you, when there is absolutely nothing but unbelief between you and perfect peace, and there is no reason why you should not, this very night, nay, this very hour, know that all your sins are forgiven, and that you are a child of God. You cannot find any reason in yourself, and surely you cannot in God. You may have been prevented by something which you saw in your own heart, which you imagine was a sufficient reason why you should not feel sure of God's forgiveness; but if God were to say that nothing that you can find in your heart is an insurmountable obstacle to your being forgiven and accepted as His child now, at this very time, would you not believe it? And this is just what God has said. He says He will forgive you out of pure mercy, because Christ gave Himself a ransom for your sins, and not because of any worthiness, or even partial worthiness, in you; for He tells you Himself that you are utterly unworthy; but exactly as you are, He can and does forgive you all your sins freely for Christ's sake, if you will only believe Him when He tells you so. But if, when you ask to be forgiven, you doubt and say to yourself, 'I cannot dare to believe that all my sins will be forgiven now, because my heart is not right, it is so cold, or, perhaps, indifferent,' are you not saying in effect that when God does forgive you, you expect Him to do it because your heart is right at the time you ask Him? If so, you are expecting Him to forgive you for your own sake, and not for Christ's; or, at best, partly for your own sake, and partly for Christ's sake.

"No wonder you feel no confidence in this hope, for God only promises to do it for Christ's sake alone, and it is by resting your hopes entirely on His promises, and nothing else, that you can really feel confidence and true peace. Are you not just keeping yourself from the joy of knowing yourself forgiven by an idea which has no foundation in the truth of the case?

" Oh, throw it aside; give up the idea of making yourself better before you come trustingly to Jesus, and do not dishonour His free mercy any longer by doubting its reality, but listen now to the glad tidings.

" ' Jesus Christ died to save sinners.' And are you not a sinner? And did He not die for you? And if He died for you, are you not, by virtue of His death, reconciled and forgiven? Oh, all you need is to believe it!

" ' He that believeth hath eternal life.' Christ is a perfect Saviour; His atonement is not only sufficient for the forgiveness of your past sins, but for the present sinful condition of your heart. Trust in it, take it to God as your plea for acceptance, and take it as your reason for believing that He has heard your prayer. Just rest all your hope on Christ. Ask and trust Him to do everything for you, to help you to trust in Him, to strengthen your faith in Him, and to make you what He would have you to be.

" You cannot think that He will refuse to hear you. Has He not said, ' Him that cometh unto me, I will in nowise cast out;' and He cannot be untrue to His word."

" MILLVILLE, *April* 3, 1860.

" MY DEAR FATHER,—

" Thy ' voluntary and entirely spontaneous letter,' written at mother's ' earnest solicitations,' was duly received this afternoon, and was read with much relish. . . . We drove out to see the old Loder-man this morning; he is still alive, though very weak indeed. He was delighted with thy old dressing-gown which we took him, and said it would keep him so warm; he is always chilly, even with a hot fire. It really seemed to be the very thing needed. He appeared glad to hear us sing some hymns. I thought even my dear father would have been convinced that it is only the abuse and not the use of singing hymns that is wrong. It seemed to soothe his feelings so when we sang Cowper's beautiful one, commencing

'There is a fountain filled with blood,' &c.

"He said it did him so much good to hear those words; they were all true, every word of them, and he thought of them when we were gone, and they seemed to go to just the right place in his heart. He has a great deal of simplicity, of course, in his way of expressing himself; but I think he has a firm trust in the Saviour. He said he could not last long; perhaps before we came again he would be gone. I asked him how he felt when he thought of dying. He replied that he was not afraid to die, for Jesus was his friend. He does love to hear all about Christ's having died to save sinners, and likes to dwell on His wondrous love and kindness to him. It really is a great pleasure to go and see him."

It gave Alice's parents much pleasure to gather all their children and grandchildren about them in the summer season for a long visit. As this was the only time during the year the sister from St John was able to come on, it was looked upon by all as a season of great enjoyment. It was on one of these visits home,

F

the first after Alice had become a child of God, that
she was made the means of blessing to this sister.
Although Annie had been a Christian for years, she
had not Alice's simple faith, and consequently not
her rejoicing confidence; and she could not be long
in the company of this young disciple without feeling
that though only a babe in Christ, Alice had an
assured confidence in Him, to which she was a
stranger.

As the trio of sisters together read and studied the
Scriptures, many passages came out in a new light.
Alice often had some forcible illustration or quotation
from a favourite author which made the subject more
plain. She frequently quoted the words : "For one
look at self take ten looks at Christ," and her sister
felt that it was just here that she needed to take a step
forward. If she would be happy and vigorous in her
Christian life she must, like Alice, look past her own
sins and shortcomings, to Christ's atonement for sin,
and His power to save to the uttermost; and it was
not long before Alice's heart was made glad in seeing
this sister, who had formerly so faithfully endeavoured
to lead her youthful steps into the narrow way,
brought to rejoice in like full assurance of faith with
herself.

Alice's quiet influence was ever after felt by Annie
to be a means of strength and establishment. The
latter thus refers to it : " Dear Alice grew very rapidly
in grace, and in the knowledge of our Lord Jesus
Christ, for in after years she became my teacher in
many things."

After her conversion, Alice felt that these family
reunions were seasons of deep responsibility, as well

as times of great enjoyment. Not only should they be able to see in each other growth and advancement since their last meeting, but the very meetings themselves should be as stepping-stones onward in their Christian life. Alice often made it a special subject of prayer, for weeks before these visits, that herself and sisters might be strengthened to put aside other things in order to devote a quiet hour every day to the reading of the Scriptures and unitedly seeking the throne of grace. She particularly enjoyed united prayer, saying that there was an especial blessing promised to it. She delighted to plead, Matt. xviii. 19, " If two of you shall agree on earth as touching anything," &c., and often dwelt upon it with a peculiar faith.

The following letter refers to this annual meeting under the parental roof :—

"TSWEDELLE, *May* 6, 1860.

" MY DARLING CARRIE,—

" I can scarcely write, I want to see thee so much. We look forward with a great deal of pleasure to seeing thee next week, if the Lord sees best to allow us the privilege of being all once more together.

" Oh, is it not a perfect rest to know that He always does everything just right, and will never deny us any privilege or happiness, unless He knows in His infinite love and wisdom that it is not best for us. Don't thee remember how afraid of the future I used to be? It is such a comfort never to have to worry about it any more. . . .

" I suppose thou wants to hear all about us, but there does not seem much to tell; the time goes by so fast without bringing much to pass, that it sometimes

quite distresses me ; but I am sure we only want to
please the Lord, so if we try each moment, we need
not worry ourselves about the whole."

" Tswedelle, May 28, 1860.

" My own Carrie,—

"A whole week to-day since I wrote thee last !
Too bad, I know, but I am sure if thou had been
here thou would not have wondered at it, for although
it was rainy nearly all last week, still there seemed no
time to spare, and we did nothing, after all, but go
three times to see a sick man. He is not a Christian,
but likes to hear us talk, though I fear he is not aware
either that he is dying or that he is a sinner. Did I
tell thee about our going to M——'s last first day
afternoon? We walked there, and, to our surprise,
they, that is the old people, seemed glad to see us.
Mrs M—— said she had been wishing I would come
again and talk to her ever since I was there last
winter, and Mr M—— seemed very cordial, and
wanted us to come again ; so last first day we went.
His sister was there. He said he brought her over on
purpose, as she said she would like to hear us talk.
I feel it to be a great responsibility, as well as a great
privilege ; but I cannot doubt but that the Lord is thus
opening my way Himself, so I leave all anxiety about
it with Him, as I am sure He never calls us to do
anything in His service without giving us the strength
and wisdom needed."

The following letter is addressed to the invalid
whom she mentioned having visited in New York
during her stay there in the second month :—

"Tswedelle, *May* 29, 1860.

"My Dear Bella Cooke,—

"It has been so long since I promised to write to you that I fear you think I have forgotten you, and the talks that we had upon the subject of holiness when I had the privilege of visiting you last February. But it is far otherwise, for I often thank the Lord for taking me to your bedside, there to learn more of the simplicity of the way of faith. You helped me very much, although you did not, I confess, clear away all my difficulties.

. . . "How often I think of what you said, that it is just trusting the Lord moment by moment, and not for the future, as I was trying to do. I was trying to grasp holiness 'for a whole year ahead,' and trying to feel sure that I should not sin all that time, instead of just leaving the past and future, and clinging to Jesus to save me from sin at the present moment, *trusting Him* also to help me to *trust Him* the next minute when it comes. Oh, what a rest it is to be thus trusting the Lord! and yet I sometimes think I am the most unfaithful child my Saviour ever had who has entered into the way of holiness and entire dedication, for I so often forget to trust Him, and, of course, fall into sin. But praise be unto His holy name, He always brings me back to wash again in His own precious blood! Is it not wonderful how good He is? It astonishes me every day to see that He can love and bless so abundantly such a poor worthless creature as I am.

"I should have written you before on this subject, but my time has been, from several circumstances, very much occupied, and all that I could spare for

letter-writing has been pretty much taken up by letters
to a number of my friends who have not yet known
Christ as their Saviour, some of whom seemed really
to be inquiring what they should do to be saved, and
to whom I felt it to be my first duty and privilege to
tell the glorious 'glad tidings' that Jesus Christ died
to save sinners."

The following letter was to one of those inquiring
friends above referred to, and to whom she had previously addressed several letters showing forth the
gospel of the grace of God, only one of which we
have before found room to insert, under date of April
19, of this year :—

"TSWEDELLE, *June* 27, 1860.

" MY DEAR FRIEND,—

"I mentioned to A—— your trouble about the text in
James, and she gladly wrote out for you a few thoughts
upon it, which I enclose.. They are very nearly what
I tried to express to you the other day, and are to me
satisfactory.

" The more I think of it, and view the chapter as a
whole, the more clearly I seem to see that this is
James' true meaning—

" 'Ye see how that by works a man is justified,
and not by faith only' (James ii. 24).

" 'Was not Abraham our father justified by works
when he offered up Isaac his son upon the altar?'
(James ii. 21).

" 'Therefore being justified by faith we have peace
with God through our Lord Jesus Christ' (Romans
v. 1).

"' For if Abraham were justified by works, he hath whereof to glory, but not before God. For what saith the Scriptures? Abraham believed God, and it was accounted unto him for righteousness' (Romans iv. 2).

" These passages being all true, must perfectly agree. Now, we have abundant proof from every part of Scripture that we are saved, reconciled, and made the children of God by faith in Christ Jesus alone, and that all works are but the natural consequence of faith, as breathing is the natural effect of being alive.

" Now, James seems to contradict and, disagree with Paul, still both are true. It is evident that Paul speaks of the sovereign act of God in justifying or pardoning the sinner, while James speaks of the man's faith being justified in the eyes of all who behold. The man is justified as a Christian, or his faith is justified: as when a man is tried before a court of justice for murder: if positive proof is found that he was in another place at the time the deed was committed, that proof justifies the man as innocent, but that proof does not make him innocent.

" James speaks to those who have a dead faith, who say, 'I believe,' 'I have faith,' and still prove by their works, and thoughts, and desires, that they have no faith. Therefore we must justify our faith by our works.

" Paul means to say—a man is saved by believing in our Lord Jesus Christ.

" James means—a man shows that he believes by his works.

" Both are perfectly true. As an illustration, James

says, 'Was not Abraham our father justified by works when he offered up Isaac, his son, upon the altar?' He could not mean here the sovereign act of God in making Abraham his child and saving him, for that was done many years before, when God called him to leave his own country, and promised He would make of him a great nation (Gen. xii. 2, 3).

"When God promised him a son 'Abraham believed God, and it was counted unto him for righteousness.' He was at that time a saved and justified man, in Paul's sense of the word. A great many years passed before that promise was fulfilled and Isaac was born, and the child was at least twelve years old before Abraham's faith was proved or justified by offering him upon the altar.

"In James ii. 14, we see an instance of a mere profession of faith: 'What doth it profit, my brethren, though a man say he have faith and have not works? Can faith save him?' or can such a faith save him? It is not the active living faith Paul speaks of as justifying a man. 26th verse: 'For as the body without the spirit is dead, so faith without works is dead also.' If we see the body of a man lying cold and motionless and stiff, we say that man is dead. But if we see a man moving and walking and talking, we say he is alive ; but we do not say that walking or talking makes him alive : they only prove that he is alive.

"In the 1st chapter, 27th verse, James says, 'Pure religion and undefiled before God and the Father is this, to visit the fatherless and widow in their affliction, and to keep himself unspotted from the world.' He here speaks of what the Christian life should be, and not what we must do to be saved. He does not say we must do this to become a Christian, but this is the effect of being a Christian."

TO A FRIEND WHO HAD LOST A BROTHER.

"MILLVILLE, *July* 19, 1860.

"My DEAR L——,—

"I have been sitting several minutes with my pen in hand, at a loss to know how to express, even in the faintest degree, the heart full of love and tenderness that has been reaching out toward you in yearning sympathy ever since I heard of your great bereavement. Dear L——, I cannot express it; it only sounds cold when I say that I give you my sincere sympathy; but I am sure if I could put my arms round your neck, and draw you close to me, I could make you feel that I do sympathise with you. I know I cannot realise half the natural grief that must fill your heart at thus parting with one so near and dear to you, whose heart has beat closely to yours for so many years, not only in the warm love of a brother, but in the closer bonds of Christian fellowship; this must make you miss him even more, and yet I know that it is in just this that you find your consolation; this tie is not severed: closer even it is drawn, for it has drawn you closer still to Jesus. In Him, emphatically, now he has his being. The bosom of Jesus is his only and perfect resting-place. And is it not the same with you? Yes, indeed, I rejoice in the knowledge that you do not sorrow as one without comfort; the thought of the sure and eternal inheritance awaiting your brother in Christ Jesus must give you great comfort. And then for yourself to know that all things are portioned out for you by the loving hand of your tender Shepherd gives sweetness to your severest sorrow, does it not? For Him you can bear it, for Him you can live, although all pleasure seems gone. To know that one all-powerful and loving is watching and guiding your feeble, faltering, and weary steps through this vale of shadows, straight upward to that eternal dwelling-place in Himself, where all joy and all love are perfected in one unbroken song of praise, must, indeed, be a comfort that no earthly sorrow or trouble can take from you. Is it not so? For however we may fail to realise or feel it, we know the fact remains the same—the glorious fact that we are numbered among Christ's own flock; and if the flock of a faithful earthly shepherd is his constant care, and its wants his continual thought, surely the Good Shepherd will not let us want."

"TSWEDELLE, *July* 31, 1860.

" My own Darling Sister Annie,—

. . . "I had a delightful and very satisfactory visit at Millville; and yet it is very nice to get home again, mother is so sweet, and everything looks so homelike.

"O Annie ! the Lord is so good to me. I do not know how to thank Him, or even begin to; but I must not stop to speak of this now.

. . . "On reaching home, I found that on the next day they were expecting C. H——, the young girl we talked to at S——, to spend two weeks. Yesterday she duly arrived, and after tea we all went to ride. C—— and I went in the buggy, which gave us a good chance for a talk. She commenced by thanking me for Malan's tracts, which I sent her. She said she had read and re-read, and liked them very much ; they seemed to make it so plain and simple (the way of salvation I suppose she meant), that while she read the ' True Cross ' it seemed as if the old man was in just the position she had been in all her life. I asked if now she felt that all her sins were blotted out, and that she was reconciled to God. She said she scarcely dared to say yes, for it seemed like presumption, and yet she did hope she believed, and so was the child of God. Thou can imagine what I said. Do pray for her, and for me, that I may not be unfaithful, but be made to do His will, for it really seems as though the Lord sent her here to hear more of His gospel.

. . . " M—— is also here. I need strength indeed to strengthen her, and I feel that I am altogether weak ; but I can say with David, ' The Lord is my light and salvation, whom shall I fear? The Lord is the strength of my life, of whom shall I be afraid ? '

. . . " I told M—— and C—— about the nice times we used to have reading our chapter every day, and proposed that we three should every morning go up into M——'s room for the purpose, which they both agreed to gladly ; accordingly this morning we commenced. I thought the Gospel of John would perhaps be the best to establish C—— in the truth, so we began with the first chapter. I felt that it would be pleasing to the Lord that I should ask His presence in a few words ; but somehow the ' old man ' did not want to ; but the new life conquered, and I believe the Lord was with us, for we had a very satisfactory time. M. M. J—— really is very clear, and brought out the gospel as I did not believe she could ; but the chapter is a very striking one.

. . . "Everything is in the Lord's hands, who knows the end from the beginning ; let us rest in that.

"While I was at Millville we had such a sweet time reading the Bible, and really studied it to find out our duty about baptism. We did not come to any definite conclusion, but have made up our minds not to stop studying God's Word until we know what is truth. I must go, darling. May our Father indeed bless thee.   THY OWN ALICE."

The young lady C. H——, here spoken of, died soon after she returned to her home, which was many hundred miles from Philadelphia, and though dear Alice never heard anything more from her, excepting the fact of her death, we cannot doubt that the all-powerful spirit of God carried on the work which He began in her heart, until faith was changed to sight.

"TSWEDELLE, *Aug.* 11, 1860.

" MY OWN CARRIE,—

. . . "Thou speaks of my needing to go away from home, but indeed it is not so.

"I went over to Germantown day before yesterday, and down to the city and home again yesterday, and my head only ached worse while I was away, and I was so glad to get home. I think it really is the best place for me.

"I had a very nice visit at A. F——'s, in spite of head-ache. She is real sweet. We went to see A. S—— after tea, and had a delightful talk. She gave me some of the most precious thoughts. She is living in the realisation of Christ as the Bridegroom, and did express so sweetly just what I have only half thought. She is a real living and truly spiritual Christian.

. . . "Do not let us allow one day to pass without making baptism the subject of prayer and meditation. The old temptation besets me to leave the subject alone, but with God's help I will not give way to it.

" May He be with thee, my darling, and with me,
"THY LOVING SISTER."

The following letter is addressed to the same friend to whom she wrote under date of June 27th of this year :—

"TSWEDELLE, *Aug.* 16, 1860.

" DEAR FRIEND,—

" Yet once again I take up my pen to write to you, for my heart has been filled with prayer for you, now that your soul is resting in Jesus in the full assurance of forgiveness and acceptance as His child, that you may indeed be filled with burning desires to glorify that precious Saviour; that you may know in reality what it is to 'hunger and thirst after righteousness;' that for yourself you may long above all things to be pure and holy, for such is His will that you should be ; yes, for this He called and washed us in His precious blood. In the 2d chapter of the Epistle of Paul to Titus, after having commanded us to live soberly, righteously, and godly in this present world, looking for the glorious appearing of the great God and our Saviour Jesus Christ, he adds, 'Who gave

Himself for us, that He might redeem us from all
iniquity, and purify unto Himself a peculiar people
zealous of good works.'   The very first impression
one gets from the Bible, I think, is, that God would
have men to be holy ; and what is so soul-inspiring
as to contemplate His way of making them so? If we
had been set to work to devise a plan for this, we
should have said to man, ' Set thyself busily to work
to cleanse thine own heart; do nothing that is evil, but
all that is good, and I will give thee an entrance into
heaven as thy reward.'   But God knew us better
than we knew ourselves, and He knew that we could
not do this ; but to convince man that he could not,
He gave the law, that by doing those things we should
live by them.   And then when man comes to confess
himself really a sinner, utterly unable and helpless to
fulfil the law, or bring himself back to holiness, or to
reconcile himself to God, then God shows him His
plan.

"Thus it is said, ' The law was our schoolmaster
to bring us to Christ.'   And just think what Christ's
plan for bringing man back to holiness is ! He takes
the sinner, all unworthy and sinful as he is ; he bears
Himself the full penalty of his sins ; He picks him
from the depths of his degradation ; He gives him full
reconciliation and union with the Father ; He places
him in the position of a dear and beloved child of God ;
and then He says to him, ' I have done all this for
thee out of mine own mercy, I have bought thee from
eternal death with the price of my own blood, and
given to thee the gift of eternal life ; and now wilt
thou not love me, wilt thou not follow in the paths of
righteousness where I shall lead thee ? '

"Who could hear that voice without replying, 'Yea, Lord, with my whole heart will I love Thee; in Thy strength with my whole heart will I serve Thee?' O my friend! if Christ has done all this for us, that we might walk in purity and holiness with Him, in the midst of a crooked and perverse generation, shall we not gladly give all our energies and our whole souls to following Him, and to fulfilling His design concerning us!

"It is through us that He would be glorified! Let us try to realise what a position we are thus called to fill. We, who were once 'dead in trespasses and sins,' are called now to be to the praise of the glory of God! We may so live as to honour Him, as to glorify His name in the sight of men and of angels.

Oh, is not this a high and holy calling? And yet how sad it is to think how many Christians seem not to realise it; that not only does the world reject and despise the Saviour, but His own redeemed ones bring dishonour on His name! But let *us* seek to honour Him, let us offer up our 'bodies a living sacrifice, holy, acceptable unto God, which is indeed our reasonable service.'

"Let us come to our Jesus, and telling Him all our weakness and our ignorance, let us cast the care of making us fit for His service upon Him. He will perfect that which concerns us, because He has promised to do it, and we may safely trust Him to supply every needed grace. If we can trust Him with the salvation of our souls, we can surely trust Him to make us ready to do His own work. We have some sweet texts for this : ' He that spared not His own Son, but delivered Him up for us all, how shall He not with

Him also freely give us all things.' But unto every one of us is given grace according to the measure of the gift of Christ. Think what a measure that is! 'And God is able to make all grace abound toward you, that ye, having all sufficiency in all things, may abound in every good work; being enriched in everything to all bountifulness, which causeth through us thanksgiving to God' (2 Cor. ix. 8–11).

"I cannot dwell longer now on this subject, though I have not said half I long to; but I can only write a very short time without getting a headache. Let me close with Paul's prayer for the Thessalonians, 'And the very God of peace sanctify you wholly; and I pray God your whole spirit and soul and body be preserved blameless unto the coming of our Lord Jesus Christ. Faithful is He that calleth you who also will do it.' . . .

"We have His own promise to be unto us wisdom and righteousness, sanctification and redemption! He alone can give us victory over our besetting sins, and draw all our affections into obedience unto Himself. But thanks be unto God, He can do it! Then shall we not, like little children, just throw ourselves on Christ as our only helper, and trust Him to do it?

"I do not mean simply for the whole future collectively, but let us trust Him to help us to please Him this moment, and each moment as it comes."

CHAPTER VI.

IN the following letter dear Alice alludes to the trial it would be to become a confirmed invalid. It will be seen in the latter part of this memoir how even such a life became a happy one to her through the sustaining presence of Jesus.

"TSWEDELLE, *Sept.* 29, 1860.

. . . "Darling H——, how often I long to see thee, and have one of our good talks. I am really decidedly better, having regained much of my strength and energy. In fact I feel as though I am getting well, and if it is the Lord's will I should be very glad. I think if it was His will, I could die; but to live on month after month, and year after year, half dead and alive, would be a trial of faith.

"I like the life of A. Newton so much; it gives one a great deal to think about. She says she longs to be a reflection of Christ in the world, and I think that just expresses the position of the Christian. Our light cannot shine if we allow any earthly object to come between us and the glorious Sun of Righteousness, from whom we must derive light if we would that men beholding us should glorify the Father.

G

"What a happy thing it would be to feel our re-flection growing brighter and brighter, as we live nearer and nearer to Him. Surely the knowledge of such a growth in righteousness would not, and could not, be accompanied by any feeling of pride or self-superiority, which might be the case if it were our own work.

"With regard to ——, it is such a struggle to keep my faith; but thou art right : 'all things shall work together for good,' though it is true not as I would have it, but, after all, at the bottom I would not wish it to be otherwise than as He wills. His love is so tender and His wisdom so infinite ; He knows better what I would have than I do myself.

"O my Jesus! what would I do without Thee? And yet how the human heart rebels against His will! Won't it be splendid when we get rid of this vile body of sin, and have our wills really and wholly swallowed up in His. .   .   .

"Thy loving little sister cousin,

"ALICE."

"TSWEDELLE, *Oct.* 1, 1860.

"MY DEAR FRIEND,—

"I have thought very often of you, and feel very thankful that you have, as I hope, been brought, by God's mercy, from a state of indifference to your soul's salvation to ask earnestly for yourself the question, 'What shall I do to be saved?' For if so, then it is to you that the good tidings are sent of a Saviour who will 'save to the uttermost all those who come unto God by Him.' Yes, the Bible has a mes-sage as directly for you as if there had never been a penitent sinner in the world but yourself; and that message is of the wonderful love and mercy of God in Christ Jesus to sinners. It tells you that though you have lived all your life in carelessness and sin, and though now you are utterly unable to make yourself any better, and are indeed entirely sinful, weak, and unworthy, that you may now, even now, this night, be a forgiven sinner, a reconciled child of God in Christ Jesus. Did you ever read in the Old Testament how God appointed that if an Israelite should bring a perfectly pure and spotless lamb, and the priest should lay it upon the altar, and should lay his hand on the head of the lamb, and confess the man's sins, at that moment they would be forgiven, as they were counted to be transferred to the lamb, which should be burned, suffering instead of the man? Now this was given us as a type or illustration of how Christ, who is the 'Lamb of God which taketh away the sin of the world,' should bear the just punishment of our sins, and how the moment we, by faith, lay them on Jesus, we are forgiven, counted free from the penalty of our sins, because Christ has already borne that penalty in our stead; and how from that moment we are God's reconciled children, not because of anything in ourselves, but because Christ died for us, and has bought us with His own precious blood.

"Yes, this is the way you can be reconciled to God this very night. Accept Christ now, no matter what you have done hitherto; accept Him now, as the perfect sacrifice for all your sins. Just cast all the weary load of your past sins and present sinfulness on Jesus, confessing that you are not able to save yourself from them, but that you believe that He is the Christ, the Son of God, and that He is able to save you from them, and forgive you; and ask Him to accept you as His child. And believe me—for it is not I, but God, who says it—at that very moment your sins shall all be forgiven, and you accepted as His child.

. . . "How can we ever be thankful enough that He has said, 'The gift of God is eternal life.' Oh, then, if it is the free gift of God, will you not come now, like a poor, weak, ignorant child, to this all-wise, and all-merciful, and all-loving Saviour, and receive it as such, and go on your way rejoicing, not in yourself, or your own goodness, but in Christ, and in the knowledge that your sins are all washed away in His precious blood; and that He is your good Shepherd, who will lead you into the paths of righteousness for His name's sake?"

"BROOKLYN, 10th mo. 8, 1860.

"MY DARLING CARRIE,—

"It is too bad thou should not have heard from us before; but now that I have seated myself to write, I scarcely know how to begin, I have so much to say.

"Last week we went up the Hudson with Uncle R——, and saw some lovely residences. I have no words to express how much more beautiful they were than anything I have ever seen; such views of the river, such mountains so near, rising in some places directly behind the house five or six hundred feet, with mountain after mountain more and more distant, until they were lost in mist. We started on fourth day, and went up to New Hamburg in the eleven o'clock train, and there took an open waggon, and drove about a mile and a half from the station, away up on the hills, five or six hundred feet above the river, where we spent about two hours at Mr F——'s place. . . . After we had looked round sufficiently, we drove eight miles down the river (a splendid ride) on its banks to Fishkill, where we stayed all night.

" The next morning we took a large open carriage, and started off to look at about a dozen places in the neighbourhood, which were 'for sale or to let,' and it was with some of these that I was so delighted. They were near the Highlands, with the 'Storm King' and the 'Sugar Loaf' in full view; but I cannot begin to describe them. . . .

" I want to tell thee about a conversation I had with —— yesterday afternoon. . . . He read some papers of his father's (who deceased when he was an infant), which he found in an old bookcase this summer. There was a paper written not long before his death, on Rom. iv. 4, 5, and it contained just the simple gospel, as clear as it could possibly be, and without any untruth mixed with it. He described a person trying to be saved by works, and then showed that he never could be saved by them, but simply by Christ's atonement, as a propitiatory sacrifice. It was perfectly lovely, and I almost cried at hearing it. —— turned to me, and said, 'That is the doctrine you preach?' I said, 'Yes.' And after talking a while he told me that those papers had been a great reassurance to him, for he thought, more than a year ago, when we first drew his attention to the subject, that this doctrine (of justification by faith) was something new; but to find that his father so many years ago had come to the same truth, had affected him very

much.   He also said that the truths of the gospel
seemed much clearer to him than they did at first;
that the new birth now seemed a very different thing
from what it did; in fact, that he had confidence that
he himself had experienced it, and was a new creature
in Christ Jesus.   Was it not lovely?

.   .   .   " O Carrie! let us pray that the Lord will
so fill us with that longing for the salvation of others
that we cannot sit still, but that from the fulness of our
hearts our mouths may speak of His mercy.   Surely
the Lord will not refuse it to us, if we ask Him.   Let
us unite twice every day in prayer for it, for ourselves,
and for each other.

" This is not all I have to say, but it is late, and I
promised to go over and spend the night with C——."

"TSWEDELLE, *Oct.* 14, 1860.

" DEAR CARRIE,—

.   .   .   " My text for to-day is, ' My grace is
sufficient for thee, for my strength is made perfect in
weakness.'   It is a lovely text, but I cannot tell thee
half as fully as thou can think for thyself all that I
have been thinking about it, and what a comfort it is
to me.   Surely we may rejoice, with Paul, ' in our
infirmities,' even in that despicable weakness which
so often makes us feel so thoroughly disgusted with
ourselves.   The text must mean *real* weakness.   What
a blessing that it does!

" Oct. 16th.—My text for to-day is, ' Jesus Christ,
who gave Himself for our sins, that He might deliver
us from this present evil world, according to the will
of God and our Father, to whom be glory for ever and
ever!'   How full it is, and what a comfort it has

been to me to-day to think that if He died to deliver us from this evil world, surely He will deliver us daily and hourly from the power of the world, under which head I think we may number all the enemies of our souls. I think I have been learning a little more of my own utter helplessness. One would say I might have learned that lesson long ago; but I am just beginning to find out how very little, in comparison to the real state of the case, I ever realised it. I can say with a great deal deeper meaning than ever before—

'I am a poor sinner, and nothing at all,
But Jesus Christ is my all and in all.'"

These two lines seem to have been the key-note to all Alice's religious experience from first to last. As she apprehended more and more the fulness there is in Jesus, she took firmer and deeper hold upon the thought expressed in these lines. Her deep and continual realisation of the truth contained in them is evidenced by their frequent quotation in her letters.

Besides the text which came in course in her daily reading, she often appropriated a certain promise to herself, such as, "Open thy mouth wide, and I will fill it," writing it down on paper, and on the strength of that promise, putting down a number of petitions, recording the day and the year. These were found in her desk, with the word "answered" written upon the margin of some of them, evidently at a later date.

"TSWEDELLE, *Oct.* 19, 1860.

"My Dear B. C——,—

. . . "My thoughts often wander back to your cosy little room in New York, and this afternoon, when I brought mother in a beautiful bunch of sweet flowers, she exclaimed, 'Oh, how I wish B. C—— could have some of these to set by her bedside, they are so sweet'—a wish which was heartily seconded by me, for I had just been thinking the same thing. But you have what is better than the fragrance of flowers—the presence of the Lord. Oh, what a precious thought it is! You seem to grasp it by faith as such an actual reality, which is just the point where the faith of most of us fails. All Christians believe theoretically that God is always with His children, but do not seem to rest in it, and realise it, as you do.

" I was so much obliged to you for giving me the text you did when we parted, for it was just what I needed. It has been dwelling in my mind ever since, and you can't think how often it has come with comfort to my heart at the moment I most needed it. 'My presence shall go with thee, and I will give thee rest;' surely a rest this side the grave—a rest in Him, independent of all surrounding circumstances—a peaceful laying of one's head on Jesus' bosom while in the din and turmoil of this tumultuous world—a freedom from all care or anxious effort while engaged in active daily warfare with sin and Satan! I would like to know whether you think we are promised that we shall always have the joy of consciously resting thus on Jesus' bosom. I do not mean to ask if we are allowed always to please Him, but whether it don't sometimes please Him that we should not realise His love so fully, or that very great nearness to Him. Of course His love is always the same, and His presence with us the same ; but if we do not have that comforting realisation of it, what must we think?

Is it our unfaithfulness, or is it sometimes a part of His wondrous dealings with us, to make us cling to Him by naked faith for our daily food? I ask you this because it seems to me you appear consciously to rest on His bosom all the day long.

"If this is the privilege of the Christian, he will always in his religion be equally happy, never knowing those mists above him, which A. S——speaks of to hide his Beloved from his sight. Are these mists clouds of our own raising, which one who 'walks with God' will never know?

"But I must not write more now, for although my health is greatly better than it has been for months, I cannot write or read more than a short time without pain."

"TSWEDELLE, *Oct.* 29, 1860.

"MY DEAR FRIEND,—

"I take this first opportunity of sending you 'The Higher Christian Life' (Boardman), which I promised to lend you, feeling deeply anxious that you may read it in that prayerful, earnest, inquiring state of mind, which, I cannot but feel confident, will lead, by the mercy of God, to your learning how you may arrive at that 'closer walk with Jesus' for which He has made you long. I have read many books on the subject, but none that I like so well. I do not altogether like the term 'second conversion.' Had the author, in speaking of the same experience, called it 'the entrance into the way of holiness,' or a 'closer walk with Jesus,' I should have liked it better. But we will not quarrel with him about a name, so long as we agree with him as to substance.

" I think he clearly proves, by the lives of Luther and others, that there is such a thing, call it by what name you please. I was struck with his illustrations of the many mistakes which the Christian is liable to fall into in seeking after the higher life, as being very instructive; particularly the instances he gives of persons who had so much trouble because they failed to realise that faith is twofold—it takes all and it gives all, as in the case of the lady of distinction and the merchant. The one, who found that she had not intelligently dedicated or given up her whole life to Christ, and thus had been trying to take all and give nothing; and the other, who was always renewing and dwelling on his own dedication to God, without taking Christ as his all-sufficiency.

" I cannot express how thankful I feel to the Lord for arousing you to seek for a closer and more abiding union with Himself; and still less can I express the deep and almost overwhelming sense I have of my utter ignorance and unworthiness to attempt to point you onward in the way; but my constant prayer is, 'May God teach thee.' And I am sure He will, and will never let you rest in a half-way dedication to His service, or in a faith that grasps Jesus as only half a Saviour, and not as your all in all—your sanctification as well as your justification."

"TSWEDELLE, *Oct.* 30, 1860.

" MY DEAR SISTER ANNIE,—

. . . "My text for to-day is in the third chapter of Philippians, 'Our conversation is in heaven, from whence we look for the Saviour, the Lord Jesus Christ: who shall change our vile body, that it may be fashioned like unto His glorious body, according to the working whereby He is able even to subdue all things unto Himself.' It is very long to write out, but I could not help it, it is so lovely. To think that 'He is able to subdue all things to Himself.' Surely even I need not despair of being sanctified, if He will do it, who is so able. . . .

"I shall keep up now regularly, if possible, the Sunday afternoon readings (at the cottages), which I think do not hurt me at all; I do so appreciate the privilege of speaking a word for Jesus."

"TSWEDELLE, *Nov.* 13, 1860.

"MY DEAR CARRIE,—

. . . "My verse for to-day is: 'Now the end of the commandment is charity, out of a *pure* heart, and of a *good* conscience, and of faith *unfeigned.*' I wish I could express all the meaning this has to me. We cannot force ourselves to charity—this charity; it must spring from a pure heart, which is in tune and harmony with the heart of Jesus, and a happy conscience free from the weight of even a moment's sin, and a faith that not only professes to, but practically and momentarily does lay hold of Jesus as its perfect sufficiency, not only to cleanse entirely and wholly from the past, but to keep for the present and future from all evil. Let our hearts be thus tuned, and we shall be filled with charity."

"TSWEDELLE, *Nov.* 19, 1860.

"MY DEAR CARRIE,—

. . . "'The times' do indeed 'look boisterous.' Father prophesies the most dreadful things;

says the troubles of '57 will be back upon us tenfold; but this is not all : disunion, the greatest of all evils, and a civil war are going to follow each other. . .

"I am reading 'The Still Hour,' and am enjoying it exceedingly. It is just what I wanted, for I am on the subject of prayer, and my text, aside from those for the day, has been for some time Matt. xxi. 22 : 'And all things whatsoever ye shall ask in prayer, believing, ye shall receive.' Is it not glorious? I am sure I don't intend to bring such mean petitions after this, when He seems to expect us to ask so much. Surely the reason we don't get more is because we don't ask or expect more."

"TSWEDELLE, *Dec.* 16, 1860.

"MY DEAR FRIEND,—

. . . "I do so long and hope to see you walk-ing very close to Jesus ; much, much closer than this poor servant of the Lord has set you the example of walking ; but, by the grace of God, from this day I will (knowing all the past forgiven) live nearer to Him. And let us both at the beginning of a new year, turning away from all beside, cleave more closely unto Jesus.

"What else is there left for us to do? Poor, weak, ignorant children as we are, yet journeying in the midst of 'a crooked and perverse generation,' with our great enemy ever watching us, to beguile us into sin and sorrow. Oh, what suffering and misery should we save ourselves were we ever to keep our hand in that of our loving and tender Guide, and yield ourselves implicitly to follow Him wherever He leads us ! For though we rejoice in the confidence that, as He has already redeemed us unto Himself, He will not let us wander from Him into eternal death, yet we know that it is often through much agony and suffering that He brings back His wandering children. My experience is, that I never left Jesus for so much as half an hour without running myself into some sort of trouble or distress. And what a mercy that it is so! For what would become of us if He allowed us to wander from Him without some sort of suffering to bring us back. . . .

"The thought, of His unmerited love is overwhelming to me to-day, but I have no words befitting such a glorious subject."

"TSWEDELLE, *Dec.* 28, 1860.

"MY DEAR B. C——,—

"Although many things seem to call my attention in other directions this afternoon, I cannot leave your last letter longer unanswered. I am now determined to push everything else aside for a quiet little talk with you on the subject nearest both our hearts, and upon which I am sure we neither of us can speak without being refreshed. I mean, of course, the goodness, the wondrous goodness, of the Lord to us in His dear Son.

"As for myself, I have indeed abundant cause to speak of His goodness and mercy, for though never in my life have I had more reason to be deeply humbled in myself, neither have I had more cause to make mention of His long-suffering and tenderness. In how many thousand ways has He not shown His presence with me, and His hand taking care of me, both spiritually and temporally!

" Adelaide Newton has a little verse in one of her hymns which is such a comfort to me !—

> ' All, all by Thee is ordered, chosen, planned,
> Each drop that fills my daily cup ; Thy hand
> Prescribes for ills none else can understand ;
>   All, all is known to Thee.'

" How true it is that He prescribes for diseases we don't even know that we have ourselves, but which nevertheless would prove fatal if allowed to go on unchecked ; but thanks be unto Him, He is all-wise, and all-powerful, and all-loving ; and although our friends around us do not understand our needs, He does understand us perfectly, but does not chide, but 'remembereth that we are dust,' and 'healeth all our diseases.'

" How strange it is that I should have been so un-grateful as sometimes to murmur at the course of medicine He has given me the past few months ; but He has graciously made me very thankful this morn-ing that He is prescribing for me, and not leaving me to myself. And it really does me good, my dear friend, to be able to sit down and express a little of the gratitude that fills my heart to you. I know you understand me, while many would think such an expression of feeling ostentatious ; for it is altogether an unexpected thing for any one, unless under some great affliction, to tell what a comfort and joy Christ is to them. Is it not a pity that it is not the general custom for Christians to acknowledge the goodness of the Lord with their lips one to another ? Not only because it would, as I think, really tend to the increase of their own gratitude, but also because not doing so robs God of what is His due, and practically gives the impression to those who have no experimental knowledge of the joys of religion that it is of very little profit to persons while in the enjoyment of worldly prosperity, although in the time of trial and sorrow it is a very desirable thing. They hear continually Christians testify what a comfort and support Christ is to them in their affliction, and how impossible it would be for them to bear it without Him; but they hear comparatively little of what Christians with equal truth could testify if they would speak of what a wealth of happiness and joy Christ is to them while in outward prosperity. To be sure they hear theoretically that there is no true happiness out of Christ, but they do not imagine that their friends are really a great deal happier than they were before they became Christians. They would really be surprised if they told them that they found the smile of Jesus to add double pleasure to their earthly enjoyments, and to take away the load of petty cares and annoyances, to say nothing of the spiritual joys and pleasures He so freely gives them; in fact, that He adds as much to their joys as He takes from their pain, and that He is as necessary to them in their prosperity as in their adversity."

TO A NEWLY-MARRIED FRIEND.

"TSWEDELLE, *January* 1861.

. . . "I sympathise in thy happiness, dear friend, but I do so realise that this very enjoyment of earthly things is fraught with great danger, although, as thou may say, it is calculated to call forth gratitude to the great Giver. Yet, darling, if we come to

Him with thanksgiving only, forgetting that we are sinners, and need a sacrifice for sin, we come in a way in which God cannot receive us.

"In the parable of the Pharisee and the Publican, it is very probable that the Pharisee came up to worship God with sincere thanksgiving, but he made no mention of the sin which stained and polluted even that thanksgiving. But the Publican, who knew himself a sinner, came crying, 'God, be merciful to me a sinner,' or, as the original reads, I think, 'Be Thou propitiated toward me.' He came bringing a plea which God himself appointed, and we read that he went down accepted rather than the other.

"I know there is a strong tendency, when we look only at that which is to us lovable and lovely in our fellow mortals and ourselves, to forget that in the eye of God we do not appear exactly in the same light, but are tainted throughout with sin, and need indeed to bring for ourselves the perfect atonement of Christ as our plea, and our only plea, for acceptance. It is such a different thing to give an assent in a general way to the atonement, and the efficacy of the blood of Christ to wash away sin, and to really appropriate it to ourselves; and know by faith that He bore the penalty of *our* sins, and that *we* are forgiven, and made the children of God by adoption in a very different way from that in which we are accustomed to consider all the human family as the offspring of God.

"I may understand thy position, but I have been wondering if thou art not striving diligently to cultivate all the noble and good in thy nature, and to resist all the evil; and for all the rest are trusting in a general way to the mercy of God. Ah, dear friend, if this is thy position, thou wilt find in it no real, lasting satisfaction ; for, after all, the very goodness thou art trying to cultivate, thou wilt find needs itself to be washed. I think this is just what the Bible means when it says that our righteousness is as 'filthy rags,' entirely worthless in the sight of God, which we must give up, and accept the righteousness of God which is by faith of Jesus Christ unto all and upon all them that believe.

"Do not misunderstand me ; I fully approve of trees bringing forth fruit, but I know that they must have the sap in their branches first ; and just so, it is useless for us to try and stifle the bad and cultivate the good in our hearts until we are joined to the True Vine, from whence we shall derive the only sap that can bring forth anything really good in us. We know that we are not naturally joined to that Vine, but must be grafted in. This grafting in is spoken of in the Bible in different places, as 'being born again, as being made the children of God by faith in Christ Jesus.' So whether thou art trusting in a general way to the mercy of God, or art by faith appropriating the full atonement of Christ to thyself, and art trusting in Him as thy perfect Saviour, is a matter of the greatest importance, and the first thing to be considered ; for it alters thy whole position, and thou starts out on thy efforts after holiness from an entirely different standpoint. Art thou very much shocked because I have said that in the one case thy efforts would be in vain ? If so, go to the Bible, for it is not I but God who says it. And surely when in such wondrous mercy God has sent 'His only-begotten Son into the world,

H

that whosoever believeth in Him should not perish but have everlasting life,' it is not strange that He should declare that whosoever will not believe cannot please Him in any other way" (John iii. 18–36).

" MY DEAR LITTLE SISTER CARRIE,—

. . . " We went to meeting yesterday morning, and in the afternoon I went down to the cottages. I commenced to read Christ's sermon on the mount at I——'s, and I think, with the Lord's blessing, it may be very profitable to us all. I asked I—— to choose a verse out of it for us to take for particular thought during the week, as we are always in the habit of taking one from the chapter of the day, and he chose the 6th verse: ' Blessed are they which do hunger and thirst after righteousness, for they shall be filled.' I had also a favoured time at M——'s.

" In the evening father, mother, and I commenced reading the life of Stephen Grellet. It is perfectly lovely, and shows as clearly as any one could wish, that it was the realisation of the full and free atonement made by the Lord Jesus Christ for all his sins that first brought peace to his soul, and filled his heart with love to God and burning desires to glorify Him.

" I do wish you would read it, for it does make one feel how half-hearted our dedication is compared with his. His life was one of so much usefulness, entered upon so immediately after his conversion, and so steadily progressive, always reaching forward, never turning back to earthly interests. O Carrie !

it ought to stir us up to live unto God and not unto ourselves." . . .

"TSWEDELLE, *March* 16.

" DEAR CARRIE,—

" I have just returned from I——'s, where I enjoyed extremely the 8th chapter of Romans, and now, after having had a short time of prayer, come to talk a little with thee, my own dear sister.

" I was so glad to hear about your Sunday-school. I can heartily join my prayers to yours that it may be blessed, and shall be delighted to do anything I can to help.

" I send thee a list of reasons why Jesus is the best Physician, Shepherd, &c., &c., which is very interesting to children, and gives room for you to enlarge on each one, and then every week you can make them remember the reasons, &c., of last week.

" I was at Germantown last week, and attended one of Mrs Guinness' Bible-classes. It was on the assurance of faith ; and what shall I say about it ? It was the most overpowering thing I ever listened to. I only wish it was written out. She treated it under three different heads.

" First.—That the Bible never contemplates a Christian who hasn't it, but always speaks to believers as to persons who have no doubt of their position before God.

" Secondly.—That no Christian can please God without it.

" Thirdly.—If so, how are we to get it ?

" She ·proved all these most undoubtedly from Scripture, bringing passage after passage to substantiate what she said. She also took up some which are commonly quoted to prove the contrary, showing what was their real meaning, and also how dishonouring to God doubts are, and, moreover, proved incontrovertibly that they generally arise from pride.

"Her final appeal to us all was very, very solemn. When she ceased speaking, a deep silence was spread over all for I suppose ten minutes."

"TSWEDELLE, *March* 19, 1861.

. . . "Do pray, dear Annie, that my intercourse with N—— may be blessed. I feel so weak; I do think the Lord never had so weak and unworthy a child, but, through the mercy and goodness of Him who died for sinners, I have a feeble hope of doing something to glorify His great name yet. Seeing Mr and Mrs G—— so good, has made me feel more than ever that I am not at all what I ought to be. But is it not a comfort that Christ is ours still? No matter how weak or unfaithful we are, He is loving us just the same, for He does not change, and He has the same reasons for loving us that He had at the beginning. He did not begin to love us because He saw anything in us worthy of love. He first loves, and then forms in us something worthy of being loved. Is it not wonderful? But it leaves no room for glorifying in the flesh." . . .

"TSWEDELLE, *April* 6, 1861.

"DEAR CARRIE,—

"Thou hast, I suppose, heard the news of our nine pound nephew, Frank. The children are delighted with him, though Nannie at first was jealous, and would not look at him, turning away her head, but when he cried, she screamed out, 'It squeaked, it squeaked, and seemed quite charmed with it. . . .

" I have had the headache almost all the past week, but at some rate have kept up, I don't know exactly how.

. . . "I am just now very much interested in a Bible-class for ladies, which seems likely to arise from Mrs B—— and myself meeting together to study the Bible. Several ladies have asked her to let them come, and, as she said it seemed a shame for us to have all these good things to ourselves, and seemed to desire that they should be admitted, I have consented. We meet this afternoon for the first time. I feel a little frightened; but it is the Lord's doing, and He will take care of it. L—— and S—— also expect to join us."

This Bible-class was carried on during all the remaining years of Alice's life, and was felt by her to be a solemn and deeply interesting responsibility. It was always much laid upon her heart in prayer, and in the last letter written before she was attacked with the illness which terminated in her death, it is spoken of as a subject of earnest solicitude. That it was blessed to others will be seen by the following reference made to it by one of its number, who had for many years been a church member :—

" How hallowed and dear to me were those hours spent in studying the Scriptures at our little Bible-class ! It was there that the glorious plan of redemption was unfolded to me. It was Alice who told me

that no efforts of my own could save my soul, but
that Jesus Christ died to save sinners, and that believing, trusting in Him, I could not perish, but had
everlasting life.   Very precious is the memory of the
hour when, listening to her words, the light of God
shone in upon my clouded vision, and I beheld Jesus,
my Saviour.   Then, indeed, peace, the peace that
passeth understanding, flowed in upon my troubled
soul."

To a Friend.

"Like the Apostle, I write not unto you because
you know not the truth, but because you know it, and
I would, like him, 'stir up your pure mind (your
new nature) by way of remembrance, that ye may be
mindful of the words which were spoken.'   All that
I shall say you already know as well as I ; but Satan
sometimes makes truth appear very shadowy, intan-
gible and inpracticable, and a simple statement of it
often helps to dispel the mists of earth which he uses
to blind our eyes.

"In the first place, then, think of what you are—
'a soldier of the Cross.'   Christ bought you when a
captive.   When you were lying helpless, sin-defiled,
dead in trespasses and sins, He took you in His arms ;
He breathed upon you the breath of eternal life ; He
opened your blind eyes to see and know Him ; He
washed you from your filth in His own precious
blood ; He clothed you in His own robe ; and even
more, He calls you son, brother ; has made all His
inheritance to be yours, and has lavished upon you
infinite love.   And then, putting into your possession
'the whole armour of God,' 'the sword of the Spirit,'

and the shield of faith, wherewith He says, 'ye shall be able to quench all the fiery darts of the wicked,' He calls you to be His soldier, to go to war, but not at your own cost; to fight, but not in your own strength; to obey His word as instantly and unflinchingly as soldiers must; to brave the foe through privation and danger; to press steadily on through darkness and trial. All this He does, not because He has need of anything, but for your sake, that He may give you a crown of joy when the work is done; and, moreover, that you may have the opportunity of showing your allegiance to Him, of proving your gratitude for all His wonderful mercy and long suffering toward you. And even more, He loves His children, and He loves to be loved by them. And as, when He came into the world to do His Father's will, He found it sweet to tell forth all the depths of His love for that Father, by the deep language of doing and suffering, His heart yearns that His chosen ones should thus show their love for Him. Is not this what He means when He says, ' As thou, Father, hast sent me into the world, *even so* have I sent them into the world?'

"Now what is the position of such an one when tempted not to obey the command, or follow where his great Captain leads? Can he prove himself to be so utterly devoid of all gratitude and love for the One who bought him? No; I know that no child of God would deliberately refuse to do what He commands; but the trouble is, Christians are not always honest with their own knowledge of what He would have them to do. They prefer to look at all the difficulties of the way, and say, ' It is impossible,' instead of looking unto Jesus, and saying, 'I can do all things through Christ which strengtheneth me;' 'Lord, what wilt Thou have me to do?'

"Another way of deceiving our own conscience is to gaze so intently at the darling 'right hand' which we are called to cast away, that our eyes are dimmed, and we half persuade ourselves that we do not really feel sure what we ought to do; although no one doubts that if he will but look the truth in the face, with a single intent to do what he sees to be right, no matter how hard, he will know right from wrong. If we did but look unto Jesus with half the earnestness with which we gaze on earthly things, we should be sure to know what He would have us to do. If we know a thing to be wrong (whether we feel it or not), we must turn our backs resolutely upon it, or else have our backs turned toward Jesus.

"It does not say, in Matt. v. 29, 30, that if thy right hand offend thee, tie it up for a season, and then unloose it. Nor does it say, cut it off all but a little, and then bind it up and seek to make it heal; but it says, 'cut it off and cast it from thee, for it is more profitable for thee that one of thy members should perish, and not that thy whole body should be cast into hell.' Here we see that He knows how dear to our human hearts the offending member often is; but still we are assured that it is absolutely profitable for us to lose it.

"'Ye cannot serve God and mammon.' And, dear friend, just think for a moment how the loving heart of Jesus must feel if we hesitate to choose for Him. He really loves us. Do not let us forget this; for is not His love worth more than all the world beside? So infinite, so tender, so everlasting! the length and breadth of which we do not even begin to conceive, and the sweetness of it, which satisfieth the depths of the soul, we have but just begun to taste. Could we give this up, and take in its stead—what? A bubble of a moment—a firefly's spark—a phantom light, that will but lead us further and further into the lake of the dismal swamp!

"Paul could say that he counted 'all things but loss for the excellency of the knowledge of Christ,' for he had suffered the loss of all things, and did count them but dung that he might win Christ."

"Do not be discouraged; remember that, 'forgetting the things which are behind,' we are to press forward for the prize of our high calling. The Lord says, 'My grace is sufficient for thee, my strength is made perfect in weakness.' He will cause you to stand, upheld by His mighty arm, if you will but trust Him for it. 'None that put their trust in Him shall be desolate,' but He will cause them to have 'all sufficiency in all things.' Think, too, of the sweet promises to such as forsake father or mother, wife, children, or lands, or anything dear, for His name's sake, Matt. xix. 19, and such as are given to obedience, in John xiv. 21, 23, 24; xv., 10, 11, 14; viii. 12; Luke xi. 34, and many more."

CHAPTER VII.

THE following letter, addressed to a young friend who was deliberating the question of joining the army of the United States to crush the Southern rebellion, is a very clear statement of Alice's views in regard to war. In enclosing it, and other letters from the same hand, the receiver writes thus :—

"What a world of consolation and instruction these precious letters contain. I shall never know all that her affectionate counsels saved me from, in the way of yielding to temptation to sin; but this I know, that she has done more toward teaching me of that 'truth that will set us free' than any other creature."

"MILLVILLE, *May* 13, 1861.

"MY DEAR FRIEND,—

. . . "You asked the other day, when we pray to God to show us what His will is, and do not receive any answer, what we are to think is the cause. I think there may be many causes. The most common, I believe, is this, that we are not really willing to know His will, that is, we are not willing to know it, if it should be opposed to our will. In other words, we ask with the hope that His will may be like ours, and a secret half-formed determination (not fully allowed, perhaps, even to ourselves) not to be convinced if it be opposite to it. I do not say that this is your case, but it is far more often the case with us than we have any idea of; for the human heart is 'deceitful above all things.' I have been deeply humbled and utterly astonished at finding something of the kind to have been working in my own heart, when I thought I had long and earnestly been seeking to know the mind of the Lord, and was just beginning to doubt His faithfulness because He had not answered my prayers.

"You see it is necessary we should be willing to receive before He can give us either the knowledge to understand His will or strength to do it. If you cannot with an honest heart look up to Him and cry, 'Lord, my one desire is to know and to do Thy will, whatever it may be,' you cannot expect to be enlightened—at least not until your heart has been changed in that respect; for the promise is, 'He that will do my will,' or he that willeth to do my will, he shall know of my doctrine.

"It could not do any harm to examine your heart with regard to this. If you should be obliged to confess that in this sense and to this extent your eye is not single, do not be discouraged, but cease not to pray for it, until the Lord himself has made it your only wish or concern in the matter to know and to do His will: for He can change even our rebellious human wills and wishes, and, thanks be unto Him, He is willing to do it.

"Another reason why we do not always get an

answer to our prayers I think is contained in the first chapter of James: 'If any of you lack wisdom, let him ask of God, that giveth to all men liberally, and upbraideth not, and it shall be given him; but let him ask in faith, nothing wavering.' Now do you really believe that it is your privilege to be given wisdom of God to know what His will is concerning you in this matter? Or have you admitted the thought that you are too young and inexperienced a Christian to expect to come to any real knowledge, from the study of the Scriptures, of what His will is, and so have not studied it with the expectation of doing so? If so, you must see that, in asking God to give you wisdom, you have not asked in faith, not expecting to receive the very thing you have asked for.

"That it is the absolute duty, as well as the privilege, of every Christian to be 'fully persuaded in his own mind' from the Word of God what His will is, is clearly taught in the Bible. In the fourteenth chapter of the Epistle of Paul to the Romans, where he speaks concerning a difference of opinion which had arisen among them about the observance of days, he says, 'Let every man be fully persuaded in his own mind,' or perfectly assured as to the right, and then goes on to say, let him that believeth one thing, and him who believeth another, each do what he doeth 'unto the Lord.'

"The case is in point, excepting one great difference, which is, that the question whether it is right for a Christian to fight is a matter of much more serious importance; but Christians differ in their ideas of right about it, and just in the same way every one must do as he feels assured the Bible teaches him he ought to. None can avoid the necessity of judging for himself what the Bible teaches on every question of duty, by thinking that what so many Christians think it teaches must be right. No; every one individually must 'search the Scriptures,' for they are indeed able to 'make wise.' They are alone infallible, and by them we shall be judged; and the Holy Spirit to enlighten us, and show us what it means, is promised to all God's children. (See John xiv. 16, 17, 26; xvi. 13; 1 Cor. i. 30; ii. 12; vi. 19 : Psalm xxv. 8, 9.)

"If we had a child who wished to do our will, would we refuse to make known that will unto him? And will God do less for us? He has said that He 'will teach sinners in the way,' for 'the meek will He guide in judgment, and the meek will He teach His way.'

"By what I have said I do not mean to infer that the views held by a majority of Christians are not entitled to our serious consideration from that fact, for I think they are ; but we should examine them by the Bible, depending on the Spirit of God to show us the truth. If we are convinced they are scriptural, then we can safely adopt them as our own, not because they are the views of most Christians, but because we believe them to be the very thing the Bible teaches.

"There is, however, one thing I would remind you of while speaking of the view upon war commonly held by Christians of the present time. It is, that far more Christians of all ages have thought it wrong for them to fight than you at first would have any idea of. During a considerable period after the crucifixion of Christ, His followers believed that He had forbidden war, and consequently refused to bear arms. This fact is established by all writers of that time. Their being Christians seemed to them sufficient reason why they could not fight; as in the case of Maximilian, who, as it is related in the 'Acts of Ruinart,' when he was brought before the tribunal to be enrolled as a soldier, replied, 'I am a Christian, and cannot fight,' and was consequently consigned to the executioner. Marcellus, who had already enlisted, abandoned his office, and the reason he gave was similar, 'It is not lawful for a Christian to fight for any earthly consideration.'

"That these were not merely the views of a few individuals, but the settled principles of the whole body, up to as late as the middle of the third century, there is abundant proof. I think a strong evidence of what the primitive belief was, is to be found in the fact that some authors of the second century declared that the refusal of Christians to bear arms was a fulfilment of prophecy, treating the fact as notorious and unquestioned.

"Justin Martyr writes, 'That the prophecy in Isaiah ii. 4, and Micah iv. 3, is fulfilled, you have good reason to believe, for we, who in times past killed one another, do not now fight our enemies.'

"Christ and His apostles delivered general precepts for the regulation of our conduct. The Christians who lived nearest to His time applied His pacific precepts to war, and believed that they absolutely forbade it, and with undoubting confidence they openly avowed this belief; and in support of it they sacrificed their fortunes and their lives.

"Afterward Christians became soldiers, but when? When their general fidelity became relaxed. It was at a time when corruption and infidelity came into the Church, and so obscured the light of truth that even the fundamental doctrine of justification by faith in Christ was almost lost. But ever since that time there have been not a few Christians in all parts of the world to lift up their voices against Christians fighting.

"I mention these things simply as a reason why we should not think that what the churches generally hold in our time must therefore necessarily be true. Had we lived in the fifteenth century instead of the nineteenth, and reasoned in that way, we should have had to believe for the same reason that we are to be saved by our own works, as that was the current belief in the Christian world at that time, and only a very few scattered individuals dared openly to avow that we are saved by faith in Christ.

"The little conversation we had the other evening on this subject was not altogether satisfactory to me, from the fact that we argued about the expediency of Christians supporting their government by taking up arms. The question to be settled is whether it is right for a Christian to slay his fellow-men for any reason. If it is wrong, then there can be no necessity or expediency for him to fight in the sight of God, no matter if there seem to be thousands of earthly reasons why he should.

"Neither did I feel prepared to argue with you about the ways and means by which a government could support itself without war, as that does not bear on the point in question. I did, however, wish very much to call your attention to some little of the evidence which I think I see so clearly in the New Testament, that it is very inconsistent and very wrong in a Christian to fight.

"This letter is already beyond all common bounds of letter-writing, but I must just give you a few of my reasons for believing as I do, in order that in taking the subject into serious consideration, as I hope you are doing, you may look a little on both sides of the question.

"In the first place, I think it is forbidden by the whole spirit of Christianity, which most emphatically teaches us to let love 'increase and abound' in our hearts 'toward all men' (1 Thess. iii. 12, 13). The Scriptures tell us to love our neighbour as ourselves, and that 'love worketh no ill to his neighbour' (Rom. xiii. 9, 10); and again, to 'do good unto all men' (Gal. vi. 10; Heb. xii. 14). When we go out to fight our neighbour with the intent of taking away that life which is of more value to him than any other earthly thing, are we fulfilling either the spirit or the letter of Christianity? When we lay low in death the husband or the son, leaving the wife and mother desolate and afflicted, are we 'working no ill to our neighbour?' I cannot but answer that such acts are a direct disobedience of these precepts, which nothing but a direct command from God could justify. I have searched in vain through the New Testament to find any command that could possibly convey the meaning that the Christian must kill his fellow-men in support of his government.

"We are told to be subject unto it, and not to resist it, for it is ordained of God, who has given to it its power. That, however, is not telling us to do what is wrong in its service; for just so we are told to obey our parents, but we do not think that would justify us in doing anything which we believe to be wrong because they tell us to. We must obey God and serve Him rather than man or any human power.

"What is right and what is wrong is to be determined by God's commands and Christ's example; therefore if from these we find it to be wrong to slay our fellow-men, we are fully justified in saying that we are not under any obligation to our country, even if she were to lay her absolute commands on us, to do so in her service. (See Acts iv. 19; v. 28, 29.)

"Secondly.—We are told to follow the example of Christ (1 Pet. ii. 21-23). He avenged not the wrongs He saw in the world, nor those done unto Himself, but went about doing good to all who came near Him, healing diseases, giving life to the dead; and finally set us an example of so loving men that He laid down His own life, in order that they might live. Can we persuade ourselves that we are in His spirit, and 'following in His footsteps,' when we ruthlessly contribute to bring desolation and want to many a fireside, and to hurry many a poor impenitent sinner into eternity, to be an everlasting witness of how we loved his soul? Christ is the Prince of Peace, and we are His lights in a world lying in darkness.

"It is the glorious mission of the Christian to carry, not death, but the light of life, even life eternal, to his fellow-men. (See Phil. ii. 15, 16; Matt. v. 14-16; 1 Pet. ii. 9.)

"Thirdly.—We are commanded not to have any fellowship with, nor take any part in, works of darkness (Eph. v. 8–11). That war in itself is a work of iniquity, every one agrees. The Bible says that all warrings and contentions arise from the sinful lusts and passions of men (James iv. 1). Therefore the only question is—Is a Christian ever justified, on any pretence, in entering into a work of iniquity? The Bible answer is very plain, 'Let every one that nameth the name of Christ depart from iniquity' (2 Tim. ii. 19; Tit. ii. 14). 'Abhor that which is evil, cleave to that which is good' (Rom. xxi. 9; 3 John ii.) If there is any doctrine strongly laid down in these pages, it is that we must take no part or lot in anything we believe to be wrong (2 Cor. vi. 14–18). Neither by any means 'do evil that good may come' (Rom. iii. 8).

" Lastly, we are told to deal with our fellow-men as Christ has dealt with us (Eph. iv. 32; v. 2). Christ deals with us in grace, and we ought also to deal with men in grace. This is not always a pleasing doctrine to the flesh, but it is Bible doctrine. We must forgive other men, even as God for Christ's sake has forgiven us. It is not the place of a Christian to avenge the wrongs done to himself, for it is written, 'avenge not yourselves' (Rom. xii. 19), and 'recompense to no man evil for evil' (Rom. xii. 17; 1 Peter iii. 9; 1 Thess. v. 15). If the commands not to avenge the wrongs done to himself are so stringent, the Christian ought to think well before he takes it for granted that it is his place to avenge those done to another, or to his government.

" If you go back to the Old Testament, you will find

that to the Israelites, war of their own will, or by their own counsel, was not lawful, for they were obliged at all times to go to the oracles of God, and get a direct command from God to go, which none do, or can do now. Nor can we make their example by itself a guide to our actions, as many things were allowable to them, 'because,' Christ says, 'of the hardness of their hearts' (Matt. xix. 8), that are not allowable to Christians. And in the fifth chapter of Matthew, He says, 'It hath been said, an eye for an eye; but I say unto you that ye resist not evil, for whosoever shall smite thee on thy right cheek, turn to him the other also.' We thus learn that those who were under the law of Moses might indeed act toward their fellow-men in simple justice, while Christians are called, by the more full and perfect law of Christ, to the exercise of that forbearance and patience and love which Moses did not command; to suffer wrong, to love their enemies, to pray for them who despitefully use them, and to seek in all ways the best and highest good for all men, even as they seek their own.

"The Bible always contemplates a Christian as called to a spiritual, not a carnal warfare. Our Lord himself says, 'My kingdom is not of this world, else would my servants fight.' And in 2 Cor. x. 3, 4, Paul says, 'Though we walk in the flesh, we do not war after the flesh, for the weapons of our warfare are not carnal,' &c.; and these weapons are described in Eph. vi. 11–17. Our feet are to be 'shod with the gospel of peace.' We are told to 'walk in the Spirit,' and we 'shall not fulfil the lusts of the flesh' (Gal. v. 16). And what is 'the fruit of the Spirit?' 'Love, joy, peace, long-suffering, gentleness, goodness, meekness' (Gal. v. 22, 23). Contrast these with 'the works of the flesh,' 'wrath, strife, envyings, murders, variance, emulations, and such like' (Eph. v. 19, 20).

"I might go on and take up every argument which I have heard urged in favour of war, and tell you how and why I have concluded them all unscriptural, but I have not the time, and I am sure if you compare them prayerfully with the Scriptures, you will come to the right conclusion. And now, with the prayer which is in my heart for you, that you may ever be kept and guided by your Father's hand, I am, as ever, your friend."

"TSWEDELLE, *June* 15, 1861.

"MY DEAR B. C——,——

"I am kept at home from my usual Sabbath afternoon duties by a toothache, which makes me feel unfit for almost everything, but I want so much to exchange a few words with you, that I am going to try and forget the pain; for on Wednesday we expect my sister Annie and her family, and with a houseful I do not generally find more quiet time to myself than I need for devotion and the study of the Bible.

. . . "I want to tell you how my visits to you have comforted and strengthened me; they seemed to be just what I needed, first in showing me very strikingly that it is the privilege of the Christian to rejoice always in the Lord, and not only so, but his absolute duty to do so. Secondly, they showed me by contrast where I have so often failed in glorifying God hitherto; and thirdly, and best of all, they

showed me the way by which even I can always rejoice in God. If I could only say that I have learned
these three lessons perfectly, you would indeed have
given me a rich legacy, but even on the first I am
sometimes tempted to doubt.

"I want to ask you a question which was put to
me the other day. I was saying that I thought we
often dishonour God by not rejoicing and praising
Him all the time as you do, when it was remarked,
'Don't you think God ever hides His face from us,
so that we cannot rejoice?' I think I hear you say,
'Rejoice in the Lord always, and again I say, rejoice;' and we are not commanded to do anything
we cannot do. Certainly it is written, 'God tempteth
no man;' and what greater temptation to despair,
unbelief, and sin can be imagined than a withdrawal
of the source of all our strength and joy and blessing
would be!

"However this may be, I will try the way you
directed me, and that is to ask and trust Jesus to
make me praise Him and rejoice in Him. So far
He has answered my prayer most graciously, and I
do enjoy a more complete rest, and joy, and rejoicing
in Him than I can express; but I would like to be
more sure that I have a right to ask to be kept so
always.

"The verse you gave me rings in my ears so sweetly
and reassuringly: 'Have I not commanded thee, be
strong and of a good courage, be not afraid, neither
be thou dismayed, for the Lord thy God is with thee
whithersoever thou goest,' and I do not know exactly
why the words always seem to be added, 'and my banner over thee shall be peace.' I believe these exact

words are not in the Bible, but they have greatly comforted me, and I can look forward to the future with so much more joy, now that I think of such a banner waving over my head.

"I send you these few disconnected thoughts, as they will at any rate prove to you that I think of you, and may serve as some slight clue to what is passing in my mind.

"And now may the very God of peace bless you richly in blessing others, and make me more like you, for Jesus' sake. Amen."

"MILLVILLE, 7th mo. 23, 1861.

"MY DARLING MOTHER,—

. . . "We get along very quietly down here, and have nice times sewing and reading. I nearly ruined one of my dresses, and have been busy keeping Miss Flora McFlimsey in something to wear. We rode out on seventh day afternoon to see old Mr Loder. To my astonishment we found him so well that he was sitting under the shade of the trees in front of the cottage, his wife and daughter both away, leaving him alone. He seemed very bright, and delighted to see us. He is very old—over eighty, I think ; but his eyes light up, and he looks the picture of happiness when he speaks of some of Christ's promises. We asked him if he was not afraid to be left so entirely alone, being so helpless. It was blowing very hard, and I asked him if he was not afraid of a loose board from the roof falling on his head, for some of them looked very like it. He shook his head, and looked up brightly and said, 'No, it might fall and kill this poor body, but it could not hurt me.' I asked him, ' Why, what gives you this confidence that it could not hurt you?' He replied, 'Jesus, Jesus will take care of me.' I thought this poor old man had learned the same secret that David knew, when he said, 'Yea, though I walk through the valley of the shadow of death, I will fear no evil, for Thou art with me.' "

To an Invalid, who was always confined to her Room.

"Tswedelle, *Oct.* 1861.

" You will probably wonder at receiving a letter from a stranger, but the other day Mr L—— gave me one of your letters to read. It was an account of your Christian life, which interested me so much that I cannot refrain from writing you a few words of Christian love and sympathy. Although the Lord has seen fit to lead us in very different ways, still I feel that it is the same loving hand that has portioned out for both of us what His loving-kindness and tender mercy sees best, and that it is the realisation of the same glorious truth, of the love of Jesus for sinners, that has made us both happy. We are both sheep of the same good Shepherd, and I know full well that we are poor, weak, foolish sheep; but have we not occasion indeed to rejoice in that we have such a good Shepherd? He himself tells us how a good shepherd cares for his sheep. Have you ever thought that the very reason why He calls us sheep is because they are such silly, helpless creatures, and are more dependent on their keeper than any other animal? It is a known fact that a horse, a cow, or even swine, can find their way home if they are lost a few miles distant; but a sheep cannot: he must be followed and brought back.

"You said in your letter that the thought that you might ever stray from Him and be lost was one which troubled you; that you knew He was faithful, but you doubted yourself. I too have often thought of that, for well I know that my natural heart is so sinful that it is capable of anything; but I have no such fear now, for I know that a good earthly shepherd does not let his sheep stray entirely away, because he knows their weakness and foolishness; and is it to be supposed that the great Heavenly Shepherd is less faithful, or will do less for His sheep than an earthly one! So now I trust Him not to let me wander, for I am far more weak than a sheep. We have His promise, 'My sheep hear my voice, and I know them, and they follow me, and I give (in the present tense) unto them eternal life, and they shall never perish, neither shall any man pluck them out of my hand;' and as if He thought some might doubt His power to keep, He adds, 'My Father, which gave them me, is greater than all; and no man is able to pluck them out of my Father's hand; I and my Father are one.' So I think from the Bible we may trust Jesus for this as well as for everything else.

"I often find myself as a foolish sheep, having become entangled in the briers of temptation, where I lie all torn and bleeding, until my good Shepherd comes and lifts me up in His arms, and carries me back on His bosom.

"Oh, is not this wonderful, wonderful mercy!

'Nothing but sin have I to give,
Nothing but grace shall I receive.'

"I did not intend making this letter so long, for my time is much occupied, and my health at present does not allow me to write much at a time. But as God has given you the privilege, among many which He has denied you, of being able to write, I would like to hear from you. I am, as a Christian, very much interested in all that interests you."

We give a portion of the answer to this letter :—

"Your kind Christian letter was received by me with a glad heart. You do not seem to me to be a stranger, although I never heard your name till I met with it in your letter. There is a pleasant familiarity among the children of God; and why should there not be, when we are adopted into the same family?

"I was doubly glad on receiving your letter, first for your Christian sympathy, next because you showed me plainly a fault in myself that I was not aware of— the sin of unbelief. You may wonder that I never discovered it in myself, but I never did, and in your letter I could see it as plainly as if I had been looking at my face in a glass. I was at the same time glad and sorry—glad that you had written to me so kindly and faithfully, and sorry that I had been doubting God's word. I thought I was only doubting my own sinful self in being afraid that I might wander from my Heavenly Shepherd, but in your letter I could see at once that it is God's faithfulness that I have been doubting. How blind I have been! And Christ has given us such assurances of security and tranquillity. . . . In Isaiah xxvii. 3, in speaking of His care of His vineyard, He says, 'I the

Lord do keep it; I will water it every moment; lest any hurt it, I will keep it night and day.' " . . .

The following letter was written by Alice, at the request of this young girl, to a friend of hers, who, though many years a great sufferer, had never found joy and peace in believing in Jesus. Indeed her distress of mind only increased as her disease seemed drawing toward a fatal termination, from the fear that her sufferings here were but a foretaste of what she would have to endure through eternity. This letter was copied before it was sent, and as no answer has been found, we can only hope that the receiver learned to say, in the confidence of faith, " For me to live is Christ, and to die is gain :"—

"TSWEDELLE, *December* 1861.

" A fews days since I received a letter from Miss S——, in which she spoke of your great bodily suffering, and also told me something of your distress of mind. I have sympathised with you so much that I have concluded to write to you, hoping that a few words from one who has found the gospel of Jesus to be indeed 'glad tidings' to her sin-burdened soul, and longs that you too may rejoice in them, may not be unwelcome.

" You say that your greatest trouble is the feeling that you are a sinner, and the fear that your sins are not forgiven, and that you are not prepared to die. Then, dear friend, the Bible message to you will be good tidings, for it says, that 'Christ Jesus came into the world to save sinners' (1 Timothy i. 15). That is, bad people ; not good people, but sinners—

those who have whole years of sins on their shoulders. And now, what does the Bible say that Jesus has done for such? 'He died to save them.' Yes! in order to save them from the punishment of their sins, which is eternal death, He came down from His bright heavenly home, and Himself died instead. Is it a reality that Jesus has died for me? That He has stooped to take my sins on Himself, and that He has already put them away for ever? Ah, if so, if this be the glad tidings, then happy am I, for the sins cannot still rest on my head which Jesus has atoned for with His precious blood. Is not this really the message of God concerning His Son? (1 John v. 9–13). And is it not His message to you? He says, 'The gift of God is eternal life' (Rom. vi. 23), and that this 'free gift' (Rom. v. 15, 16) He bestows upon sinners (Matt. ix. 12, 13). That all who will may take it 'without money and without price.' 'Whosoever will, let him take of the water of life freely' (Rev. xxii. 17). And now is it not for you? Are you not a sinner? For such Christ died. Do you not feel your need of it? Jesus said, 'If any man thirst, let him come unto me and drink.' And lastly, are you not willing to receive it? 'Whosoever will;' does not that mean you? Yes; Jesus has done all for you, and all he wishes you to do is to accept the salvation He has wrought out for you. Certainly if I brought you a rich gift, which it had cost me much to procure for you, you would not be too weak or powerless to accept it, for that would not require any skill or great exertion on your part. There would be no difficulty about it, if you had a willingness to receive it, and believed that I was in earnest in giving

it to you.   In God's great mercy, He has made the
reception of His salvation just as simple a thing.   He
tells you what He has done for you, and He wishes
you to believe what He tells you, and trust Him to
do what He says.   You are nothing but a receiver;
He sees that you are too weak and sinful to do one
thing aright, so in His mercy He takes it all out of
your hands.   He gives all—pardon, the robe of righteousness to cover your nakedness, an eternity of bless
with Him—in short, all things you need; and you
but receive, wonder, and praise.   Take God at His
word; honour Him by believing that He means what
He says, 'For through His name, whosoever believeth in Him (Jesus) shall receive the remission of
sins' (Acts x. 43).

"You say you fear that it is too late, that your
day is past.   No; your very distress about your sins
is a sure sign that God's Spirit is still working in your
heart.   Remember the thief on the cross; he was
saved at the last hour.   And Jesus is not less merciful
now.   Do not let Satan tempt you to think your
great sinfulness is a reason for believing the gospel
message is not for you.   Your sinfulness and great
need of a Saviour is the very reason that He died for
you.

"It is the sick, the very sick, who send for the
physician, and he comes quickly, just because they
are so ill.   If he hears they are not much sick, he
will delay his coming.   You know yourself that it
would be but folly to wait until you are better before
you send for your physician; and just so Jesus came
to save those who had need, great need of Him.

"If you are able, I wish you would write to me.

and tell me all, but at all events go and tell Jesus, for He is 'able to save to the uttermost all those who come unto God by Him.' Committing you to your tender Father's care, I am yours in Christ."

"TSWEDELLE, *Dec.* 19, 1861.

"MY DEAR CARRIE,—

. . . "I was so sorry, darling, that I did not think of thee on thy birthday; I thought of it the next day, and have indeed wished many good wishes for thee, and kissed thee many times in spirit. May' God bless thee, darling, and make thee to walk nearer and nearer to him each year!

"I often think how different our birthdays are to us now from what they used to be when we were children. Then they were all joyous; now, how solemnising! They make us think that it is a solemn thing to live as well as to die. . . .

"To-day will, I suppose, bring us decided news with regard to a war with England. I hope it may be averted, but time alone can and will prove. Were it not for Luther's comfort, 'God reigns,' I do not know what we should do. It all seems wonderfully like the description in the Bible of the last days."

To M. M. J.

"TSWEDELLE, *Dec.* 29, 1861.

"I have only time to say good evening to you, my dear M——, for in about fifteen minutes we are going down to sit with father in the library, and sew, while he reads aloud to us. We spend almost every evening with him, and you don't know how pleasant it is.

He generally reads in the 'Living Age,' or 'Eclectic Magazine,' and they are so interesting, containing so much general information, that the hours pass almost before we notice them.   .   .   .

"You will be glad to hear that we had a very sweet Bible-class last week, almost the sweetest one we have ever had.   It was the seventeenth chapter of John.

"I have not been regularly down to the cottages for a good while; I have been so hoarse that it is impossible for me to read or talk much at a time, even at Bible-class.   I went down yesterday just to see how they were; they seemed very glad to see me.

"I am anxious to hear all about your Sabbaths in your next letter.   I want to hear also about the Christmas tree, and the children, and about your skating; but most of all, I want to hear about the 'inner life,' and how it prospers in all the hurry of your busy life.   Not 'pushed into a corner' I trust.

'Oh, for a heart to blend with outward life,
  While keeping at Thy side !'

"May God bless you and keep you from every temptation of Satan, who, be assured, is as busy as you, seeking by what means he may spoil your work, and draw your heart away from close communion with the blessed Lord.   That we may both live on the 'watch tower,' is, my darling, the heart's desire of your loving friend,   ALICE."

"TSWEDELLE, *Jan.* 5, 1862.

"DEAREST ANNIE,—

"It is first day afternoon—lovely, clear, and cold. I walked down to I——'s for the first time for some weeks. I did not stay long, as I am hoarse yet, but spoke a little to them about Jesus, which was a comfort, as it has been so long since I have been able.

"I always now have the two girls come up and study a chapter in the Bible with me on their Sunday in. A—— evidently don't care much for the subject of religion; but she sometimes cries when I talk to her, which encourages me to go on trying, although she don't evince interest in any other way, and often gets off from her lesson by very trivial excuses. I feel much better satisfied to know that she hears the gospel at any rate. I—— is always interested, and likes to have me talk to her, but, alas! I fear her life is not altogether encouraging.

"I see mother has told thee something of the sad event which ushered in our new year [the death of H. H. L——.] It seemed very sudden to us. Carrie said it was a very solemn time. . . . I think I shall go down to see her pretty soon; the house will necessarily feel sad for a while. May we learn by this sudden removal from time to eternity to keep more before us the reality of eternal things, and the nothingness of the things of this life in comparison. Blessed be God, 'we know that if our earthly house of this tabernacle be dissolved, we have an house not made with hands, eternal in the heavens.'

"I have been enjoying so much this afternoon Mackintosh's 'Notes on Leviticus,' about the burnt-offering. How I wish thou could have these books, they give you such precious views of Christ's work in its different aspects."

After giving some quotations, she says—

" I cannot give thee much idea of how beautifully

he sets forth the self-emptied devotedness of Christ
to His Father, and the perfect pleasure and infinite
satisfaction of the Father in the Son. It seems to
give me a deeper realisation of what Christ meant
when He said, 'As thou, Father, hast sent me into the
world, even so have I sent them into the world.' As
Christ was not sent into the world to enjoy ease or
His own rest, neither are we. As His was to be a
life of pain and trial, and self-denying exertion, so
is ours. He has not sent us into the world to bear
the sins of the world, but as He came to do His
Father's will, even so are we sent to do His will.
Oh, what a picture this presents of what we ought to
be to Christ! And, dear Annie, as we know we
have the power to do that for which we are sent, we
are reanimated; for as the life of Jesus was crowned
by an eternity of glory and honour, and matchless joy
in the bosom of His Father, even so on His bosom
shall we rest for ever."

"TSWEDELLE, *Jan.* 12, 1862.

"MY OWN DEAR CARRIE,—

"It is first day evening, and thou wilt find no
difficulty in imagining us in our second story sitting-
room. . . .

"To-day has not been as refreshing a Sabbath as
this day of rest often is to me. Satan has tried a very
ingenious method to spoil what I hoped would have
been a day of much study and refreshment. Without any reasonable cause, I have been so sleepy that
I have not been able to read three words without
nodding. I really could not do a thing, and yet I
think I never longed more in my life to be fed with

the living bread. It is a dreadful feeling, this being so sleepy, and wasting the precious time for prayer or study in trying to keep awake ; but perhaps it is calculated to make and keep us humble under a sense of our utter inability to worship or to do anything by ourselves. This may be the lesson the Lord is intending to teach me.

"I had such a pleasant day in the city yesterday. I was most of the time with H——; she is as busy as ever in her Master's cause, and seems to be just as much blessed in being used as an instrument in the hands of God to bring sinners to the feet of Jesus. Her devotedness and constant fervour in the work are a real rebuke to me.

"Oh, for a closer walk with God! Won't it be lovely when we get to heaven, and are rid of this body of sin? I do so long to be rid of sin ; it is for ever hampering, and drawing down to earth, and hiding from us our great aim in life. Oh, to be able to tell forth our love to Jesus in our lives, even as Jesus told forth the depths of His wondrous love to the Father, in His life and death.

"After dinner I went with H. and S. F. S—— to see a wonderful coloured woman (Hannah Carson). I never heard of an instance of greater bodily afflic- tion, and yet she is rejoicing in the Lord. Her limbs are completely paralysed, and she has no power of motion, excepting in her eyes. She suffers great pain all the time ; sleeps but very little, and her bones are almost through the flesh. For some years she had a girl to take care of her, who added to her sufferings by the most cruel treatment. It was truly refreshing to turn from this dreadful picture of bodily

K

suffering, to behold a soul at rest, in the midst of all this, on the bosom of Jesus, quietly waiting, and suffering the will of her Father, even in joyfulness of spirit. Speaking of the new year still finding her here, she turned her bright eyes toward me, with almost a heavenly expression, and in answer to my question if she ever grew impatient to leave her poor body and fly away, she said, 'Oh no, miss, not so long as it is my Father's will for me to remain here; had it been His will, old Hannah would gladly have greeted the new year in heaven many winters ago; but I have no will but His in the matter; I can feel no wish even, apart from Him.' Was it not a beautiful answer? H—— asked her if she was not troubled by not being able to keep her mind off her suffering and earthly things. She said, 'No, it used to be so; but God is very good to me, and now I can say, in truth, that my thoughts, like my heart, are in heaven, and seldom wander.' I wish I could tell thee many things that she said. What a reproach she is to any who would murmur! She seemed so happy and calm in such an extremity of affliction. How wonderful is the grace of God!"

"MILLVILLE, *Jan.* 30, 1862.

"My Darling Annie,—

. . . "I know that all is right, and that 'all things work together for good to them that love God.' Is not this text a comfort? We use it, and take comfort in it over and over again, and still it never grows old or stale. It is just as fresh to me to-day, when I think of it in connection with thee, as if I had never heard it before. All things! That means every little thing. Oh, it is a comfort! . . .

"May God bless thee, dear Annie, and give thee a more abundant outpouring of His Spirit! Remember, darling, Blessed are they which do hunger and thirst after righteousness, for they shall be filled.'"

"MILLVILLE, *Feb.* 6, 1862.

" DEAR S——,—

. . . "What treasures are there not stored up for us in Jesus, if we would only draw largely enough! Yes, there is indeed wisdom and strength, and sweet comfort treasured up for us in the storehouse of our Heavenly Friend and Comforter. And the key-note of all comfort is found in the thought that all is in the hands of God. We must not let ourselves think of Him as a Great Creator, far away, but as a loving, tender Shepherd, bending over us, very near, hearing every unexpressed wish or longing desire, noticing every smothered sigh, and fully understanding every aggravation of trial, be it great or small; and what is better than all, taking care of everything, and making 'all things work together for good.'"

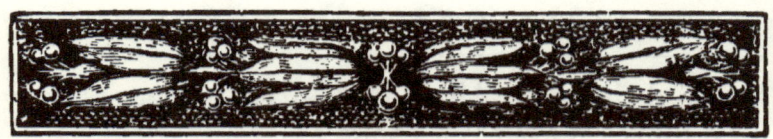

CHAPTER VIII.

THE following letter contains an account of a circumstance which deeply interested dear Alice at the time, and which gave her a source of interest for all the remaining years of her life. The little child here spoken of was the son of a young widow, who had left her father's house in Baltimore in a fit of passion, and had been reduced from one stage of degradation and misery to another, until she had ended in the wretched cellar where Alice found her. This little boy, whom she named Ernest, was always felt by Alice to be a solemn charge directly from her Heavenly Father, and she opened her heart to receive him to its loving care. During the remainder of her life she made all his clothes, supplied him with toys and books, took the oversight of his training, and often had him to spend weeks and months together at her own home, where she faithfully endeavoured to fulfil the trust she had accepted, and to train him for eternity. Her death seemed like an almost irreparable loss to him; but God so arranged it, that shortly afterward his mother, who had married again respectably, but who had concealed from her second husband at the time of her marriage the fact of her little son's existence, now made the whole story known to him, and he at once, with a noble forbearance, insisted upon taking the boy home to care for him as an own father would do.

"Tswedelle, *March* 22, 1862.

"My Dear B. C——,—

. . . "I wonder how this will find you with regard to the poor weak body; in spirit it will doubtless find you still praising the Lord. You don't know how often I think of your continual praise, ascending as it does out of your deep affliction, and it always does me good, and makes me feel like saying, with your favourite hymn—

'I 'll praise Him while He lends me breath,
And when mine eyelids close in death
Praise shall employ my nobler powers.'

"Your Methodist hymn-book, which you gave me, I often resort to. I have been learning out of it that lovely hymn commencing—

'From every stormy wind that blows,
From every swelling tide of woes,
There is a calm, a sweet retreat,
'Tis found beneath the mercy-seat.'

"It grows more wonderful to me every day, that poor sinful worms of the dust should be allowed such a refuge.

"Had I time I should like very much to tell you all about a little circumstance which has turned my thoughts and labours into a new channel for the last few days. I do not know whether you have heard about a new house of industry or female mission

which a few of my friends have been starting in one
of the very worst streets of Philadelphia, which brings
under their influence a number of the most degraded
women, who hear the gospel of Jesus, most of them
for the first time, and have an opportunity of beginning to live honest and respectable lives.

"I went down there the other day, as I often do when
in the city, and arrived just as my cousin Mrs S——
was surrounded by a number of poor women, who
were telling her in the most affecting terms about
a little baby in a cellar opposite. It had been given
by its mother to a very bad man and woman, who,
even in Bedford Street, were notorious for their
drunkenness and cruelty, and whose only object in
wanting the child was to reduce it to a skeleton, and
then to carry it about the streets begging, in order
to excite the public sympathy by its forlorn appearance.

"It was really a touching sight to see those poor
women begging us to rescue the little creature from
such a terrible fate. But what could we do? We
went over to see them, but could not make anything
at persuading the drunken creatures to give us the
child. We then went to the overseer of the poor,
but he sent us to the beggar detective police, who,
he said, would have the right by law to take the
child away by force, if he had sufficient evidence that
the man and woman were drunken, or in any way
unfit to take care of the child. We at last found the
officer we wanted, and proceeded with him to the
cellar, and in a few minutes more the child was
legally handed over to us, the mother having given
up all right and title to it.

"It was a strange feeling to think that that little fellow belonged entirely to us, and was dependent upon us.

"We took him to the mission-house, and there took off his dirty rags, and wrapped him in a clean shawl.

"A question then arose, what should we do with him? The almshouse was not the place for a baby, and not a single public institution in Philadelphia will take babies. So we took him up to my uncle's, and gave him a good bath, and dressed him in some clothes my cousin gave him, and were surprised to find him a sweet, healthy child, with a lovely smooth complexion and large blue eyes. They say he is thirteen months old, but he has a mouth full of teeth, and seems much older; claps his hands when he is hungry and sees his dinner coming, &c. We have found a private institution on purpose for little children and babies, where they have forty, all under four years of age; carried on entirely by Christians who have felt it their duty to give up their time to it, for Christ's sake, and we have put him there.

"I became so much attached to him, and he to me, that I almost wanted to bring him home; but I knew that I could not do that for many reasons.

"We have been very busy making clothes for him. Poor little fellow! it seemed strange to pray for him, and to feel that perhaps it was the first time he had ever been prayed for in his life. I feel indeed that God has made us his sponsors or guardians, without giving us the opportunity of choosing whether we will take the responsibility or not. It is a solemn

thing; nothing can relieve us from the duty of seeing that he is taught in the way of truth; and truly,
we would not wish to get rid of what the Lord himself has laid upon us.

"But I have written full enough about my baby. I
fear I have tired you, and it is time I had said good-
bye."

After a short visit from her sister from Millville,
she thus writes:—

"TSWEDELLE, *April* 1, 1862.

" MY OWN CARRIE,—

"Thou can't think how I missed thee on seventh
day. It was so dull and rainy out-of-doors, and bright
thoughts would not reign within. But I sat down
and tried to write an unusually cheerful letter to
M——, which had the effect of making me feel the
brighter.

"Yesterday we went to meeting, and I had a very
sweet time, taking home somewhat of the lesson of
Abraham to myself. In the afternoon I had a truly
favoured season at the cottages. I took the forty-first
Psalm at M——'s; I never knew how much gospel
it contained, it seemed to me I was never before
enabled to set it forth so freely and so fully."

To her other sister she writes—

"TSWEDELLE, *April* 6, 1862.

" MY OWN DEAREST ANNIE,—

"It is first day evening, and after a day of considerable exertion, I sit down to give the last end
of this lovely Sabbath to my darling sister far away.

It has indeed been most spring-like for a few days past, and after I came up from I——'s I ran down to the woods, just to see if the trailing arbutus was not out yet. I did enjoy it so much. The bright warm sun was so lovely, and the grass so green, and the birds sang more musically, it seemed to me, than I had ever heard them. All nature was praising God, and I joined with a really thankful heart. How many, many blessings does He not give us, which we seldom realise!

"I have had a lovely day, and I feel refreshed and strengthened. I do believe God will take care of me, and use me to His glory in some way. I do not know how, but with Miss Waring, I can say,

'I would be treated like a child,
And guided where to go.'

"Indeed it seems that I want the Lord to do more than that for me. I want Him not only to guide me, but to *make me go* in the right path, after I know which it is."

"TSWEDELLE, *April* 29, 1862.

"My Dear Sister Annie,—

. . . "I have been thinking lately that our everyday letters do not contain half as much of the inner life as they ought to. As for me, I seldom have anything to say of what passes within. I think my religion is deepening, rather than advancing. I am sure that Jesus, my refuge, is much more precious and necessary to me now than He ever was. I have learned much of His sufficiency, of which I scarcely dreamed before. And yet I cannot feel that I have taken as many steps forward as I ought in the past year. It is dreadful to look at my own unfaithfulness. I have wakened up to one thing, in which I have been very unfaithful, and that is in allowing myself to float along with circumstances, contented to remain in ignorance with regard to what the Lord would have me do about certain things.

"It certainly is the will of the Lord, is it not, that His children should always know, and be sure, just what they ought to do in every matter? They are surely not called to act upon an uncertainty. He has promised to be a guide to our feet, to 'lead us in a plain path,' to give us wisdom when we lack it. And is He not our 'Counsellor?' What do all these texts mean, if not that we may have confidence in all things that we may know the mind of the Lord, as to what He would have us to do? We ought not to rest short of this, for although we may be in doubt for a season, have we not cause to believe that He will give us this knowledge before He calls upon us to act?

"Now this is what in many respects I have not claimed. Beginning several years ago with the matter of baptism, I rested short of certainty with regard to what the Lord's will was, and let myself drift along with circumstances. Since then I can see the same uncertainty keeping me back in other things. Now in God's strength I have made up my mind, not in anything to rest nor to stop diligently inquiring of the Lord, until I know, and am sure that I know, His will."

"MY DEAR SISTER CARRIE,—

. . . "I am sorry I have so little time left, for I wanted to talk to thee about baptism. I am greatly stirred up about it. I have made a discovery—at least it seems like a discovery, although it is nothing new—and that is, that almost all my spiritual troubles have arisen from the fact that I have settled down to be contented with not knowing the will of the Lord about many things. It is perfectly ruinous to spiritual growth, and every time you act or stand still without being sure you are doing right, you are paving the way to more and more unfaithfulness. It is our privilege and absolute duty to know what we ought to do in every matter. I rested short of knowing this about baptism, and I have rested short of it in many things since. Now I must begin to act differently. I have begun with other things, and now I must mend with regard to baptism, as this was a sort of starting-point of my unfaithfulness. Do let us try, with the Lord's help, to be more faithful."

Shortly after writing the above two letters, after a diligent study of the Scriptures, and much prayer, Alice was settled in the conviction that baptism with water was a scriptural ordinance, and that it would be in accordance with the will of the Lord that she should submit to it. Although some of her friends, who may read this memoir, may not unite with her in her views on this subject, yet they cannot but acknowledge in her unhesitating obedience in this respect, her single eye to what she believed to be the Lord's will. Several letters, which follow, tell her feelings and experiences in regard to it.

"TSWEDELLE, *May* 20.

"MY OWN DEAR CARRIE,—

. . . "I think I have learned a lesson that is worth a great deal—a lesson in humility. I have a clearer idea of what my position ought to be. I am going to try to act like a pilgrim, and a stranger, and a traveller here. I feel somehow that I have taken a step. It is such an unspeakable relief to be settled upon some sure foundation with regard to baptism. I feel a calmness that is delightful. I am just resting upon Christ, and so I feel perfectly happy; all care, all anxiety is laid on Him.

'I am a poor sinner, and nothing at all,
　But Jesus Christ is my all and in all.'

"I am sure I never realised the first clause of this sentence so much, and I feel as though I never did the second. But I must not talk any more about this, though I believe I could write all day, I have so much to say. . . . I expect to go to New York on fifth day, nothing preventing, so am very busy.

"Kiss my nephew 'baby Fank' for me. The little darling, how I love him!

"THY OWN LOVING SISTER."

Alice went to New York to attend the yearly meeting in the sixth month, to which the following letter refers :—

"MY DEAR CARRIE,—

"Does thee think thy little sister has forgotten thee? I have been wanting so much to write, but I literally could not.

"I did not come home on seventh day, but went up the North River with Uncle W——. . . . Oh, dear, how I wish I could talk instead of writing! I want to tell thee everything. I had such a sweet time in New York, although it was a season of deep conflict and many mingled emotions. It refreshed me very much, and strengthened me in the path of duty. —— is perfectly lovely, and I was thrown with all the most interesting Friends. We had so many delightful seasons of religious and social intercourse. The first day school conference, too, was very instructive and encouraging; it quite stirred me up. . . .

" I feel that this visit has been of the utmost importance to me. I never before knew how much I loved Friends, nor how much I valued my membership, and still I feel so confirmed in the new stand I have taken with regard to the Bible. It was delightful and yet heartrending. . . . I prayed earnestly that if I was mistaken in my new certainty about baptism and the Lord's Supper, it might be shaken, and such clear doubts come into my mind, that I would not be allowed to take this step, which I feel to be one of so much importance, but if I was right, that I might be settled in it.

"The Friends were all so kind and lovely; they even told me they were praying for me that I might have clear light given me as to what was my duty

Dear —— was very sweet; she told me we should be just as near to her as ever; but I think the thought of losing us made her feel very sad; it quite distressed me to see it. We had some long conversations about taking the Scriptures simply; they were very satisfactory.

"About telling father and mother! How can I do it? I am praying about it, but I confess I am in some trepidation of spirit. I am laying in a stock of kisses from dear father; he is so good and sweet, I cannot bear to grieve him; he will feel that I am very undutiful and ungrateful. I do not want to act under any other feeling than that I am just doing an imperative duty. If we realise this, we will be willing to bear anything for the sake of it; but otherwise I know I never shall be able to stand all that it will bring upon me. . . . And now good-bye: may God bless us both, and lead us in the right way."

After telling her parents of her decision, she thus writes to her sister :—

"TSWEDELLE, *June* 13.

"MY DEAR CARRIE,—

. . . "I feel so happy about it now, so calm, and so sure I am doing right. 'If ye love me, keep my commandments.' This I believe to be a commandment, and as such I will keep it, and (God helping me) all other commands which I see that He gives. The 21st verse of the fourteenth chapter of John has been much in my mind. 'He that hath my commandments, and keepeth them, he it is that loveth me : and he that loveth me shall be loved of my Father; and I will love him, and will manifest myself to him." It is sweet to feel that you are seeking to keep His commandments."

" MY DEAR FRIEND,—

" It is one of the loveliest of Sabbath mornings, so calm and quiet; the little birds seem to be singing their praises even more joyfully than usual in the wood upon which my window opens, and my heart, too, sings praises.

" All the family have gone to meeting excepting myself, and as I could not go, I have been enjoying a little meeting here alone, and now I come to have a Sabbath morning talk with you.

" There are some precious truths, into a fuller realisation of which the Lord has most graciously brought me of late, and about which I would like to speak, for I long that you and all my friends may be more stirred up to realise with me, to what a glorious 'high calling' we are appointed in becoming the children of God through Christ Jesus.

" I know that all Christians give a passive assent when they read in the Bible that to become converted is to be made 'an heir of God, and joint-heir with Christ,' one of a 'chosen generation,' and a 'royal priesthood,' a member of the 'household of God,' even 'kings and priests unto God;' but if these truths were accepted as realities, could it help making a wonderful change in our ideas of the duties of a Christian, as well as our zeal in performing them ?

" I am now convinced that the reason many followers of Jesus do not see the inconsistency of many things, such as fighting, either in self-defence or de-

fence of their country, is because they do not appre-
hend the glorious truth of the heavenly calling of the
Church of Christ; that we are absolutely and really
'sons and daughters of the Lord Almighty,' and are
called to act accordingly. As such, we can afford to
act very differently from the way in which others do.
We are no longer to act upon human reasoning, for
we are the 'citizens of heaven,' governed by its laws
and rules; we are on the earth, but not of the earth.
Oh, what a different aspect this gives our whole lives.

" Will you not pray, dear friend, that your eyes may
be opened to realise more fully our heavenly calling,
privileges, and possessions? Think of the wonderful
names by which we are designated, and what a glorious
destiny we are told lies before us! To be the
'temple of the living God' (Eph. xi. 22), to be 'followers of God,' 'children of the light,' 'accepted in
the Beloved,' and to know that we shall be like Him,
that one day we shall share His throne and reign with
Him! We are, in short, dead and risen men; the
life we now live is resurrection life. It is as though
we had died and gone up to heaven, and taken possession of our home there, and then had been sent
back to earth for a little while to accomplish some
mission for our Lord.

" We are strangers and pilgrims on earth; we have
here no continuing city, but God has prepared for
us a city. The world hates us because we are not of
the world, even as Christ was not of the world, and
the Father loves us as He has loved His well-beloved
Son.

" You do, in some degree, appreciate what a
glorious thing it is to be born of God, do you not?

If you do, then the thought arises in your heart, as it has so powerfully in mine, 'Oh, that I could walk worthy of the vocation wherewith I am called !' The very purpose for which God has called us is that we 'may be conformed to the image of His Son.' Marvellous words ! Oh, that we may know their full meaning ! Is not this indeed the most glorious destiny of which the mind can conceive ! And shall we mar God's purpose by our disobedience and rebellion ! I am sure we do want to be made like Jesus, and do not wish even in one single little thing to come short of the wondrous destiny to which God has ordained us. Shall we not then rather give ourselves up—body, soul, and spirit—to let Him work in us to will and to do of His own good pleasure !

"And now this brings me to the second truth, the importance of which I have come to realise more than ever before. It is this—The necessity of having our minds perfectly subjected to the written Word of God. I have found that mine has not been, but I humbly hope it is now. It would be very difficult for me to make you understand exactly what my position was with regard to this ; but I never before appreciated what a gift the Bible is to the Christian, and, above all, what the Christian's position is with regard to the Bible. Just think of it, God has given us a book of written directions and commands, not only about the way by which we must be saved, through His dear Son, but about how we must walk after we are saved. We believe these are all inspired and perfect, having not one wrong direction or needless command. God himself says that they are

L

able to make us perfect, and to furnish us unto every good work. . . .

"I think I am prepared to follow the Bible, no matter where it may lead me. Such commands as those in Matthew v. 38–48, and Luke vi. 27–38, are, it is true, most unearthly and unreasonable; but they are addressed to unearthly men, to a 'heavenly race,' who do not acknowledge reason as their guide, but 'live by faith.' A child of wrath could not indeed give the cloak to him who has stolen his coat, for he has no Heavenly Father to give him another; he could not turn his other cheek to the smiter, for he has no Father to avenge his wrongs; he could not give to those who ask, and lend, hoping for nothing again, for he has no Heavenly Father to provide for all his wants; but God's children can do all this, and more, because their treasure is above. They are brought into fellowship with the Father and with His Son, and consequently are like-minded with them. God is not judging now, therefore His child must not judge; God is not taking vengeance now, therefore His child cannot avenge himself; God is dealing in grace, therefore His child must deal in grace. The world knows not God, it cannot see Him, therefore the children of God are set in the world to recommend and reveal Him. . . .

"And now let me ask you one question. Is your mind in perfect subjection to the written Word of God? Are you willing to take the Bible as your guide-book and directory, and follow wherever it may lead you? Will you give up all the traditions of men which you have been taught, and take instead the commands of God as your rule of life? Come to the Bible as a little child, willing to take every other command just as simply, and obey it, as you did the one to believe on Jesus and live. Try to forget all that man has taught you about what the Bible has said, and come to it to find out for yourself what really is there ; and remember that it is 'by reason of use,' that is, by using the light we already have, 'that our senses are exercised to discern both good and evil.' 'He that will do my will shall know of the doctrine ;' and there is no reason why you alone, with God and your Bible, should not become a 'strong man' in the things of God. It is a matter of the greatest importance to both you and me to find out what we are to do ; let us then go to the Bible, with a fresh motive and fresh zeal, to find out what the commands of the Lord are ; and what we find there we will do, the Lord helping us, will we not? for He has said, 'If ye love me, keep my commandments.' . . .

"I wish you could have met J. H. D——, a real evangelist, a 'Friend' with whom I became acquainted during my visit to New York last month. Being with him could not help, I think, inspiring other Christians with the same feelings of longing to spread the gospel. 'Freely ye have received, freely give,' has been sounding in my ears ever since. I feel so desirous that you should throw your whole soul into this work. You are not a minister, but you have 'heard ;' then say, 'Come ; whosoever will, let him come, and take of the water of life freely.'

"I could say much more on this subject, but I must not, for I want to tell you something which perhaps might have surprised you if you had not just read this letter.

"Next Sabbath my sister Carrie and myself expect to be baptized. I now see it clearly to be commanded in my guide-book, and of course I obey— yes, and gladly too; although I could not express how deeply I feel the severe trials which accompany it. Besides causing dear father much pain, it is a real trial to me to leave Friends.* It is the society of my birth, and I love it; moreover, those whose opinion I care most for are Friends. But all this is as nothing; my Saviour must be before everything, and it is His glory, not my own, that I am seeking; and, compared with the sweet pleasure of walking with Jesus, this trial seems light indeed.

"I look upon baptism as an expression of the glorious fact that I have been washed and made clean in the blood of my precious Redeemer; and also of the fact that I have been 'buried with Him by baptism into death, that like as Christ was raised from the dead by the glory of the Father, even so I also may walk in newness of life.' May He enable me to feel always that as in figure I shall go down into death, and come up again from death, so in reality I may be dead and buried to the world, but risen with Christ, and walking in newness of life. I believe that bap-

* Alice was not disconnected from the society, and she felt deeply the great kindness and consideration which she received from those who differed from her in their views on this subject. She often spoke of it afterward, and said that instead of finding it, as she had feared, to be a cause of separation from Friends she had long looked up to with respect and affection, she felt herself even more closely drawn to them in love than before.

tism is a most solemn, sweet, and appropriate figure of this death, burial, and resurrection with Christ."

On the 30th of 6th mo. Alice was baptized, and for the first time partook of the outward emblems of the broken body and shed blood of her precious Redeemer. She thus refers to it in a note written to her sister a few days after :—

"TSWEDELLE, *July* 2, 1862.

. . . "We have decided not to start for St John until a week from to-morrow, and now that we are not going so soon, I am possessed with a longing to see thee again, my own precious Carrie, but I suppose it is impossible. Sabbath afternoon was so sweet to me that I have felt better ever since ; more like living the resurrection life." . . .

About this time Alice received a visit from a young friend, for whose salvation she felt a deep anxiety. Shortly after her arrival, she sought an opportunity to set the Gospel before her. At first, there seemed to be no response, and Alice's heart sank within her, and she thought "Well, I am at least doing my duty, and must leave the result with God." After she had concluded, however, her friend threw her arms around her, and exclaimed, "Oh, I am so glad you have spoken to me on this subject ! For months I have been thinking about it, and have had no one to talk to." The result was that, during her visit, this young girl was brought to a knowledge of her Saviour, and was enabled to trust Him for the forgiveness of her sins, and, to Alice's great joy, openly confessed with her lips her faith in Him; thus adding another to the many precious souls whom she was privileged during her short life to lead to the feet of that Saviour who was so dear to her.

The next letter is from St John, New Brunswick, where Alice spent the remainder of the summer with her sister Annie.

To M. M. J.

" St John, *July* 22, 1862.

" My Dear M——,—

" I am afraid you will think your 'dewdrop' has ceased to sparkle for you, or that she has gone to Europe, or some such distant place, it has been so very long since you have heard from her. . . .

" Indeed you have been much in my thoughts, for I fancied your last letter seemed sad. I do not like to think of you as being so, although I know there must be in every life sorrows, and many trials only known to God. But is it not a comfort, dear M——, that they are all sent by Him, and that all our surroundings, and the circumstances in which we are placed, are arranged by His hand, and are working together for our good? Let us remember, for our encouragement, that we are to be living stones in the temple of the Lord, and as blocks of granite must be chiselled and carved, sometimes by hard blows and cutting, into the desired form, if they are to take a place in an earthly building, even so we are having the rough edges taken off, and are being formed into the right shape to fill just the little niche in the living temple of the Most High, which He designs for us. . . . We may have many things to make us feel careworn and anxious, but He can take care of everything, and what more do we wish? I have been earnestly praying to-day that the Lord will make me vigilant and sober and watchful; that He will quicken me by His Holy Spirit that I may be 'not slothful in business, fervent in spirit, serving the Lord.'

"My thoughts have been much occupied since I saw you in New York, by our baptism, which took place three weeks ago to-day; it was a solemn and unspeakably precious season. . . . May the Lord abundantly bless us, and shed upon us the renewing influences of His Holy Spirit."

TO THE SAME.

"TSWEDELLE, *Oct.* 12, 1862.

"MY VERY DEAR M——,—

. . . "I left St John on the 1st of September. You don't know how hard it was to leave my dear sister. I should have remained longer, but on account of the autumnal storms, it was thought best for me to leave when I did. I stayed in Salem with my friends the W——s for two weeks, and then L. W—— and Mr and Mrs O—— returned with me to Tswedelle. . . .

"I wish I could have you here for a few weeks, in the quiet! How we should enjoy it! But our dear Jesus knows best, and when that blessing is the best thing for us, He will grant it to us. In Him have we not all things?

"The 5th chapter of Romans has seemed so precious to me to-day, particularly the 10th and 11th verses. We are not only 'reconciled to God' by Christ's death, but are eternally safe because of His 'life' (resurrection), and now we 'joy in God.'"

CHAPTER IX.

THE preservation from a most sudden and terrible death, of which Alice speaks in the following letter to her friend M. M. J——, was considered by all who heard of it to be very remarkable, and to her friends it was cause of deep thankfulness that, through the mercy of their Heavenly Father, she was, as it seemed, miraculously restored to them.

"TSWEDELLE, *Nov.* 23, 1862.

"MY DEAR M——,—

"Your letters would have been answered before this, had I not been prevented by illness. I was in bed for nearly two weeks, but you will see that all danger has long since been over, when I tell you the cause of my illness. It was an accident that came very near terminating my life. I have been troubled a great deal this fall with neuralgia, particularly in my back, so about two months ago I asked the doctor if he could not give me something for it. He gave me two bottles of medicine, one for internal, the other for external use. By mistake, the wrong medicine was given to me, and it proved to be a deadly poison.   The two bottles were exactly alike, and the medicines the same colour.   It was just at dusk, and —— did not look at the label, as she felt so sure that she had left the right bottle in just that spot on the mantel, with the spoon beside it ; but some one, in dusting, I suppose, had removed it and put the aconite (which was what I took) in its place.

"I had been suffering from a severe headache for two days, and was lying on the sofa at the time I took the aconite [about the 3d of November].   In about ten minutes we went down to tea.   While at the table, I said to mother that my medicine seemed to have a very strange effect.   She immediately thought that perhaps I had taken the wrong kind. She brought the bottle, and, sure enough, I had taken sixty drops of aconite.   We looked in the 'Dispensatory,' and found it was a deadly poison ; that there were on record many cases where persons had taken twenty drops and died in less than an hour. Mother ran to order the carriage, while father and I pored over the book, hoping to find an antidote ; but nothing was said to direct us what to do.   I did not feel sick, only a burning in my stomach, and a queer drawing up of the muscles of my face.   It was a strange feeling to know that in a few short hours I might pass from time into eternity.   I knew that my life was in imminent danger, and the horrible nature of the death made me for a moment shudder ; but the thought of our perfect Saviour, and of going to be with Him, made me perfectly calm.   I got in the carriage, and we went to Dr H. C——'s, as we feared to wait for him to come to us.   He was fortunately at home, and gave me the most prompt and skilful medical treatment. It was, however, an hour and a half after taking the aconite before the emetics took effect, and by that time I was very ill. I did not lose my consciousness, though my whole body became rigid and cold : my sight left me, and even my tongue stiffened in my mouth ; the cold perspiration stood on my forehead, and I thought 'truly this is death.' For more than an hour I thought every breath would be my last. The doctor feared so too, as the effect of aconite is to contract all the nerves and muscles, particularly around the heart and lungs, thus stopping their action and causing death. It seemed a miracle that I did not die. For five hours I lay very low, suffering the most intense agony; indeed the suffering was more fearful than anything I had ever dreamed of, but I can truly say that it was worth it all to realise what a perfect Saviour Jesus is in time of trial. I wish I could tell you of the heavenly calm He granted me during those hours of dreadful suffering. I have always, from my childhood, had an almost morbid fear of death, and even since I have put my trust in Jesus I have sometimes been tempted to fear that when that trying hour came I should feel frightened, even though I knew that through a crucified Redeemer I was going to an eternal home in bliss. But when I thought each moment was my last, and the shadows of the dark valley were about me, every fear was taken away, and a heavenly joy and peace filled my soul. Jesus was with me, and I was not afraid.

"When I felt myself coming to, it was almost with sorrow that I thought of recovering, only for mother's sake. Poor mother ! She must have suffered more than we can imagine. She sent the carriage back immediately to Tswedelle for father and L. W——, who was with us at the time, and they stayed with me until morning, when they took me home. Dr C——'s family were all so kind, they were up nearly all night, four or five of them rubbing me at once to bring back vitality and allay the suffering in my limbs. I never shall forget their kindness.

"The doctor said that all danger from the poison was over by the next day, but it left me very weak, and my nervous system had received a shock which it felt for some time. I had very good nurses. They sent for Carrie a few days after, when they found how slow my recovery was likely to be. At that time I had occasional sinking turns, which seemed rather alarming; but the doctors (I only had four) said they were not at all dangerous. They all complimented me on having a remarkably strong constitution, as a weak one, they all agreed, could never have rallied.

"You don't know what a cozy little room mine grew to be during my sickness, or rather my convalescence. It always was cozy, but now it is pleasanter than ever. If you could have peeped in upon our social circle, you would have wanted to join us, I am sure; and equally sure am I that you would have been most heartily welcomed by us all, but especially by the invalid on the sofa, in the blue dressing-gown and slippers."

The trial and the triumph recorded in the above letter were to Alice cause of the deepest thanksgiving to the God of all grace, who had proved Himself to be such an all-sufficient Helper in time of need.

She often spoke of her feelings at the time, and of the perfect victory over all her natural fear of death, which was granted her. From her childhood she had always had an especial horror and dread of being buried alive, and while under the immediate effects of the poison, it seemed to her for a time that such was to be her fate; for while perfectly retaining her consciousness, she was utterly unable, by word or movement, to show any signs of life, and even seemed to herself to have ceased to breathe. She said afterwards, that at this time she realised very vividly the possibility of being supposed to be dead, and of being shut up in a coffin, and placed in the dark grave, with her consciousness remaining as vivid as ever; but she was not frightened or troubled, for she felt that the presence of Jesus would sustain her even there.

" TSWEDELLE, *Dec.* 2, 1862—3d day.

" MY OWN DEAR CARRIE,—

. . . " Mother told thee, I believe, that I had another ill turn on fifth day evening. I very foolishly over-exerted myself, and brought on a bad headache and chill, accompanied by some of the old symptoms, which left me weak. Yesterday I came out into the sitting-room for the first time, but did little but lie still on the sofa. To-day I am better— that is, stronger, but have a very bad headache; don't know that I ought to write, but am quite tired of doing nothing. These neuralgic headaches make me sometimes a little cast down, because I have to sit still in a world so full of action; but it is very wrong, and in the depth of my heart I do love to have Him do with me just what He pleases.

. . . . " I must tell thee before I go any further how much pleased they were at the B——
Home (the home where she had placed Ernest) with
the things we took them ; the fruit of our 'sewing
bee,' one week long.   My zeal for making things
for the children increased tenfold ; indeed the more
you do, the more you want to do.   We took them
over a royal Thanksgiving feast—cakes, apples, &c.
H. B—— entirely lost her heart over a dear little girl
named Mary, and a dear little Lizzie has haunted my
dreams ever since.   She is a new-comer, entirely
friendless, only thirteen months old, and as sweet a
looking child as you ever saw.   They all enjoyed the
good things so much.

" I have been thinking we have been very zealous
getting their bodies something to wear; now it is,
I am convinced, necessary to the proper develop-
ment of their characters that they should have something beside their little thin fingers to play with.
Children learn as much through their bright picture-
books and playthings as we do from our books.   I
have not been able to sleep, thinking of my different
plans for, in some degree, filling this want.   Just
think of Frank shut up in a big square room, without ' Lu Lee ' or the bag of spools, or blocks, or
in fact anything for his active little fingers to busy
themselves with ; no chairs even, to put together for
' chu chu cars,' only long benches to sit on.   Now
Christmas is coming, and I am determined they shall
have some Christmas beside eatables.   I do not believe
there is a doll in the whole establishment.   I am going
to buy and dress some, but my capacity for rag babies
is, I fear, very small, and rag dolls are just the best

things. Christmas is near at hand; we must be up and doing.

"I can't make up my mind which would be the nicest way of giving the things—to take them over on Christmas day, or before, and have the rows of stockings hung up on Christmas eve, and found full next day when they get up. An apple, a little candy, cakes, and one plaything—doll, or book, or something of the kind—would fill a stocking.* Dear little things! They need home pleasures to look back upon. . . .

"My last visit to the city was of great use to me. Our talk about the guidance of the Holy Spirit stirred me up very much, and I have enjoyed more direct communion than for a long time past. It is a very sweet thing to feel that we have, absolutely have, His guidance about even little things. Every step ought to be guided sensibly by Him; that is, we can and ought to be sure that this minute we are doing the exact thing that He wishes us to do. . . .

"I enclose H——'s letter; do send it back to me; but first get all the good out of it thou can; it is lovely. Since I have received it I have been praying that prayer ['That Christ may dwell in our hearts by faith, that we, being rooted and grounded in love,

---

* A Christmas tree was finally decided upon for the children at the Home, and a noble one it was, reaching to the ceiling, and loaded with cakes, apples, tarlatan bags of candy, dolls, and brilliantly-coloured picture-books; while at its foot lay wheelbarrows, waggons, and other toys, enough to gladden the hearts of these little friendless ones, who were seldom, after that, forgotten by her at Christmas. Little Ernest shared largely in these gifts from "Aunt Alice."

may be able to comprehend with all saints what is the breadth, and length, and depth, and height, and to know the love of God, which passeth knowledge, that ye might be filled with all the fulness of God' Eph. iii. 17–19], and have had such glorious views of Christ's love, that I feel almost afraid to mention it, lest I should tread on holy ground. I had no idea that He loved me so much as I am now sure He does, and I am very sure I never enjoyed loving Him so much. I feel as though I love Him with all my heart, but I am afraid I don't act as though I do. May the Lord help us to acknowledge Him in all our ways ! "

"TSWEDELLE, *December* 3, 1862.

"MY OWN DARLING SISTER ANNIE,—

. . . "Father and mother have gone to G——, and I have settled myself down for a cozy day all by myself. I am lying on the sofa—a peculiar position for writing—in the sitting-room, and pussy blue, my only companion, is curled up by the flue.

"My heart turns toward thee in loving thoughts while I lie so still. For the last week I have had to keep to the bed or sofa most of the time, and it gives me a great deal of time to think. I have been particularly blessed with a sense of the presence of Jesus, and have enjoyed His love wonderfully. How sweet it is, and how much better than anything else ! And it makes us feel our sinfulness and unworthiness more than anything else, does it not? I have enjoyed a fuller understanding of what it means to be 'brought nigh' by the blood of Jesus than ever before.

Strange how words fall on our ears, and we do not take in their meaning until, at last, the Holy Spirit shines down their full import into our hearts. I have been wondering how it is that we feel in our hearts that we love Him so much, and yet our lives show forth so little of that love. I am sure I feel as though I love Him better than ever I did before, and with my whole heart, fervently; yet dozens of times a day do I forget, and do what does not please Him. Do pray for me, dear Annie, that my life may tell forth to Him that I love Him."

"TSWEDELLE, *December* 28, 1862.

"MY DEAREST ANNIE,—

. . . "Thou asks if the neuralgia has been increasing on me. I had more of it almost immediately after my return home in September, but I do not know that it has increased much since then, only, as I have not been quite so strong since my accident, I have suffered more. But enough about my health, I am well enough to consider it an insult to be called an invalid, although I take the petting with a very good grace.

"The sweet season of Christmas has passed. I have been wondering how it passed with you. I know that to thee it brought sweet thoughts of Jesus. How did Charley and Annie spend it? I never had so much of the fun of Christmas before. We had a right merry time, and enjoyed fixing Frank a tree very much. Father said we were like so many grown-up babies. Frank thoroughly entered into the pleasure. I wish thou could have seen his dear little face as he walked round and round the tree, pointing up

M

with his fat little finger, first to one thing, and then to another, asking his stereotyped question, 'What's ems?'"

"DEAR S——,—

. . . "The love of Jesus is what we shall feast on in eternity. We may imagine what a glorious feast it will be, since the little glimpses we have of it here are so indescribably sweet. I long to know more of it, and who can tell what depths of His love, if we ask earnestly and constantly, He may not show us?

. . . "I long to love the will of God, and to have it for my treasure; and it is so sweet, is it not, to know that this is His wish also? 'This is His will, even your sanctification.' I believe He rates a man's sanctification (in the sense of growth in grace) by the degree in which He sees that his will is subjected to God's will. It is our will that He looks at, for it is the mainspring to our actions. If He sees that our will is always unreservedly to do His will, and to have His will done in us, and by us, and through us, He will look very leniently upon our external performance of it. How much, how very much, we must grieve Him by withholding from Him this simple constant desire to do His will."

"MY DEAR S——,—

. . . "It is not for external or glaring sins that He most chides His children, but for a wandering of heart, a turning away from Him, a seeking of pleasure or satisfaction in the world instead of in Him. 'Where your treasure is, there will your heart be also.' Jesus is the centre. We have life and peace only because we are in Him, and when our heart and mind cease to revolve around Him as the One most to be desired and altogether lovely, we lose our strength and are in a position of most imminent danger. Jesus has said, 'I am the vine, ye are the branches, without me ye can do nothing.' Every moment the sap must continue to flow from the parent stalk through every leaf and fibre. If it is interrupted, the leaves wither and die, unless the obstacle be removed, and the union between the branch and the vine becomes again a practical reality. Just so it is when the communion with the great Source of our life and strength is interrupted, our spiritual life begins to ebb away, our strength and all our heavenly peace is gone, and Satan, taking advantage of our position, redoubles his efforts to reign in our hearts. Satan is strong and we are helpless, but there is One mightier than he. If you will be like the little shell-fish clinging to the mighty rock, all the storms, all the powers of earth and of darkness, cannot hurt you. Your danger is when your clasp of Him is loosened."

To M. M. J.

"MILLVILLE, *March* 22, 1863.

. . . "I cannot tell you, dear M——, how glad, unspeakably glad, I am that you have been blessed by the realisation of the nearness of Jesus. It is just the thing we want, for if we have Jesus near us, all else goes right. I, too, have been richly

blessed lately by a sense of His presence, and I long,
darling, that we should live near to Him all the time.
I am sure we can do it, and I think we want to ; why,
then, should we not?   Surely He does not withdraw
His Spirit from us, for He says, 'Lo, I am with you
alway, even unto the end of the world.'   And again,
in the 16th chapter of John, He says, 'If a man love
me he will keep my words, and my Father will love
him, and we will come unto him, and make our abode
with him.'   Oh, I am praying that I may not grieve
that Holy Presence away from my heart.   He can
teach us how to live very close to Him, and give us
the strength to do it; and, moreover, He has promised
that if we ask, we shall receive.   We want more faith
and earnestness in asking.

"If this is life, to know the only true God and
Jesus Christ whom He has sent, is it not growth to
know more and more of Him?   I am thoroughly
stirred up to pray for it, and I think I am receiving
gradually sweeter and sweeter, closer and closer
knowledge of His love, and the best of it is that the
deepest draught of His love is only a taste, for what
infinite depths are there which no human being has
ever fathomed ?

I am having such an interesting visit with Carrie.
There has been a great revival here.   Hundreds of
the most careless seem to be roused earnestly to inquire the way of salvation ; and very many, I really
believe, have passed from the old life into the new.
. . .   Carrie and I have had the privilege of talking
to quite a number of these inquirers, and we have
indeed found it a blessed field of labour, they are so
glad to hear the 'glad tidings.'   Several very inte-

resting cases have come under our observation, and made our hearts thoroughly enlisted in the work. This has made me lengthen my visit considerably, for I feel that such openings ought not to go unimproved. There has also been a great interest manifested in the Sunday-school; quite a number have made a profession in the Methodist church, and others seem desirous of becoming Christians. We have been visiting them in their homes, and, as is naturally the case, the more we do, the more opens before us to be done. Our time is thoroughly occupied, for, besides our out-of-door duties, we are very much interested in studying the Scriptures together."

Dear Alice always seemed to find work for the Master wherever she went; but especially at Millville, a wide field of labour opened before her among the families of the workmen on the place, and those connected with the Sabbath-school.

She was very sympathetic and loving in her ways, and the poor and sick always rejoiced to see her coming to their homes, more for her kind and gentle words of sympathy and comfort than for the delicacies or necessaries of which she was so often the bearer. She never liked to go empty-handed to visit the poor, for she often used to say, "A half pound of tea or some sugar opens the heart wonderfully to receive the gospel." Many a poor woman has received some article of clothing or a nice bonnet, made by her busy fingers, to enable her to go to church. She would speak most faithfully to them, too, of their souls' best interests, for she never seemed to feel any fear or false delicacy in a matter which she felt to be of so much importance.

Once when visiting with her sister a sick person, they found with him another young man, a neighbour. He seemed perfectly indifferent when Alice spoke to him of the importance of having *his* sins forgiven and washed away in the blood of Jesus; but she, seeing his hardened state, and the uselessness of talking to him unless the Holy Spirit took her words home to his heart, kneeled down, and in the most earnest manner besought God to open his eyes to behold his own sinfulness, and his utterly lost and undone condition without a Saviour. The man seemed entirely overcome, and was melted to tears; but it remains for that last great day to reveal whether the word spoken brought forth fruit unto eternal life.

She was also a great help in the Sabbath-school. It was always opened with singing, and the reading of a portion of Scripture followed, which was generally the subject of a few remarks, or a short address. When Alice was present she used often to speak to the children. Her sister writes, "I never shall forget the day she took the cleansing of the leper as her subject. She brought out the type most beautifully, and the words of our Saviour—' I will, be thou clean'—never seemed so precious to me before." She was very fond of the typical teaching of the Old Testament Scriptures. The burning of the leprous garment (sin in the flesh) and the law of the Nazarite (a separation within a separation) were with her, to a great extent, practical realities, and having thus received their teaching into her heart, they came from her lips with twofold power.

"TSWEDELLE, *April* 30, 1863.

" DEAR FRIEND,—

. . . "It is hard for our natural hearts always
to realise of how very little importance all earthly
things are compared with spiritual; but I am sure
that the more we grow in grace and in the knowledge
of the Lord Jesus, the more we shall realise that 'the
things that are seen are temporal, while the things
that are not seen are eternal.' A man on important
business to a foreign land cares little for the trials
and inconveniences of the way, for he thinks, 'Ah,
if I only accomplish the end for which I came, it
will be worth all, and far more!' The thought of
settling himself down in ease and comfort in the
pleasantest village he can find there, never enters his
mind, for he has not started out for *pleasure*, but is
intent on some earthly object, and is in a hurry to do
his work, and go home with a fortune, perhaps. If
the scales of earthly-mindedness were withdrawn
from our eyes, we should live in the realisation that
our position is like that of such a man. This world
is, in truth, a strange land to us, for our citizenship
is in heaven—our mission here is not enjoyment, although true joy, like many other things, is oftenest
found when we seek it not.

"Our mission here is to do the will of our Father
who sent us, and to accomplish the work which he
has given us the privilege or honour of doing for Him,
whether it leads us into pleasure or pain. Surely our
glorious mission should be a far more powerful motive to self-denying exertion than the desire for riches
or any temporal good.

"I am glad that you have been thinking about our

heavenly calling, for I know it will make the rough way easy to you, especially if you add to the realisa-, tion of this great truth the constant remembrance of the sufficiency of Jesus, our strength, for all things whereunto we are called.

> 'Jesus, my strength, my hope,
> On Thee I cast my care.'

How little we appreciate what He would be to us if we would only let Him. I often think of what Ryle says, somewhat in these words, "Why will ye remain hungry, when there is such a rich feast of the living bread spread on purpose for you? Why grow faint from thirst, and refuse to take but a few drops from the living Fountain? Are you poor? It is because you will take a few pence only from your boundless treasury in heaven, from whence you might draw the endless treasures of grace.' I do not pretend to quote him word for word, but the thought seemed to me to be a striking one.

"What lovely promises those are you spoke of; they have often comforted me, particularly that one, 'Call upon me in the day of trouble, and I will deliver thee, and thou shalt glorify me.'

"Since I last wrote you I have been to the 'Border Land.' I have stood on the very brink of the river of death, but it was not my Heavenly Father's will that I should yet pass into the glories above; so I have returned to the battle of life, stronger and better, I hope, for that glorious experience of the power of Jesus to support in a dying hour. . . . In looking back, it seems to me that one reason why the Lord spared my life may be that I may testify to

others of the power of the gospel of Jesus to support
one of the weakest and most unworthy worms of the
dust in the face of a sudden and most frightful
death. More than ever before did I realise the deep
meaning of the words—

> 'Nothing in my hand I bring,
> Simply to Thy cross I cling.'

Oh, there is no use in our trying to be worthy of eternal life ; if we receive it, it must be as a free gift—
freely given in mercy for Christ's sake, and not because of anything in us, or which we can do. . . .
It seems to me that to live aright in order to get to
heaven is deeply dishonouring to Jesus, and spoils
all acceptableness, of such service, for the motive is
more than the work in God's sight.

" Our Lord certainly gives us strong enough motives
to a holy life without this, and if they are not sufficient for us, then indeed is the loss our own. I think
the Scriptures plainly teach us that there is an abundant recompense of reward given unto all those who
will serve Him in sincerity ; and that those who will
not be obedient shall suffer loss both here and hereafter. We are not told that the reward is a title to
heaven, for we can only enter there by the blood of
Jesus ; or that the loss that the unfaithful child sustains
(who, remember, is still a child, though a naughty one)
is the forfeiting of heaven. In 1 Cor. iii. 11–15, it
says, ' Other foundation can no man lay than that is
laid, which is Jesus Christ ;' but ' if any man build on
this foundation, gold, silver, precious stones, wood,
hay, stubble, every man's work shall be made manifest,' for 'the fire ' (which in the Scriptures is often used

to symbolise the judgments of God) 'shall try every man's work of what sort it is. If any man's work shall abide he shall receive a reward. If any man's work shall be burned, he shall suffer loss; but he himself shall be saved, yet so as by fire.' You will notice that the foundation was the same in all these cases, so an entrance to heaven was alike sure to all, for they all were redeemed children; but when it speaks of their works there was a vast difference, as great as between hay or stubble and precious stones, so great is the difference in the rewards.

"I have been looking out some of the promises given to obedient children, and they are just perfectly sweet, and make me feel as though I would be willing to do or suffer anything to be obedient. Take, for instance, the 21st and 22nd verses of the fourteenth chapter of John. If we have ever tasted the heavenly joy of communion with Jesus; if we have ever known what it is to have the sensible realisation of His being very near to us, then indeed we will feel that to have Him come in and abide with us is the richest reward He could possibly offer.

"We all know how far we feel from God when disobedient, and sin is sure to rob us of all our enjoyment in religion here, and, doubtless, if habitually indulged in, will materially lessen our capacity for enjoying the eternal glories of heaven.

"Have you ever noticed that there are blessings promised, not only to those who obey, but to those who have his commandments? I have been much struck with this; for are there not few comparatively who take the pains to study, and have clearly before their minds each and all of the commands given to

Christians in the New Testament? I have commenced to read it through, with the idea of picking
them all out and learning them, and I am astonished
at finding so many which I have never before looked
at in the light of commands; for instance, 'Fear ye
not, therefore, for it is your Father's good pleasure
to give you the kingdom.' I always looked upon
this as a very comforting assurance, but I did not
realise that the 'Fear ye not' was just as much a
command as 'Love your enemies.' It is a great
thing to be on the look-out for the imperative mood;
we shall find it oftener than we think. 'Comfort ye
one another with these words' (1 Thess. iv. 16–18)
is another text I never thought of as a command, and
so I have never tried to comfort any one with those
words. I could not be said to have that command,
for I never recognised it as such. So it is with many
other words of our Lord, and I am convinced that
the loss we sustain in not having His commands is
only second to our loss in not obeying them.

"The first thing to be done in this most important and interesting search after truth, is to make up
your mind that, with all the strength God gives, you
are going to obey every command you find there,
no matter how hard or even unreasonable it may
seem to the natural man; believing that as we think
God means to do exactly what He promises, and
wishes us to take Him at His word, even so when He
commands, He wishes us to take Him at His word
in the same simple way, and really to do what He
tells us to do. When this step is taken, the next
difficulty we meet is to decide which commands are
spoken to His disciples, only to be acted on at that

particular time, and which apply to all Christians. This at first seems hard; but prayer and a little meditation will always bring us to a conclusion on each text as it comes; for surely God gives us our guide-book in order that we may know His will, not in order to hide it from us. I find great benefit in taking each command and making it a subject of prayer, that I may be taught just what it means, and be made to keep it in just the sense in which it was given. We ought also to pray that we may learn to love each one, and keep it gladly as a privilege, and not merely as a duty.

.　.　. " May He ever encircle you in His everlasting arms, and keep you from all evil, drawing you closer and closer to Himself! "

To M. M. J.

"Tswedelle, *May* 1863.

" My Dear Little M——,——

.　.　. " I long to see you so much; what nice talks we will have, and how delightful the thought of studying the Bible together once more! I never enjoyed studying it so much as I have lately. I am making such a nice text-book on all different points of doctrine. I find the texts and put them together, and it brings every subject out so beautifully. You must begin one when you come, for I am sure you will like it, and I have felt that a real blessing has rested on mine.

" My Heavenly Father has led me through some very interesting experiences, about which I have sometimes longed to sit down and tell you, but I know that a quire of paper would not contain half.

. . . "My heart re-echoes your longing. It will indeed be a glorious time when we shall lose our vile bodies, and be free from sin. My longing to be rid of sin increases every day, for I feel so constantly that it is the only thing between us and God. How sweet that we constantly have that washed away in the blood of Jesus, and so there is really nothing left to separate us from Him in spirit. But, oh, the treachery of our nature! I often think of what somebody says, that no matter how slight the sin, or how transient the foolish thought that we indulge in, it as completely shuts us out from communion with God, for the time, as a greater sin." . . .

CHAPTER X.

HE following letter was written to a young girl who had been spending a week or two with Alice :—

"TSWEDELLE, *July* 20, 1863.

"MY DEAR FRIEND,—

. . . "I cannot tell thee how much I long that thou shouldst have that settled confidence toward God which will make thee sure at all times that He has redeemed thee, and 'blotted out as a thick cloud thy transgressions,' for in this way canst thou best honour and please Him. 'He that believeth hath set to his seal that God is true.' Thou wilt remember that the first sin that came into the world was unbelief. Before Eve disobeyed God by eating of the forbidden fruit she doubted His word. Satan told her, 'Ye shall not surely die,' and she believed what he said rather than what God had said. First, she lost her faith in God's love towards them [in denying them what seemed to her good for them], then, after thus doubting His love, she was ready to doubt His truth, and the natural consequence of this was disobedience.

" Thus the first sin was unbelief, and in God's supreme ordering, faith, or belief, is the first thing in the sinner which He can impute to Him as righteousness (Rom. iv. 16–25). The natural mind cannot realise the exceeding sinfulness of unbelief toward God, or the blessedness of faith in Him ; but ' His ways are not our ways, nor His thoughts our thoughts,' for He tells us in the Scriptures that unbelief is the condemning sin (John iii. 18, 36 ; John. viii. 24, 46 ; John xvi. 9 ; 1 John v. 10). And again, that ' He that believeth on the Son hath eternal life, and shall not come into condemnation.' But it is of great importance to remember that our faith, apart from its object, has neither value nor existence. It is what we believe in that makes our faith valuable, and the ground on which we believe it that determines its stability.

"And what is it that the sinner must believe? Simply that Jesus is the Christ, and that He died to save sinners, and that he himself is a sinner (Acts xiii. 38, 39 ; 1 Tim. i. 15 : 1 John v. 1). If he believes God's testimony concerning Christ—and either we do believe it or we do not : there is no middle place between faith and doubt— if he believes this, then God says of him that ' he is justified '—he ' hath everlasting life '—he ' shall not come into condemnation '—but that he ' is passed from death unto life '—and to doubt this is to make God a liar (1 John v. 10, 11). Christ is the Saviour ; faith only apprehends Him. Do not try to find out whether thou hast faith—look at Jesus, not at thy faith. If we want to know whether we can see, we look at something ; we do not begin to feel our eyes, or go to the doctor to have them examined. So it is with faith ; if uncertain whether we ever believed, no matter, let us believe now. The Bible says, ' He that believeth ' —not did believe or will believe, but he that believeth—' hath '—not did have or will have, but ' hath eternal life.' It is Jesus, not our faith. Remember when a beggar comes to take the bread you offer, it is the loaf he looks at, not his hands which he stretches out to receive it. Hold, dear friend, ' the beginning of thy confidence steadfast unto the end,' for so are we made partakers of Christ (Hebrews iii. 14)."

"TSWEDELLE, *August* 4, 1863.

" MY DEAR B. C——,—

" I cannot tell you how much we have thought of you since the dreadful riot in your city (New York). . . . I feared lest it might be too much for your poor body, even if your house was preserved from fire or the depredations of the mob.

" As for your spirit, I felt sure you would be able to say with the Psalmist, ' In the time of trouble He shall hide me in His pavilion ; in the secret of His tabernacle shall He hide me ; He shall set me upon a rock. And now shall mine head be lifted up above mine enemies around about me ; therefore will I offer in His tabernacle sacrifices of joy ; I will sing, yea, I will sing praises unto the Lord.' . . .

" I have been enjoying the last part of the 4th chapter of 2d Corinthians so much lately. ' Our light affliction, which is but for a moment, worketh for us a far more exceeding and eternal weight of glory, while we look not at the things that are seen, but at the things that are not seen, for the things that are seen are temporal, but the things that are not seen are eternal.' I never noticed until lately how the whole sentence hangs on that 'while we look,' for we know that sorrow and affliction do not always work for us a far more exceeding weight of glory, and this explains how it is. If we look at the seen thing, which is the affliction, it crushes us down to earth ; but if we keep our eyes fixed upon the unseen thing, which is God's love in sending it, and power to support us through it, then it worketh for us a far more exceeding weight of glory. It has been very interesting to me to notice how everything in this world has a seen side and an unseen side to it. The seen side we look at with the eye of flesh, while the unseen side is only beheld by the eye of faith. Death, to the eye of flesh, is terrible and appalling, but faith sees that it is only the gate to heaven." . . .

To M. M. J.

"Tswedelle, *Oct.* 8, 1863.

" My Dear Little M——,—

. . . "I am so glad that you have been blessed by a fresh outpouring of the Spirit of the Lord. How these heavenly glimpses of His beauty and His nearness strengthen and reanimate us for the fight! It is indeed sweet to feel the lovely robe of Christ's righteousness wrapped about us, and when we realise it thus, what presumption and folly all our former efforts appear to pin some of the rags of our own righteousness on to this perfect mantle!

"I have been trying to make that idea of Madame Guion, about having the will of God for our treasure

N

a practical matter, and I find it very sweet. If it is our treasure, no trial nor trouble nor sorrow can rob us of it. No circumstance but has its sweetness, though to the natural eye it seems most trying. . .

"I cannot begin to tel. you what nice times we have with Annie and the children : they are too sweet to speak of; particularly Master Thomas Frederick, a young gentleman of eleven months old, perfect in form, feature, and behaviour, the very most playful, sweetest, and cunningest little rogue that ever lived, and, best of all, he is quite devoted to his Aunt Alice. Annie expects to start for St John day after to-morrow, and I shall probably go as far as Boston with her. . . .

"And now I must close, although I have much more that I would like to say. May our dear Lord draw us both very close to Himself in the path of self-abandoning obedience. How I long to live nearer and still nearer to Him each day !"

"TSWEDELLE, *Nov.* 28, 1863.

"MY DEAR CARRIE,—

. . . "I arrived at home last second day, after a most interesting and delightful visit at Brooklyn. I sincerely hope it will be blessed.

. . . "I am sorry to hear of thy perplexities, but it will no doubt be all arranged as is best. Is it not a comfort to feel that our Lord's hand is in the everyday matters of life ? I am sure that if we do not believe in His having the arrangement of these, it is folly to think that He arranges anything for us. . . .

"I am enjoying the subject of the ' second coming'

very much. I have gone back to my old plan of taking an hour every day for reading and devotion, and I find the greatest comfort in it. We cannot be healthy and strong on little snatches of spiritual food, any more than we can on just little bits of earthly food taken irregularly, instead of our meals. Do let us watch and pray against the temptation to push our time for devotion into a corner. Satan is so subtle and our hearts are so deceitful. . . .

"I had a very satisfactory talk with —— this morning. His conversion seems like a real one; he rejoices in the full assurance of faith, and says life and the Bible seem new to him. . . .

"I want to come down and see thee very much, but I really think I cannot until just before Christmas. I have so much that must be done. Poor little Ernest has nothing but his blue merino dress and some light calicoes. He is here on a visit now. Last Thursday was Thanksgiving-day, and we drove over to the Home, to take them some thanksgiving. We gave each child a red apple and a cake, besides some other substantials which we left for them. We brought Ernest home with us, as I wanted to fix up his clothes. He is a dear little fellow, as good as a kitten. He calls me 'Aunt Alice' nicely now, and often comes up during the day for a kiss. He is so affectionate, I am really enjoying him. . . . I pray that the Lord will make him a good Christian man, and then, whatever becomes of him, he will live to the glory of God, and that is all I want. But I must not spend the time talking about him when I ought to be sewing for him.

"It is quite too bad that I should write a long

letter like this, and not one word about the things in
which we are most interested.   I will give thee a text
from Psalm xxxii. 8, 9, a sweet promise which I have
been enjoying, 'I will instruct thee and teach thee
in the way that thou shalt go, I will guide thee with
mine *eye*.   Be ye not as the horse or as the mule,
which have no understanding, whose *mouth* must be
held in with bit and bridle.'   What a loving appeal
to our spiritual nature !   My heart goes up in earnest
prayer that both thou and I may be guided by His
loving eye, and not make it necessary for Him to
drive us with His chastening rod."

"Tswedelle, *Dec.* 1863.

"My Own Precious Sister Carrie,—

.   .   .   "I have been as fully occupied this week
as ever.   I had such a refreshing day last Sabbath.
Nothing outward, but a refreshing outpouring of the
Spirit in my soul.   How wonderful a thing is communion with God !   It seems too glorious for such
sinful mortals as we, but still we do taste it sometimes.
How different everything looks when we see it from
God's point of view !   Of how little consequence do
all earthly things appear, and how sweet to yield ourselves to His care and guidance !   Oh, to live always
so, would it not be sweet !"

"Tswedelle, *Feb.* 17, 1864.

"My Own Darling H——,—

"I have wanted inexpressibly to see or hear from
thee, but I have been too sick to write, until within
a few days.   I was in bed for ten days, suffering
most intensely, though not dangerously, and since

then have been too tired and weak to do anything but sleep.

"I was so glad to get thy letter last evening, only it made me long to see thee, my precious sister cousin.

"I felt disappointed at first about ——, but it only lasted for a moment, for it is so evidently of the Lord's arranging; and when you once begin to rejoice in the Lord's will, because it is His will, you can't bear to lose the chance, can you? It is so sweet a pleasure. I would not say this to any one but thee, dearest, for it might imply to some that I thought my will broken ; but thou knows full well that subdued for the present is a very different thing from dead." . . .

"TSWEDELLE, April 1864.

" MY DEAR S——,—

. . . "Oh, for real friendship we must not stop short of Jesus. There is none like Him. Why are we always seeking to rest in the hearts of our fellow-men? I think one reason may be, that we do not have that realising faith in His humanity that is our privilege. We are so apt to exalt the love wherewith Jesus loved us into something so high above our comprehension, that we cannot rest in it as we do in human love. Yet does He not love us with the fulness of a human heart, only perfectly pure and unselfish, and infinitely deeper and sweeter than anything in this world ever can be? It seems to me that if we are really satisfied in Him, we shall be more thoroughly independent of our fellow-men than we now even dream we could be."

"Tswedelle, *May* 9, 1864..

" My Dear M——,—

. . . " I have so much to say to you, darling, that I scarcely know where to begin. I have been thinking a great deal about you, and wanted to write; but you know sometimes when the wish is strong the energy is lacking. . . .

" We have been having considerable company staying with us, which is very engrossing, as, of course, some one had to be with them, and we had not very good servants. Then Carrie's nurse left her, and she had to pick up her baby and Frank and come up to look for one. She was here over a week, during which time the baby (Marion) was our constant care—just as sweet as she could be, but determined not to let us do much but pet her. Then came house-cleaning, that bugbear of all housekeepers ; and then all the vines had to be trimmed, and the gardening attended to, which, you know, takes time. I tell you all this that you may imagine a little how your friend has been occupied.

" As for spring clothes, do not speak of them ; the warm weather is down upon us, and I have not done a thing for myself, but am suffering in winter clothing. One thing I am not behindhand in ; I believe I have Ernest almost all ready for summer.

" S. S—— and I drove over to the ' Home ' on Saturday, and took him some things, and a dozen broad-brimmed straw hats, all lined and trimmed for the children to wear out in the sun. They were perfectly delighted with them. Coming home we stopped

on the Wissahickon at Krieshcim Creek, and walked
to the 'Devil's Whirlpool.' We had a lovely time.
I thought of you, and gathered a few wild flowers,
which I have put in press for you. I wish you could
have enjoyed with us the exquisite beauty of the
place. It is just like summer here, the trees so very
green, and all the fruit trees in blossom, and the
whole face of nature wearing such a full bloom.

"And now, my darling, I have told you a little of
external things ; what shall I say of spiritual? My
heart is full of much that I long to tell you, but a
letter seems too short to attempt it. . . . I
have been enjoying a piece of poetry about the 'Will
of God' so much. It expresses what it is—just to
rest, like a little child, upon His will, and be satisfied.
In one place it says :—

> 'I run no risks, for come what will,
> Thou always hast Thy way.'

"Is it not blessed to hold a position where we may
feel that even in this uncertain world we run no risks?
. . . "My text is Heb. iv. 16: 'Let us
therefore come boldly unto the throne of grace,'
&c. Is it not sweet?"

"TSWEDELLE, *May* 16, 1864.

. . . "I long to tell thee, dearest H——,
everything that interests me, but, after all, I have not.
much to tell. Of that matter about which we spoke
when last together, nothing, only that the Lord is
taking care of it, and I fully believe that He will
make me, weak and sinful as I am, to do just His
will about it. . . .

" God is *so* good. If it is His will that I should
lie down, and let Him use His scourge of small cords,
I think I could not help lying still, for I do realise
that He loves me so."   .   .   .

                          " TSWEDELLE, *May* 1864.

" MY DEAR SISTER ANNIE,—

" I have just come from down stairs, where I have
been reading to our old cook.   Poor old thing ! she
cannot read, and she likes me to read to her so much.
She is not a Christian, but I had a very solemn time
with her this evening, over the fifty-fifth chapter of
Isaiah.   How lovely those words are, ' Ho, every
one that thirsteth.'   It has seemed to me that they
apply very often to my soul, for how often do we go
empty and thirsty, when He is calling us to come and
drink, to buy wine and milk without money and without price ?   How different is the wine which He gives
from the wine of earthly joy which intoxicates !   We
may well say, in the words of the Canticles, ' Thy
love is better than wine.'

" Life seems to me such a solemn thing to-night.
Perishing souls all around us, and Satan trying his
best to lull us into forgetfulness of their great danger
and our deep responsibility.   But, oh, how sweet it
is to feel that we rest on an everlasting arm which is
about us, and a sovereign power that worketh for us,
and in us."

                          " MILLVILLE, *June* 3, 1864.

" DEAR S——,—

    .   .   .   " The steady, unchanging light of the
Sun of Righteousness is a far better thing to reflect

and bask in than any brightness of earth. A cloud may have dissipated the glow of earthly brightness even now from your spirit; but I know that the glory of the grace of God is, and ever will be, shining down in a flood of everlasting light upon your head. May no cloud of earth ever hide it from your eyes!"

From this date very few family letters can be found. Those written by her, during the succeeding two or three years, to her sister in St John, do not seem to have been preserved, and the removal of her sister Carrie and family to the cottage at Tswedelle referred to in the following letter, brought them into daily companionship, thus removing the necessity of correspondence.

To M. M. J.

"TSWEDELLE, *June* 20, 1864.

"My Dear Little M——,—

"Your letter received at Millville would have called forth an answer immediately, but that I have scarcely had time to breathe slowly since I came home. I had to finish some things in a great hurry for the Sanitary Fair, and then we have had a great deal of company, and, as I am the only young person at home, I drive them about, and entertain generally, which you know runs off with time wonderfully.

. . . "That promise never wears out, 'All things work together for good,' and particularly when we lay all the arrangement of things on Him by faith, how can we ever doubt that He is managing for us?

To rest our will on His, is the *sweetest* thing on
earth. I will copy a lovely hymn on this subject
for you. I have learned it, and repeat it to myself
continually, and do take such satisfaction in it that I
want you to have it too.*

. . . "I have a piece of news to tell you.
My sister Carrie is coming here to live. The old
farm-house is being fixed up for them, and they expect to move the first of July. Will it not be splendid to have them so near?"

Dear Alice's reference in the above letter to driving her friends about, recalls many pleasant associations. She always very much enjoyed showing her
friends the beautiful country in the vicinity of her
home, pointing out to them with animation, as they
rode along, spots of interest or of especial beauty,
while at the same time she managed a pair of horses
with graceful ease, driving fearlessly, and yet carefully, up and down the steep Pennsylvania hills, to
the decided disquietude of some of her companions,
who were quite unused to so fair and delicate a driver.
Sometimes she would drive on an unfrequented
road to a retired spot, and then, fastening her horses
to a tree or a fence, lead the whole party through
the woods in search of moss or wild flowers.
A few miles from Tswedelle is Valley Forge,
where Washington and his troops were quartered for
many months, and where the earth-works thrown up
by them are still to be seen. Here on one occasion
Alice conducted a party of her young friends, and,

* See Hymn, page 304.

selecting a wild and shady spot under the branches of an old pine tree, they spread upon a large flat rock a simple repast which they had brought with them.

No earthly pleasure, however pure and simple, was fully enjoyed by Alice unless sanctified by the presence of the Lord, and, at her request, before partaking of their little feast, they rendered unto Him an offering by singing a hymn of praise. Scarcely had they finished when a drunken man appeared upon the scene, and approaching them familiarly, placed his bundle and jug upon the ground, and, seating himself beside them, asked the little group in rather incoherent tones for a song. Alice replied, "We will sing for you if you will then go away and leave us." This condition appeared to make the man very angry, and he answered, in coarse and threatening language, that he would do just as he pleased about that. Alice felt frightened and worried, but, casting herself and friends upon the protecting care of her Heavenly Father, she began to sing—

"Guide me, oh Thou great Jehovah,"

her friends joining in. As they proceeded it was most interesting to watch the softening of the expression of his hard features. Perhaps the sacred strain touched a tender chord in his not utterly hardened heart, recalling some touching memories of childhood. Be that as it may, when they had finished he arose, and, with a gentle "Thank you," took up his bundle and jug, and proceeded quietly on his way.

CHAPTER XI.

IN the early part of 8th mo. 1864, Alice accompanied her brother-in-law and Sister Carrie on a trip to the White Mountains, and St John, N.B., of which the following letters speak.

"REVERE HOUSE, BOSTON, *Aug.* 8, 1864.

. . . "I come again to talk with my little S——, but it is not in the gray morning light on the steamboat, but under the brilliant chandelier of a brilliant drawing-room, in this dear old Yankee city. How entirely separate from the world does this make me feel! I feel particularly to-night as a 'stranger and a pilgrim,' who has no part with the world in its vanities, for such sweet *rest* in Jesus is in my heart. How good of the Lord to give me this!

"I pray that He may keep my eyes from turning to gaze upon earthly objects, for I know that just as truly as one look at Christ dispels the clouds of earth, *just so* one backward longing look dims the brightness I now see in the things which are eternal!

. . . "The disappointment is quite lost in the thought that He whom our soul loveth is having

His way about it. Can we not say in little things, as well as great ones, ' God's will is *sweetest* when it triumphs at our cost ? ' I think we can."

" St John Boat, 8th mo. 18th.

" Dearest Mother,—

. . . "Our trip to the White Mountains was a perfect success. We had a most delightful time, and I do not like to think it is all over; but I am sure I shall never forget those splendid views. Oh, they are grand ! more beautiful than anything I ever saw before.

" H—— seems to be enjoying himself very much, and it is no doubt doing him good. He and Frank are *a pair*, they do have such fun together. I think it has improved Frank very much ; he is not half the little mischief he was at home. He is a great amusement to persons we meet ; he makes such old-fashioned speeches, and talks so wisely about matters and things.

" H—— and I went up Mount Washington on horseback from Crawford's. It was thoroughly enjoyable ; not too warm on the way, nor too cold on top. The views going up were magnificent, but it grew misty toward the top, and we did not see much from its stormy summit but a sea of fog, with here and there a dim outline of a lofty mountain range, faintly shadowing forth what it would have been had it been clear.

" I am very glad we ascended Mount Lafayette, and had such a fine view from there, as we were disappointed at Washington.

" 8th mo. 21st. Here we are safely in St John,

after a most prosperous voyage from Portland. The sea was as smooth as a mill-pond, and we were none of us at all sick.

. . . "Annie was perfectly delighted to see us. Charley and Nan have changed very little, and as for 'Toots,' he is just as sweet and cunning as he can be. He calls Marion 'baby,' but looks at her rather suspiciously when his mamma takes too much notice of her; but on the whole seems to like her very much, and gives her 'um-a-num-a-nee,' as he calls water, out of his 'sil-cup,' of which he is very fond.

"Charley and Frank have splendid times together, and play in the nicest manner possible. Charley is a dear boy; he is still as much of a comfort to his mother as ever. Frank too has had on his good cap ever since we started from home; and as for May, she is as sweet as ever, and that is saying a great deal when it is old maid Aunty that speaks."

"St John, *Aug.* 21, 1864.

" Dear S——,—

. . . "I have been praying much for you, that you may be kept moment by moment, and led step by step upward and onward. The hand that is leading the way can never fail nor make a mistake. I never so fully understood A. S——'s piece, where she alludes to our journey,

' Up the steep mountain side,
    Where we must follow,
    Slow where we fain would soar;
    That *step by step*, thus onward,
    Our Guide must go before,'

until I saw the full force of the illustration in our journey up the rugged and rocky sides of Washington and Lafayette. It is 'a slow thing,' as the guide remarked, this climbing a steep mountain, and cannot be done in a minute; but it is only a step at a time, after all, and the way is simple if you have a good guide with you, and do not turn to look backward and downward, and become dizzy, as I did several times, before I learned to *look up*, and not be afraid.

. . . "Indeed, there was much that was teaching to me in our journey, and much to enjoy, which I did not anticipate. The mountains are far more wonderfully grand and sublime than I expected, and speak so powerfully of the might and majesty of Him who created them with His word—of Him upon whose encircling arm we rest—that it was sweet to gaze and wonder and adore, while thinking of the love that made all this our own."

"St John, Sept. 3, 1864. . . . The glorious rays of the 'Sun of Righteousness' indeed make glad the heart, and brighten the life, as no earthly sunshine ever can. Is it not strange, dear S——, that we should ever hang our heads to earth, when there is *always* such brightness above to gaze upon and delight ourselves in? '*Delight* thyself *in the Lord*, and He shall give thee the desire of thy heart. Commit thy way unto the Lord : trust also in Him, and he shall bring it to pass.'

"That verse of A. L. Waring has been such a comfort to me to-day, and has seemed so *new*—

' Father, I know that all my life
  Is portioned out for me,
And the changes that are sure to come
  I do not fear to see;
But I ask thee for a present mind,
  Intent on pleasing Thee.'

.   .   .   "If loneliness and heartaches did not
come, the joy and peace of resting an aching heart
upon Jesus never could come either."

"TSWEDELLE, *Nov.* 1864.

"DEAREST H——,—

.   .   .   "I am praying that the Lord will show
me just what will please Him best, for that I want to
do.   .   .   .   I have experienced all the mortification
of feeling myself looked upon as self-righteous and a
religious fanatic.   .   .   .   Dear H——, I do not believe thee *can* understand how keenly I feel this mortification of the flesh, for to thee I do not believe it
would be any trial at all; but I am not like thee; I
do like to be thought well of, and, in short, *to be
respectable.*   However, it gives me a chance of bearing for the Lord's sake, and I do absolutely enjoy
doing it for Him, more perhaps than if I felt it less.
Surely heavenly strangers upon the earth should not
have any fear of man.   I can only trust the Lord to
deliver me from it.

.   .   .   "My heart longs so for thee and thy
strengthening influence.   Satan is so strong and I am
so weak; but there is One who dwelleth in me who
is all-sufficient, and I try to remember it, but we do
love outward supports so much; at least my old nature
does.

"One thing I want to ask thee, whether thou thinks

our Lord loves all His children alike, or whether He gives to those who walk with Him, in His fellowship and communion, a peculiar tenderness of affection. I have thought this was at least implied in some of the texts under our heading—'Peculiar blessings promised to obedient children,' for instance, John xiv. 21: 'He shall be loved of my Father, and I will love him.' But the other day, when I suggested the thought, the person with whom I was speaking was shocked at the idea that God loves some of His children more than others, and thought it entirely inconsistent with the doctrine of free grace, which teaches us that God loves us freely, with a perfect love."

" Dec. 3, 1864. . . . As for myself, all that I have been living upon is that same old 23d Psalm. 'The Lord *is* my shepherd,' I say to myself many times a day. When we yield to His leadings, it is by *still waters* that He leadeth us, and into *green* pastures."

"Feb. 8, 1865. . . . But, after all, as Luther says, 'God still reigns,' and God is God, and strange and dark and wrong as anything may seem to us, down in the depths of our hearts we *know* that He has done just what is right. And this is our only resting-place. God is all-powerful, and *He cannot err.* Our Bible tells us this; it says, ' He doeth according to His will in the army of heaven and amongst the inhabitants of the earth, and none can stay His hand, or say unto Him, What doest Thou?'"

"March 1865. . . . I feel as though it would be all fixed by the same loving hand that never denies

O

me anything I want, unless it is absolutely necessary. It is so sweet that He sympathises with all our desires and longings, for He is human as well as divine, and He knoweth our frame, He remembereth that we are dust.' Then if He does deny us anything, we know that it was absolutely necessary for our good that He should do it."

"Sabbath morning. . . . I know that in many phases of our inner life we must fight and suffer alone : ' Fight and suffer *alone*,' did I say? I know you will understand what I mean, but I cannot let it stand unqualified, for it is too blessed a thought that we can never be alone—without Jesus.

"I have been feasting on that lovely passage this morning, 'Neither life, nor death, nor angels, nor principalities, nor powers, nor things present, nor things to come, nor height, nor depth, nor any other creature, shall be able to separate us from the love of God, which is in Christ Jesus, our Lord.' These words came over me with as much freshness as if I had never heard them before. Oh, what an inexpressible comfort it is to know that whatever comes, although the heart may ache, and the storms pass over our heads, yet nothing can rob us of the *rest* we have in Christ !"

> " We rest in Christ, the Son of God,
>   Who took the servant's form,
> His love is our abiding-place,
>   And refuge from the storm.
>
> " At peace with God, *no ills we dread*,
>   In Christ is our repose ;
> Our life is hid with Him in God,
>   Secure from all our foes."

"Tswedelle, 1865. . . . What and if the world *is* dark! *This* is not our home; we are not here to *enjoy* the world. We come as pilgrims and strangers, in reality, and not only in song, to do His will who sent us, even as Jesus came to do His Father's will, and then ascended to *joy above*. That we cannot see anything pleasant before us and around us in life, ought not to discourage us, seeing it will not in the slightest degree make it harder to be entirely devoted to the service of God. On the contrary, it will make it much easier to set our affections on things above, and not on things on the earth!"

In the early part of the sixth month Alice left home to visit some relatives in Brooklyn, and from there went to Newport. At each of these places she very much enjoyed attending some of the sittings of the New York and New England yearly meetings, then in session.

"BROOKLYN, *June* 10, 1865.

"DEAR CARRIE,—

. . . "On fourth day I went over to meeting in the morning. It was a meeting for worship, and a very interesting one. . . . After several sermons ———— arose and spoke very sweetly, saying that she had been praying that the whole gospel might be preached that morning, the forgiveness of sins through a crucified Redeemer, as well as the bearing of the cross. Then followed a lovely prayer from some one I did not know, and then R. D——— arose, and we did indeed have the glad tidings of the gospel preached. . . .

"I went in the afternoon to the regular yearly meeting, and was much edified; the feeling of love and unity was so sweet. It only held three hours and a quarter! I came home pretty tired, thou may imagine, and found F—— and L. B—— here to see me. . . .

"The next morning I went to see B. C——, and found her daughter H——'s little boy, just Marion's age, dying of cholera infantum. He was in his cradle, close by B. C——'s bed. He looked so sweet, and reminded me so much of baby Alice, that I could not take my eyes off from him. His dear little dimpled fat hands and soft light curls made me just realise, as I never did before, how we should feel if our little pet lamb were lying at the point of death. Do take especial care of her till I get back. I cannot tell thee how I long to see her; kiss her a dozen times for me, and tell her Aunt Alice is going to bring her something when she comes home. Ask her what she thinks it is; a little white sugar lambie on a cake, won't that be nice?"

A peculiarly tender tie existed between Alice and the little niece spoken of in the above letter. From her earliest infancy her Aunt Alice had claimed half the proprietorship of this little one, and her parents felt that their precious child was rich indeed in the wealth of affection thus lavished upon her, as well as in the sweet example daily before her in her "own Aunt Alice," as she so often called her.

"NEW BEDFORD, *June* 14, 1865.

" My DEAR S——,—

"You see by the date I am at New Bedford. My visit to Newport is over, and seems most wonderfully like a dream. The beautiful views of grand old rocky shore, and grander ocean, the long avenue of splendid country seats, and the crowded hotel life, all seem unreal, and blend and run into one another, like the reflections on the surface of a rippled stream.

"The life here seems very quiet by comparison, but none the less pleasant. This morning we have been reading aloud Gail Hamilton's last book, 'A New Atmosphere.' I like what I have read of it very much. She says some things which I have at times fairly gasped to give utterance to, but never before had the satisfaction of seeing put in words. . . . Did you know that those who know her say she is a very religious character?

"But enough of this. I want to tell you about my text for to-day. 'This charge I commit unto thee, . . . that thou mightest war a good warfare, holding *faith,* and *a good conscience,* which some having put away, concerning faith have made shipwreck.' I do not think I have ever sufficiently considered the subject of a good or clear conscience before, and it has come home very clearly to me to-day as being connected so closely with faith. Notice 1 John iii. 21-23, how they are joined. A good conscience is a thing we always *ought* to, and might possess by faith, and still the fact which my heart is obliged to confess is that I do not always have it. I want to think and pray more about this subject, and understand it better."

During the visit to Newport referred to in the above letter, Alice had some conversation, on her way to a first day school conference, with a gentleman to whom she had just been introduced. Finding that he was a first day school teacher, she spoke with much earnestness upon the objects of such teaching, and that nothing short of the conversion of his scholars should satisfy the teacher. She soon found that her companion had no settled confidence that his own sins were forgiven through the mercy of a crucified Redeemer, and she tried to set forth the gospel of the grace of God as fully as the time would allow. No other opportunity offered for conversing with him on the subject, but he was much laid on her heart in prayer, and after her return to Tswedelle she wrote him, enclosing a list of texts on this important subject. The Lord opened his heart to receive the blessed truth which it was Alice's privilege thus to set before him, and after some correspondence and further conversation on the subject at Tswedelle, he was enabled to rejoice in conscious acceptance with God through Christ his Saviour.

In enclosing the following letter, he writes :—

"Many times since I first met Alice at Newport have I blessed God that He turned her steps toward New England. The recollection of my first acquaintance with her will ever remain the most impressive of any era in my life. . . . Never in my brief · experience have I met with a person who could so forcibly and clearly state the great plan of redeeming love, as could that dear sainted girl. . . . She placed the truth as it is in Jesus so powerfully before my mind that eternity cannot efface it."

" My Dear Friend,—

. . . "It seems to me a fearfully solemn thing to be drifting down life's stream, with the question of our soul's position before God wrapped in a mist of uncertainty ; for it is not uncertain whose we are, however we may feel about it, for there is no middle ground, no such thing as being '*partially* a Christian.' We are either Christians, washed and accepted of God, through the blood of the Lamb—or else we are not Christians, not forgiven, not reconciled to God.

" Many, through unbelief or indifference, or a fearful educational error, settle down satisfied not to know where they stand. That it is not the will of our Heavenly Father that we should be in this state is plainly manifest. We are told, 'Examine yourselves whether ye be in the faith.' Again we are told in John, 'These things I write unto you that believe on the name of the Son of God, that ye may know that ye have eternal life.' He does not say 'that ye may *hope* some day to have it,' but 'that ye may *know* that ye *have* eternal life.'

" The realisation, however, that it is not only our privilege but our duty to have an assured confidence toward God, does not lessen the feeling of the importance of having this confidence founded on something which will stand the great judgment day. He who has a false hope is as badly off as he who has no hope at all. But, thanks be unto our Heavenly Father, He has made the true ground for confidence so plain and easy to be understood that a child may see it, and distinguish the difference between it and the false as easily as he can see a difference between rock and sand.

"Some persons imagine that their peace is made with God because they have dedicated themselves to Him. They have been roused to see the importance of their eternal interests, and have made up their minds to serve God with their whole strength, by the aid of the Holy Spirit, and therefore they think they have become Christians. But will this bear the test? Does God promise to save us because of our dedication to His service, or to forget our past offences because of our good resolves for the future, even if these good resolves are not broken? This confidence is not founded on Christ and His promises, but on *our own efforts* and the aid of the Holy Spirit. Such persons make our Lord Jesus Christ 'a helper,' not 'a Saviour.' But Jesus never promised to help any man to save himself. Such a thing would be a practical denial of His work of atonement finished eighteen hundred years ago.

"He does indeed proclaim that 'the *gift* of God is eternal life;' that He has paid the ransom money; that He has become 'the Lamb of God that taketh away the sin of the world.' This is 'glad tidings' to the truly convicted one, who feels that he cannot do anything acceptable in the sight of an all-pure God, and that unless dealt with in pure mercy he can never be saved. It is by accepting what the Saviour has done for us, not by doing anything for Him, that we are to be saved.

"It is the duty as well as the privilege of the Christian to make an intelligent surrender of himself to his Saviour, but it comes as the consequence, not the cause, of his conversion. Man would reverse God's order, which is salvation *first* and service *afterwards.*

"If we notice the 'therefores' of the New Testament, we shall find that they are almost always an exhortation to earnestness in service, *based on* the possession of salvation. 'Ye are bought with a price, *therefore* glorify God in your body and in your spirit, which are His.'

"As an eminent Christian once said, 'We have nothing to do in order *to be* saved, but a great deal to do because we *are* saved.'" . . .

In the fall of this year Alice went to St John, to visit her sister Annie. In relation to this visit she writes :—

. . . "I never remember having felt so badly at leaving home before, but after a while a strong feeling came over me that the Lord had some especial work to accomplish by me in this journey. I cannot tell you how sweetly and solemnly it came. Of course I do not know what, or when, or how; but it is sweet to know that though

'I know not the way I am going,
Yet well do I know my Guide.'

Oh, that I may keep my hand close in His, and ever be on the watch-tower! There is something so very sad in the thought that we may, if not watchful, let the opportunities God throws in our way of glorifying Him slip by unnoticed."

"MY DEAR S———,—

. . . "I would like to tell you about Thomas Frederick F———, who has completely stolen my heart just now. He is the laughing little beauty and mischief of the family. I would not dare to begin to tell of the funny speeches he makes, or my last page would be gone before I knew it. He is very charming, but I do not feel that he takes the place of my little lambie Marion, they are so totally different. . . .

"I did not get any further than Salem in telling you of our journey; yet that, to me, seems the smallest part of it. We went from there to Portland in the cars, and about five o'clock went on board the boat for St John. The sun was just setting as we left the harbour, and the broad ocean spread out before us. Mother and I sat on the forward deck, admiring the clouds, which were glorious, and the rosy dreamland light, which added an unearthly beauty to the scene.

"While I watched, as I dearly love to, the soft line of the horizon, where the sea and sky meet, broken only by the white sail of some distant ship, all my enthusiasm was kindled, and I felt my spirits rise to almost a sublime ecstasy. I drew my breath softly, not to break the spell that seemed to raise me nearer heaven. But alas! alas! as H. B. Stowe says, 'The one step from the sublime to the ridiculous is never taken with such alacrity as at sea!' Just as a beautiful white sea-gull came floating near, to add still another charm to the scene, we became painfully aware that the 'stiff breeze' which had made old ocean so beautiful, with its myriad white-capped waves, had made it '*rather rough*,' as the captain said, and we mutually agreed 'that we had better go in.' Ah ! that 'going in' is significant. Suffice it to say, that was the end of all sentiment for that night !

"Next day, toward evening, it seemed calmer, and I sat on deck for an hour, to see the beautiful rocky coast we were passing. The sunset was accompanied with as rich a wealth of clouds as the night before, and this time I could enjoy it."

"St John, *October* 8, 1865.

"My Dearest Carrie,—

. . . "I have just returned from the stone church, where we had a lovely sermon from Mr S——, the simple glad tidings spoken from a loving heart. It did me good, and I felt that it must any who took it into their hearts. . . .

"Yesterday Mrs B—— came in the morning to ask us to go to drive with her in the afternoon and get some ferns; she was so delighted with our fernery that she wanted one at once. So she bought an elegant large glass shade, and about half-past one o'clock yesterday afternoon we went—mother, Annie, Mrs B——, Charley, and myself, forming the party—in their open carriage. We went to Lily Lake, and rambled about for two hours on the beautiful hills which surround it. In the woods it was one sheet of moss and ferns, and the lovely little views we came out upon every once in a while were charming. There was such a beautiful rosy light over the distant hills, and the little quiet lake, nestled among the peaked firs, looked so calm and peaceful.

"We rambled a great distance, and you should have seen us returning to the carriage with our treasures!

"Mrs B—— would have us go back to their house to dinner at seven o'clock, which we did, and spent the evening very pleasantly, arranging the fernery."

                           "TSWEDELLE, *Dec.* 31, 1865.

"My Dear B. C——,—

    . . . "I too felt that my last visit to you was not all I wanted that it should be, but I enjoyed meeting the Jewish brother in Christ; and as the One who planned it 'doeth all things well,' I felt it must be for the best.

    . . . "I cannot tell you how nice it was to see your handwriting again, and to know that I have been 'much on your mind.' I have not been sick, however; on the contrary, I never was better in body in my life.

"As to the spiritual life, what can I say, but that I am a poor sinner resting on Christ? I think that expresses it all. Self — sinful, weak, unfaithful; Christ—loving, tender, faithful!

> 'Jesus, sun and shield art Thou,
>   Sun and shield for ever,
> Never shalt Thou cease to shine,
>   Cease to guard us never!'

"I have just come up from Sunday-school, where I have been telling my scholars about Jesus' love, and it seems to me I never felt it so great and sweet before.

> 'Oh, to grace how great a debtor,
>   Daily I'm constrained to be!'

. . . "You kindly ask after Ernest. He is growing a large boy, and I think a very nice one, although not at all handsome or brilliant in any way. I hope he will make a good man, which is far better."

To M. M. J.

"MILLVILLE, *Feb.* 11, 1866.

"MY DEAR LITTLE M——,—

. . . "The prayer that God may keep you clinging very closely to Himself, and shelter you under the sweet shádow of His wing, has sprung from my heart for you very often. Trust Him in everything, dear M——, as you have begun, and He will sustain you, and bring you out victorious over all your rough billows. 'None of them that trust in Him shall be desolate.' 'Be of good courage, and He shall strengthen thine heart.'

"I have been miserable for two days, but feel much better to-night, and am going to try to go to Bible-class. . . .

. . . "Surely our Father is plenteous in mercy. I have been thinking all day of this text: 'Can a woman forget her sucking child, that she should not have compassion on the son of her womb? Yea, she *may* forget, yet will I not forget thee.'"

"TSWEDELLE, *Feb.* 18, 1866.

"DEAR FRIEND,—

. . . "I hope that you may be a blessing to those around you. Were it not that I know how strong He is whose arm is about you, I should be almost afraid of the Unitarian influence upon you; it is so insidious, and works away in the dark be-

fore you know that it is having any effect upon you.
The only way is to keep so near Jesus all the time
that it cannot touch you. He is our 'hiding-place'
from every temptation, as well as from every snare,
trouble, or sorrow. It has seemed to me the last few
days that His love is perfectly wonderful. Why
should He love us so when we are so unworthy?

. . . "Last Saturday was father's birthday.
Mother had a large turkey of her own raising roasted,
and, as it was a bright day, Carrie and the chits
came over to dinner, and we had quite a pleasant
time. My cap made its first appearance duly, at the
dinner table, on dear father's head. Frank wrote
him a nice letter, with a great deal of exertion, and
enclosed his photograph, which he had taken especially for the occasion, and which was a perfect surprise to his grandpa.

. . . "If this letter is not readable, you must
excuse it for Marion's sake. She stayed with me last
night, and has been doing her best to make me give
more attention to her than to my letter. She insists
on my holding her doll for her, and puts all her
play-things, one after another, on my writing-pad for
me to look at, which is all very charming, but does
not agree with letter-writing.

"And now I must go, as the carriage is here for
me to take this to the P.O., and visit those two poor
sick women, both of whom I believe you know.

"May God ever bless and keep you by His own
mighty power, and in His most tender love." . . .

CHAPTER XII.

N the early spring of this year a young man, a connection of the family, who was engaged in business in Philadelphia, was taken with hemorrhage, and, having no relations in that city, was invited to Tswedelle until he should have gained sufficient strength for the long journey to his distant home.

Alice, although but slightly acquainted with him, knew of him as gay and worldly, seeming to care only for a merry life in this present world, without a thought of one to come. He was much laid on her heart in prayer as soon as she heard that he was to become an inmate of Tswedelle, and, almost immediately after his arrival, she sought an opportunity of presenting the gospel to him.

She found that the Lord had been preparing the way, and that he was ready and anxious to talk on the subject, desiring, more than anything else, to know what he must do to be saved. Although very reserved, he opened his heart freely to Alice, and she said that she had never in any one seen such deep conviction and sorrow for sin. At first he could see nothing but his own sins; but gradually, as she dwelt on the 'glad tidings,' that 'Jesus Christ died to save sinners,' his eyes were opened to behold 'the Lamb of God which taketh away the sin of the world,' and ere two weeks had elapsed he could rejoice that he had found a Saviour who was 'able to save them to the uttermost that come unto God by Him.'

How little Alice's friends imagined, as they saw her daily performing all the many kind and thoughtful attentions which are so much needed and appreciated by an invalid, that before another spring-time came they would be performing the same for her, who was now the light and joy of the household. It seemed to be her greatest pleasure to minister to the wants or by her ready sympathy to lighten the sorrows of others. She would often steal away from the parlour, even when the company of dear friends from a distance made it a real sacrifice on her part, that she might by her cheerful conversation and reading of the Scriptures enliven what would otherwise have been the many weary hours of her invalid friend. He was much strengthened and settled in gospel truth by this constant intercourse with one who had long known and proved the faithfulness of the Saviour of sinners, and who rejoiced from a full heart to speak of Him to others.

This young man died some months after reaching his home, in the full confidence of faith in Jesus.

To M. M. J.

"TSWEDELLE, *June* 18, 1866.

"MY DEAR LITTLE M——,——

.   .   . "Alas, the hurry, hurry of Tswedelle is still the same as ever! We are so busy all the time, that it don't seem as if we have half a chance to settle down and enjoy Annie.

"Saturday we had a children's party, which went off finely, and all the children seemed to enjoy it very much, but it pretty well tired out the old folks.

. . . "Don't neglect to pray that our visit to P—— may be blessed to us all, and that we may be comforted and strengthened in our heavenward journey by being together." . . .

Dear Alice found her great strength for service in the closet, in communion with her Divine Master. To Him she took all her cares and troubles, as well as her daily needs, and she always found rest for her aching head upon His bosom. It is to be regretted that she did not note down some of these more intimate communings in the form of a journal, but her life has left a fragrance to all those who knew her intimately which words can never describe.

Hers was a thoroughly active, busy life, always occupied for others, never thinking of self. God gave her in an eminent degree what she often used to pray for—

> " A heart at leisure from itself,
>   To soothe and sympathise."

She was seldom thrown with any one for any length of time without speaking personally of religion, endeavouring to find out whether they were living in the present possession of eternal life. She always laid the matter first before the Lord, asking Him to open the door, and her prayers were often wonderfully answered. Even when the person addressed seemed entirely indifferent to the solemn warning or the

P

gospel message, the word spoken in the name of Jesus would often, like bread cast upon the waters, be found after many days.

A coloured servant boy, whom she had taught of Jesus, was converted some time after leaving Tswedelle to join the navy.

He always retained a most affectionate remembrance of Alice's interest in his eternal welfare, and, among many other expressions of gratitude, he thus writes to her in the fall of this year :—

" I am so glad that you spoke to me about the love of Jesus Christ. When I first came on board this ship, I tried to banish the thought of Jesus from my memory, but there was one Christian man who spoke to me, and asked me if there was not some one who had taught me to love Jesus. . . . Miss Alice, I have often wondered how it was that preachers have ofttimes talked to me on that subject, but they never made any impression on my mind, and no one ever did but you. When you first mentioned it, I thought that all my sins looked me in the face. . . . Oh, if you had not spoken to me, I was on the road to ruin, and I can never repay you for it. Ever since those evenings when you spoke to me I have always thought that if by giving up my life I could repay you, I would do it."

About the 1st of 7th mo. Alice accompanied her sister Annie and family as far as Boston, on their way to St John. From there she went to Salem and Pittsfield, to visit some friends.

"MY DEAR S——,—

. . . "What a comfortable feeling it is that He is arranging everything for us. It brings such a quietness with it, such a calm to the restless spirit. O S——! what would we do without this confidence in Jesus? He may not, He does not always arrange things as we should have wished, but He doeth all things just right, and that is better, far better. And although our poor, weak hearts may not always rejoice in it now, because we cannot see or realise it, we shall hereafter, praising Him eternally. Oh, to say with the Psalmist, ' I will praise the Lord at all times, His praise shall continually be in my mouth !' I feel like praising the Lord to-night, but I do not always feel so. I have been asking Him to keep me always praising Him, for I am sure this is what He wants, or He would not tell us to do it."

"PITTSFIELD, *July* 23, 1866.

"MY DEAR S——,—

. . . "It was a very warm morning upon which I started from Salem, and I was filled with not a few misgivings ; I always dread going among strangers, and this was so entirely an untried field. However, I thought of the strong arm I had to lean upon, and of His sweet words, ' My strength is made perfect in weakness,' and so seated myself in the cars for Pittsfield in a quiet frame of mind, prepared to see all that was to be seen, and bear all the dust and heat in as philosophic a manner as possible.

" The ride to Springfield was just as warm and un-

comfortable as it well could be.   Then we began to
enter a beautiful mountain district, and the three
hours' ride from there was fully worth all the discom-
forts of the first part of the journey.   The views which
we had were lovely, as we wound round amongst the
hills, and by the banks of little streams, now swiftly
gliding through a fertile valley, surrounded by hills, .
and now dashing through a gorge in the mountains,
to come out on the other side to still more beautiful
views beyond.

"I wish I could describe to you the perfect beauty
of a thunder-storm coming up among the mountains;
but it is useless for me to begin.   These lovely scenes
make me long so to have the power of giving some
faint idea of them to those I love, who cannot see
them.

"But I must go back to my story, and tell you
how kind the clouds were to me on the day I was
speaking of.   They came up in great rolling masses
about noon, and not only shielded me from the great
heat of the sun, but, by casting their ever-varying
shadows upon the valleys and mountain sides, gave a
perfect charm of light and shade that I enjoyed intensely.   At last, just as we entered the beautiful
valley in the midst of which Pittsfield is situated, we
could see, miles away among the mountains, the
black thunder-clouds rolling toward us, first envelop-
ing one, then another in its darkness, while the valley
in which we were was still smiling in the bright sunlight.   For the first time in my life I saw the effect
which Bierstadt gives in his 'Storm in the Rocky
Mountains.'   It was almost too aggravating in such
a scene not to be able to stand still, but to be whirled

along, whether you would or not, at the same head-long speed.

"A few minutes more and we were in the midst of the shower, and almost at the same time we stopped at Pittsfield. The change was so sudden that I stood like one bewildered for a moment on the platform. I did not expect to find M—— or L—— out in such a shower, so called a hackman, and committed my check to his tender care, telling him that I wanted to go to Dr R——'s, upon which he replied that the doctor was looking for me, and in a minute brought a pleasant-looking gentleman, who very politely and heartily welcomed me to Berkshire.

"In a few minutes more we were before the door of the 'Pill-box.' The sun looked out just then, and I thought it was about as pleasant a place as I have seen. The house is situated on a broad street, lined on both sides with elms, and a broad strip of velvet grass between the road and sidewalk, which I think is one of the prettiest features of many New England towns.

. . . "Saturday we had a splendid drive among the mountains to Windsor Falls, about six miles from here. We had lovely views all the way, and enjoyed our ramble through the woods to the falls very much. They are picturesque and beautiful. We then drove through the Gulf, a wild gorge in the mountains, which brought us out on the top of a hill, where we had a fine view of old 'Grey Lock,' which is the king of the mountains hereabouts; in-deed Dr R—— says it is the highest point of land in Massachusetts."

"TSWEDELLE, *September* 26, 1866.

"O S——! how kind our Heavenly Father is! Why can't, why *don't* we trust Him more, and not be afraid? . . . I guess all Christians find that when the joy of earth first leaves them, the joy of their religion seems also to be shadowed. But it is out of just such battles that our real appreciation of God's peace grows. I do wonder if any one has ever satisfactorily expressed the difference between the first fresh joy of the buoyant gushing childhood in the Christian life, and the deep, inexpressible joy of those who have been tried in the fire, yet have found in Jesus more than even their most sanguine dreams had pictured, and yet so different. He is so very good, and gives so bountifully of His good things. He does not take us through dark places for nothing, it is always to bring us into brighter regions above."

"TSWEDELLE, *Jan.* 1, 1867.

"MY DEAREST ANNIE,—

"All my letters lately have begun with excuses for not having written before, but this shall not, although I might tell thee of all the letters I have had to answer since Christmas.

"This is the first day of a new year, and I have made several resolutions, differing, I hope, essentially from those I used to make and break right away when I was a child, because made in my own strength. How true it is that the Christian's vital breath is prayer!

"I have been refreshed lately by reading 'Mary, the Handmaiden of the Lord,' by the author of 'The

Schönberg-Cotta Family.' It is sweet. I think the little sermon she preaches on that part of the angel's message to Mary, 'The Lord is with thee,' is as lovely as anything I ever read. She says our Christian growth depends on our realisation of God's presence. To live in His presence consciously is the one thing that will keep us or make us heavenly-minded. I do so long to be more heavenly-minded, don't thee?

" I have been spending every other sixth day night with A. S——, in order to attend some meetings for young Friends. I wish I could tell thee all about them. I enjoy A. S—— so much, she is such a satisfactory Christian. She is so entirely devoted, and full of love and zeal for the cause of truth, that it seems impossible to be with her without catching some spark of the heavenly fire.

" I promised H. W. S—— that I would make her a visit as soon as our Sunday-school closed for the winter, and now that it is satisfactorily wound up with a festival, which went off very nicely on Christmas day, I feel at liberty to go to-morrow. . . .

" I wish I could have peeped in upon you on Christmas morning to see the opening of the stockings. Our children enjoyed themselves exceedingly. We were too busy to make them a tree, so Frank went out and got a little one of his own, and arranged it himself for his 'little sisters,' and although it was, of course, a rather crude affair, still I do believe they all enjoyed it more then any we ever made for them. I advise thee to try it. Let them do it themselves, and it is very little trouble, as you have no character to sustain in the matter. The tree must be small, so that they can reach, and they feel so proud of their work when it is done.   But I hope to see thee before another Christmas.   .   .   .

" A happy New Year to all.

" Thy own loving

" ALICE."

CHAPTER XIII.

O N the second of 1st mo. 1867, Alice went to Millville to pay the visit referred to in her last letter. The first evening of her arrival her cousin had a long conversation with her, in which Alice expressed a strong desire to know a deeper and more abiding work of grace in her soul, and to realise a closer union with Jesus, and a fuller baptism of the Holy Ghost.

There was staying in the house at the time a dear minister of the gospel,—one deeply taught in the things of God,—and the next day was a day of feasting to Alice, as she sat with her open Bible, listening to his expositions of divine truth. God had so ordered it that he dwelt mostly on the subject of "walking in the Spirit," and taught very emphatically the wonderful truth that those who did thus walk need not and would not fulfil the lusts of the flesh. It was just the teaching Alice needed, and the Lord opened her heart to receive it. During the course of the day the question was asked of this minister whether Christians ought to expect to live in the condition described in the seventh chapter of Romans all their lives, longing to do good, but finding it impossible because of the weakness of the flesh? His reply was emphatically "No," and then he showed very clearly that the eighth chapter of Romans describes the true Christian experience, and one which may be realised by every child of God, since it is the purchase of the death of Christ, and is all treasured up in Him for those who believe on Him.

Alice was very much struck by this answer, for although she had in a remarkable degree lived a life of faith in Christ, yet there was one point in which her faith was lacking, and therefore she did not realise so complete a victory over the evil tendencies of her heart as her soul longed for. The difficulty had been that, while trusting Christ fully and entirely and alone to deliver her from the *guilt* of sin, she did not trust Him fully and entirely and alone to deliver her from the *power* of sin. She knew she had no strength of her own, and it was her constant prayer that Christ would give *her* strength, whereas *she* was to have no strength at all, but, like a little child folded to his father's bosom begs his father to drive away his foe, so she was to hang helpless on to Christ, and ask Him to fight the foe in her heart, trusting Him practically to be her strength.

The glorious possibilities of the full salvation of Jesus began to dawn upon her, and her soul rejoiced. In the evening a Bible-class was held, and the subject of walking in the Spirit continued with many forcible illustrations. The true secret of a life of faith was opened to Alice's understanding ; that it is to cease from all efforts of our own, and to commit to the Lord Jesus our whole life and our daily living, trusting Him to work in us to will and to do of His good pleasure, so that we can say in very truth, " I am crucified with Christ; nevertheless, I live ; yet not I, but Christ liveth in me." She at once acknowledged in the depths of her heart this to be the true way, yet for a moment she shrank from such a complete abandonment of self, as a yielding to it involved. Then, instantly frightened at her own rebellion, she breathed a prayer for God to take her in hand, and make of her just what He pleased. At that moment the veil was lifted, and the Lord Jesus was` revealed to her enraptured soul as her all-sufficient and perfect Saviour, in a way she had never before even dreamed possible. As she described it, she seemed to be as it were *extinguished in Jesus.* She realised her absolute oneness with Him, in a way no words could describe. Indeed she felt as if He entered into her soul and became her very life. At once she was enabled to adopt as her own the words, " Yet not I, but Christ liveth in me," which but a little before had seemed so impossible for her. Her whole being was overwhelmed with the glory of the revelation. She said nothing, but tears rolled down her cheeks, and she soon found that the depth of feeling could no longer be repressed, and asked to be excused. She was obliged to lean on her cousin for support, as she left the room, and sat down on the first chair where she could be alone. There some time afterwards, she was found weeping and praising God. "Oh, what a Saviour Jesus is !" "Oh, what a complete salvation ! " "What a perfect Saviour !" "Oh, how precious ! " Such were some of the ejaculations that continually burst from her lips.

The next day found dear Alice still filled with the

Spirit, and overflowing with unspeakable joy. She listened with eager delight to the further expositions of the way of faith, which all that day and the next it was her privilege to hear from the dear minister above referred to. He dwelt much upon that text, "I do not frustrate the grace of God, for if right-eousness come by the law, then Christ is dead in vain," and he showed plainly that the frustrating here meant, was the legal striving of the soul, after being justified, to keep itself pure and holy, and to "work righteousness," as the Scriptures express it, by its own efforts. This striving, he said, could not but hinder the full acting of the grace of God, by which Christ would be made unto it sanctification and righteousness, in the same real and practical sense as He was its justi-fication. Alice was delighted with the new light thus thrown upon this text, and at once said that it should be henceforth her own especial text. "I ask no more blessed experience than this,"-she said, "not to frustrate the grace of God." And constantly she might be heard repeating to herself, under her breath, the words, "I do not frustrate the grace of God, no, I do not, I will not!"

Many other precious lessons were learned during those days, which cannot now be recalled, but the Bible seemed to become almost a new book to her, and her favourite hymns acquired a new and glorious meaning. Those two precious lines which had so long been a comfort to her, seemed, she said, never to have been understood before,

> "I am a poor sinner, and nothing at all,
> But Jesus Christ is my all and in all,"

and she repeated them over and over with the greatest

emphasis, trying to show to all around her the blessedness of realising their utmost truth.

There were several little social meetings for worship during the course of these few days, and Alice
took part in them, praying with great power and nearness of access. All who were with her took knowledge of her that she not only had been, but that she
was then, with Jesus. During this time a very severe
temptation beset her, and she learned experimentally
the secret of victory over it. She no longer tried in
her old legal way to resist it, praying for *help*, but
she handed it right over to her mighty Saviour, committing to Him the whole care of resisting and con-
quering it for her, while she stood by and held her
peace. And to her unspeakable joy she found He
did deliver.

In this manner several days passed. They were
her last well days on earth. The weight of joy was
too much for her delicate frame; and on the third
morning she was unable to leave her bed. She lay
there too weak to speak much, but her countenance
was expressive of a peace that passeth understanding. She soon rallied, however, sufficiently to be
able to start for home. A day or two before leaving
her cousin's, she thus writes to her mother and sister :—

. . . "I think I will write you both in one,
as my time here is too precious to spend much of it
in writing. I can talk when I get home. I expect to
come out from Phila. on seventh day, and I thought
it would be nice to have Bible-class that afternoon,
in which case I could meet Carrie there. Do let us

pray, dear Carrie, more earnestly for a blessing on our Bible-class. I so long that Christ may be more exalted there, and that we may really be fed from the fountain of all truth.

"How I do wish thee and mother could have been here with Mr —— ; he is a most wonderful teacher, such an one as I never met before. It was just one Bible-class all the time he was here. Every evening we all collected round the large table in the parlour. F. D—— and five or six others beside our own family were generally there. I cannot begin to tell you how much I enjoyed it. It really seemed that the Holy Spirit accompanied his words, and brought them home with power to our hearts, so that we could say in truth that we never saw the fulness of our possession in Christ before. Oh, the realisation of the love of God toward us in Christ Jesus is indeed worth more than all the wealth of all the worlds. What *unutterable* joy and peace it gives! Not only the peace of knowing that our sins are forgiven, and joy in the prospect of an eternal inheritance with Him in light—these are ours when we come and lay our weary load of sin at the foot of His cross, as Pilgrim did, and go on our way rejoicing—but He gives us *His* peace. 'My peace I give unto you, not as the world giveth give I unto you.' It is different in its very nature and essence from any earthly peace, because it is the very peace that God feels. He is the Vine, we are the branches; just as the sap runs through the vine to the branches, just so His peace flows from Him unto us. It seems as if my words were powerless to touch anything so glorious, so wonderfully "——

It is very much to be regretted that the last sheet of this letter, in which she spoke more fully of the experience through which she had just been passing, has been lost.

She came to Philadelphia on the 16th, intending to spend the night with her friend, A. S——, and go to a gathering of Friends, according to a previous agreement. Dear Alice's usual energy led her to go through with this exertion, but it was more than her health was equal to. The rooms were crowded, and a window was opened near where she sat. She thus added to a cold which she had taken several days before.

The next morning found her too ill to leave her bed ; but, although the flesh was so weak, her spirit was rejoicing in God her Saviour, and the two or three days she was obliged to remain in Philadelphia, before she gained sufficient strength to reach her home, were days of sweet communion with her friend, who cared for and watched over her with loving tenderness. When able to join the family at breakfast, after their morning reading of the Scriptures, she prayed very sweetly and fervently. In mentioning it afterward, she said that before she received this outpouring of the Spirit, the cross, in such an effort, would have been great, but that now she did it joyfully, feeling it a privilege.

On the 19th of 1st mo. she reached Tswedelle, and was thankful to be again at her dear home. At first it seemed as if a little quiet and good nursing would soon restore her to her usual health ; but as she continued rather to grow worse, the family physician was called in, who at once pronounced her disease acute bronchitis. She was troubled with a severe cough, and great weakness, which prevented her speaking much to her beloved family of the blessing of the fulness of Christ which had been bestowed upon her while away from home.

She was able, however, to tell her sister something of the revelation of Jesus which she had experienced, saying she knew Christ as a mighty power within, in a far higher sense than ever before. She had often felt her Saviour to be very near to her, but never before so fully enjoyed the consciousness of His dwelling in her, and walking in her. He was more to her now than ever a present help outside of her, for she realised Him to be dwelling in the inner citadel of her heart, and doing all for her, instead of helping her to do it, as heretofore.

The day after her return she wrote the following note to her cousin, from which something may be gathered of her experience at this time :—

"TSWEDELLE, *January* 20, 1867.

"MY OWN DARLING H——,—

"I expect thou wonders why I have not written. The reason is that the flesh (literally) is very weak. It seems that my body has almost given out under too much joy. I feel so exhausted to-day, that I can scarcely move : but the goodness of the Lord is just the same as ever, and it is just as nice to rest on Him. Oh, what a comfort to have such a loving Saviour to *do* everything for us, and to *be* everything for us ! In my present languid and good-for-nothing state it is such a rest to feel that He has taken my will into His own hand, and that there is no crossing of my will with His. May He in His pitying mercy keep it Himself. I have such a realising sense that if He let go of it for a moment it would spring up in all its old force, and the old fight, to do God's will against my own will, would begin. It seems to me we have enough to fight with, without fighting our own wills. What a mercy that there is One who will bind them for us with the chains of love! It seems to me that the great thing the Lord is fighting in me—I do indeed speak reverently—is my old habit of mind. A habit of mind, I suppose, must be harder to overcome than habits of life, for one is the spring of the other. My old habit of thinking that I must fight my besetting temptations in the old legal way is so strong, that I try it many times each day, because I forget that there is a better way, and, of course, fall into sin as often as I try it. The more I think of the glorious truth of what Jesus is, the more wonderful it seems.

" It is so sweet to think of thee, darling, as in the hands of One who is so loving, so powerful, and so true. He put many sweet prayers into both A. S——'s heart and mine for thee, while I was there. My visit to her was confirming, and very sweet, although my head was very naughty. . . .

"As ever, thy loving little sister-cousin,

"ALICE "

A week or more after her return she became much worse, and for three or four weeks was very ill. Several times she seemed to be getting better, and gained strength enough to sit up a short time, and then without any perceptible cause became worse again.

During the third month she seemed to gain strength

Q

more steadily, and was able to sit up a part of the day, and even walk into an adjoining sitting-room. Her recovery, however, being very slow, it was thought best about the first of fourth month to call in a consulting physician, whose opinion was found to be decidedly unfavourable. This was a terrible blow to her family, but the Lord graciously enabled them to submit their wills unto His.

Her sister, whose privilege it was to be her constant companion and nurse, writes concerning this period in her journal :—

4th month 11th, 1867.—Dear Alice's room is as bright and cheerful as possible, but everywhere else the house is as sad as if there had just been a funeral. We have carefully kept our fears from her, but it seems that although outwardly as cheerful and bright as usual, she has for the past week been realising for the first time her exceedingly critical condition.

She has often said when in health, that she thought for the Christian a sudden death was much more to be desired than one from consumption; to have no time to think of the parting, or the death struggle, but in a moment to be ushered into the immediate presence of Jesus, to go no more out for ever, would be glorious. She spoke to-day for the first time of her present feelings with regard to it, saying, " For days past the thought of dying in consumption has been very painful to me, but it was glorious when I felt that Jesus was able for this also. He will bring me through, and even make me triumph over it, and now the thought of a lingering death is not painful, it even looks cheerful."

I said, " He has enabled me, darling, to give thee

up into His hands, to do with thee as seemeth best to Him."

She replied, "Thee need not have told me that, my precious one, for I knew it, I felt it, and I think it is so sweet thee can give me up so entirely. It is lovely to feel that others are laying you into His arms, for He is so good, so precious. For myself I have no wish, no choice; but when I think of father and mother"—and her eyes filled with tears—"it goes to my heart. What would they do without me? Sometimes I think that it may be God's will that I should live to cheer and comfort them in their declining years; but He knows what is best."

Her characteristic forgetfulness of self, and thoughtfulness for the pleasure of others, were beautifully shown in her planning a little surprise for her sister Carrie on the anniversary of her wedding, which occurred only a few days before the conversation above recorded, and while a death by consumption was looking so painful to her. Outwardly she was the same bright, cheerful "Aunt Alice," who must be taken into the counsels of the children, as to what presents to get for mamma. With her own hands she made them a wreath of beautiful flowers from her conservatory to crown their mother on this the tenth anniversary of her wedding-day, and herself came down-stairs that nothing might be wanting to the enjoyment of the occasion, which to the children was unmixed with sadness.

As the spring advanced, Alice continued to gain strength, driving out almost every day, and was able really to enjoy the society of her sister Annie, who had been sent for from St John in the early part of the fourth month, as the physicians then feared that she might not last until summer. Although thus steadily improving, dear Alice did not encourage the hopes of her family and friends as to her recovery, as will be seen by a little note written to her friend M. M. J——— in the fifth month.

.   .   .   "I see by your letter that you do not realise how feeble I am. I still have to be carried up and down stairs when I go to ride, which I do almost every fine day. I have been as far as five miles, when feeling very bright, the horses walking most of the way, but on my sick days a little exhausts me. In short, dear M———, it is scarcely worth while for you to make any calculations about my going away, as it is very uncertain whether I shall be able to leave home at all, until I leave it to go to that better home prepared for us above.

"I ate my tea on the portico last night, and walked out a few steps to look at the flowers. Wasn't that an achievement? It was all so wonderfully beautiful; it was a great treat to me. Oh, Jesus has been so kind to me! I feel His strong kind arm just underneath me; it is such a resting-place! How tender and gentle our precious Saviour is to us!

"Do not feel too anxious about me, dear child; my disease is not one of immediate danger; but I feel that the future is very uncertain. My desire and prayer is, 'Thy will be done, and make me *love* it.'"

The following extracts are from the jottings of one of her sisters in the fifth mo. :—

"Dear Alice replied to my exclamation that I really believed she was getting better, 'I don't think it is best to think whether I am getting well or not, but patiently wait God's time and will, living every day and hour so that we shall not regret it either way. We know that whichever way He orders it, it will be best. I am so thankful that the choice is not left to me, for I had far rather leave it in His hands, to do as He wills. I should not be half so happy if I did not know that *His* will, and no one else's, will be done. I could not enjoy getting better if I did not know He is doing it for His own glory; and if He sees fit to raise me up again, I know that it will be for some wise purpose of His own.

" In speaking afterward of the visit of a dear friend, D. T——, who had prayed most sweetly with her, she said, 'And for me she did not ask for " length of days," but she asked for just what I wanted her to ask for '—rich spiritual blessings, and the joy of uninterrupted communion with the Lord.

" She realises the power of Jesus to save from yielding to temptation, and said the other day that she frequently prays that she may see *sin in its approaches*, so that she need not be hastily overcome, before she has time to flee to Jesus for deliverance.

" A few mornings ago she told me that she awakened suddenly in the night from a distressing dream. She thought that she was being placed in a coffin, and all the physical horrors of death came over her. She felt weak and without strength to resist such feelings, but she just cast herself upon Jesus, and in a moment He brought promise after promise to her mind, and all her fears vanished, and she could say, ' Though I walk through the valley of the shadow of death, I will fear no evil, for Thou art with me.' She said, 'Afterward I was really glad of the temptation, for it showed me how able, how strong Jesus is to deliver.'

"At another time she said that in a dream she seemed to be a soul wandering in darkness and distress—when Jesus appeared to her in the form of a man wrapped in a large cloak, and folded her to His bosom. She added, "Dreams are sometimes so queer; but it was lovely, after my weary wanderings in the dark, to feel myself clasped to His loving breast, and completely hidden and sheltered by His large cloak from cold and darkness.'"

It was particularly trying to Alice's naturally independent disposition to be indebted to others for the supply of all her wants; but, recognising her Lord's hand in this also, she bore it with great sweetness, often calling herself "Grandmother," and playfully giving her age as "one hundred and ten."

The following letter to her mother, who had at Alice's urgent request taken one of her little grandchildren from St John, to consult Dr T—— of the New York movement cure, about a paralysed limb, breathes her usual bright and cheerful spirit :—

"June 14th. . . . As for this little old grandmother, she is getting on nicely. Every want I could possibly have is supplied, and I seem stronger and better than when thou left home. I am wonderfully blessed in not suffering much pain. I enjoy so much going out on the lawn, and sitting on the piazza toward sunset.

"It is Marion's birthday, and I expect the dear

pet over here for four kisses shortly. I walked quite a distance on the lawn yesterday afternoon, and sat on the portico, and took my tea in fine style. I enjoyed it more than I can tell, everything looked so lovely. The only thing that I could have wished for was to have the sweetest of little mothers here to see me. But I am very glad it is as it is. Everything is in the hands of our Father, to arrange for us better than we could do ourselves. It gives me such a sense of rest when I think of it. May He, in whom we trust, richly bless thee, precious one, and bring thee back to us at the right time."

At times Alice suffered from alarming attacks of oppression, in which it seemed to her as if she could never recover her breath; but the heavenly expression of her face showed that, although outwardly so distressed, He whom her soul loved was hiding her in "the secret of His presence."

After one of these attacks, speaking of them to her sister, she said, " They are, of course, very distressing, but then I only have to bear it one moment at a time, and I always feel more then than at other times the near presence of my Saviour, and that more than makes up for the suffering. I do not believe that there is any trial or suffering that the presence and support of Jesus would not more than compensate for. I had much rather have the pain with His presence, than to have that withdrawn and be at ease."

During all this time dear Alice's blessed experience of abiding in Christ continued unclouded; of the first five or six weeks of her illness, when confined almost entirely to her bed, and often too weak to sit up even for a few moments, she thus writes under date of Feb. 28th :—

"DEAREST H——,—

. . . "How wonderfully kind our Heavenly Father is! He has been so good to me; indeed I can say with M—— that my sick-bed has been the most perfectly happy place I ever knew or conceived of. I never before thought of its being possible to live hour after hour, and day after day, in such consciousness of His presence; indeed I did not know what perfect joy one moment of such companionship is. It seems to me now it would kill me to be left without it. O H——! how incomparably lovely our Jesus is! It seems to me even the subject of trying to glorify Him in our lives becomes insignificant compared with Jesus himself."

And in the third mo. to another friend she writes :—

. . . "How much, how very much, I have to be thankful for! Our Father has dealt so tenderly with me. I cannot tell you of the sweet stream of peace that has flowed through my heart like a river. Jesus has seemed so very near. I never realised before how close Jesus is to us every moment, whether we realise it or not, and oh, the realisation of it is such intense joy! May He henceforth keep us both in the constant consciousness of this! Is it not wonderful that this is our privilege?"

And again, in a note dated July 19th, 1867, she says :—

"DEAREST H———,—

. . . "I think often of thee, and long for a
sight of thee, but am more than content with what I
have; for really, H———, it does seem to me no one
ever had so many blessings. Our precious Saviour
is so kind; He knows what a weak baby I am, and
'tempereth the wind to the shorn lamb.' He is my
rock, my sure resting-place; in Him, indeed, do I
put my trust, and yet sometimes I dishonour Him by
looking away and getting discouraged. He brings my
eyes back, and all is bright again; but, oh, H———! I
never did have such views of myself as I have had
lately. Sometimes it has been dreadful; but, oh, what
a salvation we have!"

Dear Alice, during her hours of weary suffering
and physical langour, had no friend more firmly
established than herself in a life of daily faith, to encourage and strengthen her against the wiles of the
adversary. Those by whom she was surrounded
knew little experimentally of the life of entire
abandonment of self, and of complete trust in Jesus
upon which she had so lately entered. Some were
inclined to question whether the salvation of our Lord
Jesus Christ provided for such an abiding in Him as
to give a continual deliverance from the power of
inward and outward sin, and whether it was the privilege of any one to rejoice always in the Saviour's presence and smile. It was suggested that the joy and
triumph which Alice had realised for the past few
months were only a little fresh sense of divine love
and mercy, which would after a while become dim,
and leave the soul as before. Alice was at first too

sure of her own experience to pay much heed to
these questionings. She knew that Jesus was able to
keep her trusting Him, and she could not be persuaded that she had ever experienced His indwelling in anything like the sense she now realised it.
But she was weak and nervous, and, at last, the
doubts of others began to find an entrance into her
soul. She said afterwards that she remembered
the moment when the first thought of unbelief passed
through her mind.

A dear Christian friend was conversing with her,
and expressed his doubts whether such joy and nearness of communion as she had lately enjoyed could
last, saying that he had often had seasons of very
blessed communion, but had never found them to
last any great length of time. The thought then
flashed into Alice's mind—"Must this be so? must
I give up the blessed consciousness of the presence
of my indwelling Saviour?" A few days after this a
friend was sitting beside her, and she looked up
and asked the question almost imploringly—"Does
thee think a Christian may have the conscious presence of his Saviour with him *all* the time?" The
friend addressed did not know experimentally, and
could only say that she thought the Scriptures taught
that they might; but her words were too doubtful to
comfort or help dear Alice much.

It happened also, that two ministers of the gospel,
entirely unknown to each other, visited her at different times, and, with the intention, doubtless, of
preparing her for the dark hours which so often visit
invalids, spoke of God sometimes hiding His face
from us, and that such seasons of desertion must be

endured with patience and resignation. After one of these visits, she was found in tears, and, upon being urged to tell what troubled her, replied, " I cannot bear to think of my Heavenly Father withdrawing His smile from me, for I feel so utterly weak, that I think, without it, I could not bear my physical suffering."

She was pointed to the unfailing love of Jesus, and reminded that it certainly is His will that we should always be happy in Him, for we are not only commanded to " rejoice evermore," but our Saviour himself told us to " ask, and receive, that our joy may be full." To this her only reply was, " The thought will come that perhaps my Heavenly Father sent —— here to warn me of a dark season ahead, and, oh ! I am so weak. I do not think I can bear it." This dread of a dark season in store for her was doubtless aggravated by physical causes, as she, at that time, had the additional suffering of a succession of abscesses in her side, and her mind taking particular hold of this thought, she overlooked the truth that her Saviour would be with her through it all, although the clouds might prevent her realising His presence so sensibly, as lately it had been her privilege to do. Thus Satan found room to enter a wedge of unbelief, and he never ceased his efforts until he had deprived her of all her joy. She lost the precious realisation of her life being hid with Christ in God. She could no longer say, as she had once said with such depth of meaning, " Not I, but Christ." It became again to her as it had been in old times, " I, and Christ," and this was soon fol-lowed by the " I," without " Christ." Even her old

assurance of faith in the forgiving mercy of her
Saviour failed her, when she lost the precious sense
of His presence, that had so filled and satisfied every
need of her soul.

For a few weeks her view of the Sun of Righteousness was interrupted by these clouds of unbelief.
But she felt that it was so dishonouring to her Saviour
thus to doubt Him, that she spoke of it to very few,
and seldom referred to it even to them. She was not
long suffered by her loving Father to wander in this
wilderness of doubt. She grew so much stronger
that she was able to leave home, and was taken to
Atlantic City for a few weeks, and there she met the
same cousin at whose house she had been so blessed
in the winter. To her she disclosed the state of her
mind, and asked her help. "Tell me," she said,
"the old, old story of the gospel, just as thee used to
tell me at first. Treat me like a child, and talk to
me about Jesus as the Saviour of sinners." "I want
the milk for babes," she would say over and over.
"Just show me the places in the Bible where Jesus
is revealed as able to save the chief of sinners."
Then she began to question whether she was not
commanded to trust, and not be afraid; and she listened eagerly to text after text on the duty of believing, on the sin of unbelief, and on the preciousness
of faith in God's eyes. Gradually her doubts were
conquered by the promises of God, and again at
the end of the year, as at the beginning, dear Alice
could say the precious words, "Not I, but Christ,"
and could feel, as she often expressed it, that she was
"*just extinguished in Jesus.*" She thus wrote concerning this period of darkness to her friend A. S—— :

" MY VERY DEAR FRIEND,—

. . . "I have so often thought of the day dear
A. F—— and thou came out to see me. How kind
it was of you to come, and how sad that the shadow
that hung over my spirits should have saddened you.

"I cannot think of the experience through which
I was then passing without a shudder. Oh, what a
fearful thing is unbelief! I do believe, A——, it is
the blackness of darkness itself. We cannot come
near to its borders even, without feeling the gloom of
its deep shadow. How awful, then, is the thought of
being plunged into its depths!

"But thanks be unto God, we are called to be
'children of the light;' we are to have nothing to do
with darkness. He has brought us 'out of darkness
into His marvellous light.' Our place is to bask in
the light of the Sun of Righteousness, and so let fruit
ripen unto His glory. How preposterous it is to
think for a moment of its being His will that any of
His children should, even for a season, go back
under the old shadow from whence He brought them
forth. And, oh, what a price He paid to bring them
forth! The idea that it could be His will to try any
of us by taking away our rejoicing confidence in Him,
is one which I am sure He has never given us the
least ground for in His Word, but, on the contrary, it
is entirely opposed to all His teaching. He wishes
us to trust Him at all times. It grieves Him when
we doubt His word, for He has commanded, 'Have
faith in God,' and still further, 'Rejoice in the Lord
alway.' How, then, could He take away our power
to believe and rejoice, since He does not contradict

Himself, or do evil that good may come? I grieve
that such a God-dishonouring thought could have
found even a transient lodging in my breast, even at
an hour when too weak and nervous to think coolly
or reasonably. The language of faith answers all such
suggestions : ' God only is my rock, and my salvation ; He is my defence, I shall not be moved."

Later she thus writes to her cousin :—

"*January* 7, 1868.

.   .   .   " Indeed I have longed to write to thee,
dear sweet sister-cousin. I long to have thee know
just how it is with me ; but writing is in fact the
hardest thing I have to do, as it always gives me a
pain in my side, and besides I begin to cough when I
sit down to write, and generally keep it up until I stop
and lie down.

" Thou asks if I am at rest in Jesus. I can say, in
truth, my soul is at rest in Him. My visit at Atlantic
City did me a deal of good ; it cleared away so many
dark shadows of unbelief, and I have realised much
more of the sweetness of trusting in Jesus. In short,
I have had to trust Him more than I ever did before,
because I am so weak, such a coward, I could not
bear for one minute the ' pressure of my care,' without resting it on Him. Oh, it is such a comfort to
have Him to rest on !

" My experience last year was real ; I learned to
trust and to know Jesus a power *within*, which I find
a great comfort."

CHAPTER XIV.

DURING the previous summer, Alice's little namesake, Alice W. S——, opened her blue eyes upon the world, and when she was four weeks old Alice had the pleasure at Atlantic City of holding her for a few moments in her arms. A sweet picture they made ; the one so soon to leave the cares and joys of earth for her home in heaven, the other just entering upon life, with all its uncertainty as to earthly joy and prosperity.

Upon first hearing of her birth and name, Alice thus writes to the little one's mother, her "sister-cousin :"—

"Ain't I proud, though, to have a namesake ! I am delighted. May the dear little pet be a great comfort to her mamma, and may she early know, love, and glorify our precious Lord and Master, is the prayer of her loving Aunt Alice."

In the fall of this year Alice's health seemed so much better that it was thought advisable to try a journey northward, and she was taken to Saratoga, Pittsfield, and New Bedford. During her two months absence from home she continued to improve, slowly but steadily. Long rides over the mountains seemed to agree with her, and she often spoke with pleasure of these delightful excursions, some of which required the day to accomplish.

She returned to her home the last of eleventh month, so much stronger and better, that hopes were raised in the hearts of her friends that she might ultimately recover. But it was not the will of her Heavenly Father that she should tarry on earth much longer. About the first of first month, 1868, her appetite again began to fail, and she grew rapidly weaker, until all became apprehensive that she could not remain longer than the spring. She had lost her voice some weeks previously, and from that time was never able to speak above a whisper, but her energy and cheerfulness continued undiminished, and she wished to be carried down-stairs and out to ride until a few days before her death.

Although so weak in body, she still neglected no opportunity of speaking to others of their souls' salvation.

Since her death, M——, a girl who sometimes waited on her, acknowledged that her first serious thoughts on the subject of religion were consequent upon personal appeals made to her by Alice, during her illness.

One of her sisters writes : "I remember now, her telling me at the time, of the first conversation she had with M—— on the subject. It was one morning when I was unable to assist her in dressing. When M—— came in the room, although she really longed to say something to her personally, it seemed like a great undertaking, a perfect mountain before her.

Satan suggested that she needed all her little strength for dressing, which always so much exhausted her; and in reference to her weakness she said, ' I never felt more entirely without strength, and unfit to say a word; indeed I seemed not to have a word to say; but I knew that God could speak through me, supplying all needed strength; so I just cast myself on Him, and asked Him to open the way for me to introduce the subject easily and naturally; and I don't think I ever spoke with less effort to any one, or with more conscious power of the Holy Spirit.'

" I remember the animation with which she spoke of this way of faith, saying that it made hard things so easy, removing in a moment mountains of difficulty.

" How my heart rejoices that the precious seed sown by her in so much weakness, has been made fruitful by the Holy Spirit to another heart. How rich will be her reward as she meets these redeemed ones at that last great day! Many, we believe, will be gathered through her words and prayers, that we shall never know of here, but they will shine as stars in her crown of rejoicing."

Often during Alice's illness a few of the disciples of the Lord Jesus gathered in her room on the first day of the week, as did the early Christians, to break bread in remembrance of their Lord. Several weeks before her departure she wished once more thus to show forth her Lord's death, but she evidently felt that it was the last time she would meet with His children, thus to remember Him on earth. Her eyes filled with tears, and although she said nothing, it was one of the very few occasions on which s'ts

R

seemed to feel the coming separation from all earthly ties and fellowships.

Many times during those last months she spoke of her departure. She seemed to be quietly waiting by the river, clinging to nothing on earth, but ready at any moment for the summons. She often said, " I am very happy; Jesus keeps me in perfect peace, resting upon Him," and upon several occasions remarked, " It seems almost wrong in me to be so happy at the thought of going, when I know it makes you all feel so sad."

Her sister from St John was not able to reach Tswedelle before the last of third mo. on account of severe storms, and at times it seemed doubtful whether Alice would live to see her. In speaking of it, she said, " I would love to see dear Annie again, and I know it would be a great satisfaction to her to be here, but I feel no clinging to it ; I know it will be just right."

Several weeks before they met, Alice wrote her the following little note :—

"*March* 12, 1868.

" MY OWN SWEET SISTER,—

" I feel as if I could not stand it another minute without writing to thee ; it makes thee seem so much further off when I don't talk to thee myself.

" Carrie has told thee, of course, how much worse I am in body ; but I am *very* happy. I think the thought of just falling asleep in Jesus is perfectly sweet. It is so different from my old view of death : and this is all that death is to him who trusts in Jesus —just falling asleep on Jesus' breast to awake at the glorious resurrection morn.

" Yesterday, and indeed for two or three days, I

seemed so prostrated, I thought the end must be very near, and I longed to write thee a love-greeting once again, my precious one. But I feel so much revived after a better night, that when I found I could eat a little breakfast this morning, I almost felt as if I might last until thou comes; but whatever is His will, darling, we know He will make sweet to us.

"Jesus is so strong and so loving, we haven't anything to be afraid of while He is near. And He *is* very near to sustain me, and I trust He will be so to the end, and I trust Him, too, to sustain all of you, my dear ones.

. . . "I am thy own sister; best of all, one in Jesus, and soon, oh, how soon, we shall together 'hail Him triumphant descending the skies!' It will only be a little while at longest. Lovingly,

"ALICE."

After embracing once again this dear sister, it seemed as if Alice had nothing more to desire in this world, saying that her Heavenly Father had mercifully given her all, and more than she could have asked. She had taken a last farewell on earth of almost all her friends, many of whom came from a distance to see her once more. For most of these she had some parting token of her love, some of which were presented by herself with tender words of farewell; and although these partings were inexpressibly sad to her family and friends, they cannot be looked back upon as mournful. It was as if she were going on a pleasant journey, and had prepared these as tokens of loving remembrance during her absence. Those who received them made great efforts not to sadden her peaceful spirit, by manifesting in her presence the grief of their own hearts. A happy smile often rested on her face, and several times she made such remarks as the following: "What a blessing it is that almost all my friends are Christians! Some of them do not enjoy the full assurance of faith, but it is very sweet that I can say to nearly every one, 'We shall meet in heaven.'"

To others of her friends these memorials came not until Alice had gone to her home above, and then the message accompanying them—sometimes a peculiarly appropriate text—came like a breath of inspiration from the spirit-land, impressing, in her well remembered and loving accents, the word of truth upon the heart.

She sent the 14th verse of the 27th Psalm, which was a great favourite of hers, as a farewell message to a friend who was unable to come to see her. To another she wrote a few parting words, closing with :—

"My dear friend, cleave close to Jesus; let Him be your all in all. The joys He gives are far better than what the world can give, and I pray you not to let it draw your heart away from heaven, from Jesus, our Jesus, who loves us so much, and longs to have us live very close to Him, because He *does* love us so much. Oh, the wonderful depths of that love! I am just revelling in it now. The love and the mercy and the grace are all true, and our King changes not. What a resting-place is the bosom of Jesus for the dying sinner!

'I am a poor sinner, and nothing at all,
But Jesus Christ is my all and in all.'"

The following extracts are taken from memoranda made by one of her sisters during the last month of Alice's illness :—

" 4th mo. 6th. Dear Alice is too weak to say much, but every member of the family receives at all times a loving smile and hearty welcome to her room. When dressed for the day, and occupying her usual reclining position on the sofa, she enjoys much having us all gather in the room, and listens with interest to the cheerful conversation, sometimes taking part by a few words, or a smile of assent. All that she says is spoken in a whisper, and a few words at a time, as she finds breath.

"She seemed quite surprised to-day when I told her that A. T—— (a very skilful nurse, who had been much with her, and to whom she was much attached) thought that in two or three weeks she could come to be with her through the summer if she needed her. She looked up and said, in her old quick way, ‘I *should* like to know how much longer she thinks I am going to live.’ I replied, ‘She told me she thought thee might be with us for weeks, or even months.’ I knew that Alice was hoping that the summons would come unexpectedly and very soon, and that this was far from good news to her; but in an instant she checked the little impatience of her manner, and, although her eyes filled with tears, she said, quickly, ‘I would not have it any way but the Lord's way; still I feel so weary sometimes,—I just long to fall asleep in Jesus.’ I told her she must remember what a precious boon every added day and hour of her stay was to us, while she was not suffering more than at present, although we could only say with her, 'Thy will be done.'

"4th mo. 11th.   This evening, when Annie kissed her good night, she said, 'Such a happy thought has been filling my mind to-day,—I do not think any of us realise how near I shall be to you,—when I have left this body, and am with the Lord.—In all your communion with Him I shall be there!'

"4th mo. 15th.   Dear Alice suffered much from oppression to-day; but when Annie told her that, although we can do so little to show our sympathy, we do feel for her from the depths of our hearts, she said, 'You must not sympathise with me, for I don't feel as if I need any sympathy.—I do not want you to feel sorry, but to praise the Lord that I am kept in such perfect peace.—It don't seem as if I have to bear my suffering;—I seem to be *carried through it.*'"

The preceding extract gives evidence of dear Alice's thoughtfulness for others, which was a most touching feature all through her illness, and which shone conspicuously as her life wore to its close. She kept hidden, as much as possible from her beloved friends, the suffering she was enduring, that their feelings might not be wrought upon by perceiving its full extent; and, indeed, it really seemed as if she so entirely cast herself upon her Saviour for bodily relief and comfort, as well as for spiritual, that she realised in a degree the literal fulfilment of the prophecy spoken of by Matthew : " Himself took our infirmities, and bare our sicknesses."

Two of the little band of cousins before spoken of

made a farewell visit to Alice on the 22nd of the 4th
mo. They thus write about it :—

"We found darling Alice very weak, and unable
to speak above a whisper. She was lying on the sofa
in the large front room ; the soft spring air stealing
in through the open window. Everything about her
wore a bright and cheerful aspect, and all her surroundings, even to her little round table, with its
vase of delicate flowers, glass of ice-water, and
dainty little saucer of gum arabic, bore witness to
the refinement of her taste.

"The gentle invalid herself never looked more
lovely as she welcomed us each warmly with tender
kiss and pressure of the hand. Her soft hair, turned
back from her sweet pale face, revealed an expression of almost heavenly loveliness. She looked only
too ready to depart.

"Our conversation soon turned upon heavenly
things, and for the few short hours of our visit
we enjoyed the privilege of holding with our precious cousin sweeter communion than we had ever
known when all in the buoyancy of health. The
glory and joy of the resurrection were themes upon
which Alice dwelt with delight, and vividly did she
seem to realise that she should be a partaker of the
coming of Christ, and of the glory that should follow ; that as she had suffered with Him, so also she
should reign with Him. While she thus fully entered
into the enjoyment of all the glorious future as revealed in the Scriptures, she was not dismayed because
there is so little direct revelation with regard to the
intermediate state of those who sleep ·in Jesus, but
had intense comfort in the assurance that she would

immediately see and enjoy her Saviour. ' I shall be with Jesus, and that will be enough,' she said, and these words, so full of reality to her, were to us words of great solemnity.

" It was remarked by one present that as she lay there so patiently suffering she was permitted to glorify her Lord. She replied, with evident feeling of her own nothingness, ' How wonderful that a *worm* can glorify Him ! '

" The thought was suggested to her, that as she was the first of the group of cousins who had thus tried the power of their Saviour, she was the means of greatly strengthening the faith of the rest in manifesting that He took away all fear of death from one who simply trusted in Him for salvation. She replied, stopping after every few words to take breath, ' What a privilege it is to *prove* Him ; it has been my privilege to do this both for a sudden death and a lingering one.—When I thought myself dying (from poison)—four or five years ago,—I felt no fear, for I could just cast myself on Jesus,—and now I can trust Him in the same way for a lingering death,—although it takes much greater faith to keep trusting Him for so long a time,—for Satan never wearies in tempting.— Sometimes he comes in the night and says, " You know you would be dreadfully frightened if you should have to die now,—to-night."' On being asked how she met such suggestions : 'Oh !' she said, ' I tell him to be gone.—If I depended on *him*, I *should* be frightened at the thought of death,—but my dependence is placed on One stronger than he,—and I know that He will never leave me nor forsake me.

" In reply to one who remarked what a comfort it

was to see her so happy, she said: 'My heavenly
Father is so good ! it seems almost too good not to
let any clouds come in ; '· and afterwards, 'I know
what it is to abide in Christ; I feel *extinguished* in
Him.'

"Dear Alice's voice was so low, we had to be
very quiet to catch all she said. She kept her eyes
mostly cast down, but now and then she would look
up, with a kindling glance of earnestness and love,
as she said something of her Jesus, or responded to
His praises from another. We did not let her see
the anguish of our hearts as we thus looked upon her
for the last time on earth. Once when she noticed
the tears that would not be withheld, she said that
she did not dare to let her thoughts dwell upon the
separation from her loved ones; it would be too
agonising for her to bear ; and hearing her mother's
step outside, she said, 'There's darling little mother;
I can't think about her.'

"When we bade her farewell she kissed us again
and again, and said, 'It won't be long.'"

Another dear cousin about this time made her a
parting visit. He writes :—

"Never shall I forget the impression left by this
visit. Dear Alice appeared like one about to start
on a pleasant journey, which she had long looked
towards, and now that its realisation was near, she
seemed unable to conceal a certain exuberance of
joy. As I was about leaving, she called me to her
side, and said, 'Dear cousin J——, I want to give
thee the words of the Psalmist. 'Wait on the Lord,

be of good courage, and He shall strengthen thine
heart.'   How often since her death has this promise,
given of the Lord, and confirmed by her angelic de-
parting spirit, come to me with power.   'She being
dead, yet speaketh.'"

One of her friends who visited her at this time
writes :—

"I remember how dear Alice, characteristically
drawing a spiritual significance from little things,
called my attention to an odorator which had been
given to her.   As her sister gently breathed into it,
and diffused its perfume through the room, she said:
'Isn't it like the Christian?   He may have Christ in
his *heart*, and enjoy the *possession* of the gospel, but
it is only when breathed on by the Holy Ghost that
he has power to convey to others the blessing of it.'"

One of dear Alice's greatest enjoyments and com-
forts was to hear portions of Scripture and familiar
hymns repeated.   This was done many times a day.
She did not weary of repetitions of the same, but
wanted to hear them again and again, each time
seeming to receive fresh nourishment and strength.
At one time, when taken suddenly in the night with
a spell of suffocation, one of her sisters being alone
with her, was so anxious to relieve her physical distress, by getting ether, fanning her, &c., that she
forgot to repeat texts, as Alice had before requested
her to do at such times.   But Alice, who seemed to
value spiritual comfort more than that intended only
for the body, afterwards begged her never to forget

it again, saying that at such times it was impossible for her to think—mind and body seemed a chaos of suffering ; and, she added, " You don't know how the precious words and promises of Scripture fall upon my ear, as if Jesus himself were speaking, and they seem to do me more good than anything else."

When at all able, she requested to see every one that called, silently and cheerfully bearing any additional suffering their presence in her room might cause, being anxious to gratify their desire of seeing her once more, and wishing to neglect no opportunity of witnessing for Jesus, even with her latest breath. Although daily and hourly growing weaker in body, her spiritual strength seemed to be continually increased, and her mouth opened by the Lord to speak constantly of heavenly things.

On the 25th of 4th mo., twelve days before her death, one of her sisters writes : " When suffering a great deal from oppression and nausea, so that the tears would come, she said : " I seem to you to be suffering a great deal—and I am so weak that even a little pain will bring the tears—but underneath it all I take a great deal of comfort ;—I have been having such a sweet, happy time to-day.'

" In the evening, when Annie bade her good-night, wishing her sweet and comforting thoughts, she said : ' You cannot know how full of happiness I am within. I want you to know—so that you may not mind so much seeing me suffer.'

" 4th mo. 29th. On reading the forty-sixth Psalm to her, and remarking how she had marked and underscored it in her Bible, she said : ' Yes, I love that Psalm—I want you to say it to me when I am dying.'

She asked me to còpy a favourite hymn, entitled 'Lean Hard,' for her to send to a friend, saying—'It is beautiful; it grows upon you.'

" This evening, after her position had been changed, and she was, consequently, much fatigued, I repeated a little verse which had been a favourite during the past winter :—

> ' Pilgrim of earth, who art journeying to heaven !
>   Heir of eternal life, child of the day !
>   Cared for, watched over, beloved, and forgiven,
>   Art thou discouraged because of the way ? '

"She answered me at once with a very emphatic 'No,' adding, 'God has been so good to me !'"

"5th mo. 1st.　This morning, when the eighth chapter of Romans was read to her, she said with a heavenly smile, 'Is not that glorious?' and later when physical suffering caused the tears to roll down her cheeks, she said, 'These tears have no business here ; but they are only outside tears,—for my heart is not crying,—when I think where I am going,—and "'tis but a little longer,"' referring to A. S——'s verse :—

> ' 'Tis but a little longer ;
>   Methinks the end I see :
>   Oh ! matchless love and mercy,
>   The Bridegroom waits for me,—
>   Waits to present me faultless
>   Before His Father's throne ;
>   *His* comeliness *my* beauty,
>   His righteousness my own.'

She could only follow these lines with her lips, excepting the last, which she said aloud.

"Later she said : ' Tell me the old, old story.' We thought she meant the story in verse, and upon search being made for it, she said : ' You know it ; I want it from the Bible.' Many verses were repeated to her, but she said : ' About Moses lifting up the serpent.'—When it was finished, she said : ' That is it—when you want to comfort any one—point to the *object* of our faith—Jesus Christ crucified.—The nearer I approach to death—the more clearly I see the glorious truth,—that we are justified by faith in Jesus alone, and that works have nothing to do with it,—excepting as the fruits of faith.—I feel that my works are nothing,—nothing but filthy rags—

> " Thy righteousness, O Christ !
>   Alone can clothe and beautify,
>   I wrap it round my soul,
>   In it I 'll live and die." '

"After passing through a severe turn of difficulty of breathing, she said : ' When I was suffering so much from oppression a while ago,—that verse was such a comfort to me—" He that trusteth in the Lord shall never be confounded." '

" 5th mo. 2d. This was a day of peculiarly sweet and heavenly intercourse, although dear Alice's weakness prevented her taking part in the conversation, excepting in broken sentences, and by expressive looks and words of assent.

" The 53d chapter of Isaiah and the 8th chapter of John were during the morning particularly the subject of our conversation. In dwelling upon the precious truths contained in these portions of Scripture, the communion of spirit that was enjoyed we felt to be more precious than if it could have been expressed in words.

"She took pleasure in looking out of the window for the first time for many days at the beautiful landscape which lay smiling in the sunlight; but the beauties of earth seemed only to make her think of the transcendent joys and glories of heaven.

"When it was remarked how sweetly the birds were singing, she said: 'Singing praises,' and added, looking lovingly at father, who with several others of the family were gathered round her, 'I wish we could sing a hymn of praise *all together.*—I want to die singing praises;' and indeed I think we could have sung a song of thanksgiving and praise even then, for the atmosphere around our precious one was such that the unseen and spiritual seemed the only real things in life, and for the time we could share her joy at the thought of so soon entering into the unveiled presence of her Beloved. Jesus seems very near to her; she said: 'I used to rest in the promises, but now I rest in the Beloved.'

"She sent a message to Aunt M. E———. 'Tell her that in the hour of trial I find Jesus all sufficient—all is peaceful, and I know that I am going to be with Him who died for me,—and my great comfort is that Jesus Christ did *all* for me,—and all I have to do is to rest and trust in Him.—Tell her I long to meet her among the glorious company of the redeemed at the resurrection.—I send her for a text, John iii. 14–18, 36.'

"To dear mother, who with tears was speaking of what her loss would be, and saying that Alice had always been to her all and more than her heart could have desired in a daughter, she replied,—'It is the greatest comfort to me that you all give me up so sweetly, and the more precious and lovely I am to thee, darling mother,—the greater will be the sacrifice to give me up to Jesus;—and it is so sweet to give our *most* precious things to Christ.'

"5th mo. 3d. A lovely first-day morning found our precious one still lingering in the 'border land.' She said—'Before another Sabbath morning I shall be in heaven.' I drew her reclining chair toward the window that she might look out, involuntarily exclaiming, as my eyes rested on the green fields and distant blue hills spread out as a panorama before us, 'If this world is so beautiful and fair, what must heaven be?' She kept her eyes closed, and replied as in a murmur from the spirit land: 'And how fairer than all is He, the source and centre of all blessing.' *I* was looking at the fading beauties of *this* world; *she* was beholding, although as yet through a glass darkly, the matchless beauties of the eternal, invisible One.

"About noon, when asked if she was much oppressed, she replied, 'Yes, but I don't mind it;' and afterward, when somewhat relieved, said, 'I feel better now.'—'How sweet it is,—so many kind friends.'

"Very much that she said we could not hear, only words occasionally, as, 'beautiful,' 'lovely.' When asked if she felt more comfortable, she said, 'Nothing would be suffering—while realising His near presence, as I do now.' She always endeavours to direct our thoughts from herself to the Saviour, saying at different times, when asked how she feels, or if she is suffering much, 'I am resting on Jesus,' or 'The Lord is so good.'

" During this day 1 Cor. xv., and 2 Cor. v., and the four last verses of the fourth chapter, were read. Also, among many others, the twenty-seventh Psalm. She requested the first verse of this to be repeated to her several times, saying, 'I was trying to remember that verse this morning, but I could not quite get it.' Many sweet hymns were also read to her. She enjoyed particularly, 'Rock of Ages,' 'How firm a foundation,' and 'Jesus, lover of my soul.''

" In the afternoon she expressed a wish to see her nephews and nieces, feeling that her departure was hastening, and the time of her leave-taking getting very short. They were brought in one at a time. She kissed all very lovingly, and to the older ones said a few parting words.

" 5th mo. 4th.   2d day. This morning early dear Alice remarked, 'How sweetly the birds sing—they began just at four o'clock ;' and then reflecting on the mercies of God toward herself, and her near prospect of entering upon an eternity of happiness, said, 'We will shout and sing praises to the Lord.— Oh, it is glorious !—I wish you would all shout for joy and sing praises.'

" After a while she said, ' The name of Jesus is so sweet to me,—say, " How sweet the name of Jesus sounds." ' She followed with her lips the last two verses :—

> ' Dear name ! the *rock* on which I build,
>   My shield and hiding-place ;
>   My never-failing treasury, filled
>   With boundless stores of grace.

> ' I would Thy boundless love proclaim
> With every fleeting breath ;
> And may the music of Thy name
> Refresh my soul in death.'

And then added, ' Indeed it does refresh me.'

" Again and again she asked for familiar passages of Scripture, and often when thought to be asleep would say, ' Go on ; it does me so much good.' Once she said, ' Be sure you say some of those passages when I am dying.'

" Early in the morning she asked for the hymn, ' Anywhere with Jesus,' and a few hours afterward asked for it again. Dear Alice, who was resting with her eyes closed, remarked on the sad tone in which it was read, and, looking up, seemed much surprised at seeing us all in tears ; then, as if suddenly remembering the cause of our grief, said, ' Let the Lord strengthen your hearts so that you will not cry ;—it makes me feel as if I ought to be sorry too.'

" When Annie spoke of her suffering, she said, ' It is little I can bear for His sake ;—it is the only way I can show I appreciate what He suffered.' "

On the morning of the 5th, third day, it was evident dear Alice's departure was near at hand. Her sister writes, " We thought this would be our darling's last day on earth. In the morning her pulse seemed to be growing weaker, and she called us all to come close to her, one at a time, and gave us each a loving farewell." It was, however, her Heavenly Father's will that she should have another day and night of suffering. She revived somewhat and fell into a doze for a few moments, and on awaking said,

s

"I hoped I was going to rest when I went to sleep that time." Some time after, knowing how she longed to go, her sister Carrie leaned over her and said, "Darling, don't thee ever ask the Lord to take thee home *soon?*" She replied quickly, "No; I leave that to Him; He shall do just as He pleases about it."

She took her mother's hand, and said, "Dearest mother, thee ought to rejoice,—it is so sweet,— Heavenly Father, bless dear mother—and comfort her, for Jesus' sake." And later, when a sudden thought of the future led one of her sisters to exclaim, "How shall we ever live without thee?" she replied, "The Lord—trust Him;—let Him be your all."

In the afternoon she said, "I am suffering greatly; but I rejoice to suffer, as He gives me strength." And again: "Mine is no ecstatic vision,—it is simple faith, —just resting and trusting in Jesus. I am so happy, —but it makes no difference how I feel, does it? His love is always the same,"—then adding with more energy, "It is an absolute duty to have faith in God."

A friend, for whose salvation she longed, was admitted for a few moments to her room. Dear Alice said, as she gave her a parting kiss, "I want to tell thee, dear, that all we have to do is just to trust in Jesus—He has paid all our debt;—He has done it all; —we have only to trust in Him, and be happy." To another, who came from a distance scarcely hoping to see her, she said, "I want to add my testimony to those who have gone before,—that the blood of Jesus Christ cleanseth from all sin."

Later in the afternoon she said, "Tell everybody

what a Saviour Jesus is; and then, with her characteristic energy and warmth, added, "He's such a *splendid*
Saviour!"

Toward evening she said, "All is peace;" and
then quoting the two lines which had been the expression of her earliest Christian feeling,

> "I am a poor sinner, and nothing at all,
> But Jesus Christ is my all and in all,"

she set the seal thereto with her dying lips, saying,
emphatically, "That's true;" and then, "Where
should I be now if I trusted in anything but Christ?"

She seemed much pleased to see her aunt M.
W——, who came from Philadelphia to stay all night,
and see dear Alice once more. In the evening the
last nine verses of the seventh chapter of Revelation
were read to her, and many comforting texts repeated.
Prayer was also offered by her side for her release in
the Lord's own time; "for," writes one of her sisters,
"we could not but feel with her, in the language of
one of her favourite hymns—

> 'I know not what my soul might lose
> By shortened or protracted breath.'"

Late in the evening she asked for the first chapter
of 1st Peter, but by mistake 2d Peter first chapter was
begun. She said, "That is not it; I want the one
where it says, 'All flesh is as grass, . . . but the
word of the Lord shall stand for ever.'"

All night she lay upon her large reclining chair.
At her earnest solicitation her parents left her for a
short rest, and those who remained in the room said
little to her during the hours before midnight, hoping
that she might be refreshed by sleep. She lay most

of the time with her eyes closed, for her weakness and oppression were such that she could say but little. Occasionally the upward glance of her pleading eyes, and the clasping of her hands as if in prayer, revealed the communion she was having with her Beloved. So peaceful she looked, so little trace was there upon her countenance of the suffering she was enduring, that her aunt could hardly realise she was otherwise than comfortable, and, bending over her, asked with affectionate solicitude, if she was suffering much. With clasped hands she replied, " Agony ! agony !" All praise to her covenant keeping God, who so strengthened the frail tabernacle as to let the taking down of the pins thereof be known only to Himself.

After midnight, finding that it was impossible for her to rest or sleep, her sisters endeavoured to comfort and strengthen her by reading or repeating portions of Scripture. She seemed to feel very grateful for this, saying, " You don't know how much good it does me." In her very weakened condition she could not, without effort, recall the whole of the texts which arose in her mind, and these she brought to their notice for them to take up and finish, by repeating, in a whisper so faint as sometimes to be scarcely understood, the first two or three words, as, " The Lord is my shepherd ; " " God so loved the world." These comforted her much, and she liked to hear them again and again, saying, " You need not mind repeating the same texts many times, for I like to let my mind rest upon them."

Her sufferings every hour became much more acute, but not one word of repining escaped her lips. She many times clasped her hands, and moved her lips in prayer, exclaiming, "Come! come!" Once, when in great distress, she said, "Father, my times are in Thine hand;" and again, when almost in agony, and realising the pain it gave those around her to see her in so much suffering, and fearing they might be tempted to doubt the goodness of the Lord, she said, "Don't let it shake your faith,—there is some good reason." Her sister writes, "And we who were privileged to watch her in these hot fires, could see how the gold was being purified, and she was every hour growing in likeness to her dear Master. Never shall we forget the heavenly beauty deepening in her face, and the meek, loving, trustful look which grew in her patient eyes." And another sister adds, "I never could realise before how our Saviour must have looked when He was led as a lamb to the slaughter, meekly willing to suffer all His Father's will. It was only the reflection of His image in our darling's face that was so lovely. Truly her prayer of last summer was fully answered—'Thy will be done, and *make me love it.*'"

Several times the beautiful verse was repeated to her—

"And welcome, *precious*, can His Spirit make
My little drop of suffering for His sake;
Father, the cup I drink, the path I take,
All, all are known to Thee;"

when her eyes always gave the full assent which she was too weak to speak.

She asked for the second chapter of Songs of Solomon, but being so low, she fell into a doze as it was read, and on awakening she said, "Did you read it

all?   I did not hear about the spring-time coming,—
and the singing of birds."—It was read again.

About four o'clock her sisters began to sing some
of her favourite hymns.   This appeared greatly to
relieve the feeling of bodily distress, and she followed
the words whenever she was able with her trembling
lips.   After singing one or two, fearing she might be
tired, they would stop, when, looking at them affec-
tionately, she would say, " When you are rested sing
it again."   The one she seemed most to enjoy was

"REST FOR THE WEARY."

"In the Christian's home in glory
    There remains a land of rest,
There my Saviour's gone before me,
    To fulfil my soul's request.
        There is rest for the weary,
            There is rest for me,
        On the other side of Jordan,
        In the sweet fields of Eden,
        Where the tree of life is blooming
            There is rest for me.

"He is fitting up my mansion,
    Which eternally shall stand ;
For my stay shall not be transient
    In that holy, happy land.

"Pain and sickness ne'er shall enter,
    Grief nor woe my lot shall share,
But in that celestial centre
    I a crown of life shall wear.

"Sing, oh sing, ye heirs of glory ;
    Shout your triumphs as you go ;
Zion's gates shall open for you,
    You shall find an entrance through."

This they sang again and again, Alice asking for it many times, and their dear Saviour, who was manifestly present with that little band, enabled her beloved sisters to sing these touching lines with steady voices, and to join with her in looking forward with longing hope to the time which was soon to take their darling from them.

Thus through the still hours of the night from that chamber of death, instead of the voice of weeping, arose hymns of faith and hope, mingled with songs of praise.

Early in the morning she was removed from the chair to the sofa, which was placed in the centre of the room that she might have air from the open windows. The rosy light crept over that landscape upon which dear Alice's eyes had so often delighted to linger, but for her another and a fairer vision was opening into view.

About half-past five she seemed to be passing away; her breathing grew faint, and her colour faded, and those of the family who were not present were called. Her father held one hand, her pulse each moment becoming more feeble and fluctuating. Her sister bent over her and said, " Weeping may endure for a night, but joy cometh in the morning." " Into Thy hand I commit my spirit; Thou hast redeemed me, O Lord God of truth." Her face lit up at once with a sweet heavenly smile, and she bowed her head in token of assent.

One by one the little group around her bent over her for their last kiss, and to each she gave a sweet, loving look and smile, and then closed her eyes and said, " It is so lovely to be going."

But, although her pulse had nearly ceased, it was
her Heavenly Father's will she should again revive.
Feeling herself getting stronger, she looked around
upon her friends, and said, " Are you sure I am not
reviving?" and in a few minutes, with an appealing
glance to her father, " Father, am I dying?" He
could not bear to tell her—what he knew would be a
disappointment to her—that he thought she might
live many hours—but one of her sisters, who during
the night while praying for her, had been impressed
with the belief that she would soon be released, said,
" Yes, darling, I am sure the Lord will take thee
home this morning." But she still repeated, " Father,
am I dying?" He told her her pulse was getting
stronger. She said, " It is all right; I want the
Lord's will done."

When feeling somewhat better, she asked for the
story of Stephen; and later said, " Read me about
the crucifixion." She seemed much strengthened
and comforted by these Scriptures, and other portions which were read to her, particularly the fifty-
third of Isaiah. She repeated, " He was oppressed."
The hymn

> " I know not the way I am going,
> But well do I know my Guide,"

was repeated to her, and several times, when emotion
caused a short pause, dear Alice went on with the
next line, thinking it was forgotten.

The valley of the shadow of death was so lighted
by the presence of Jesus, that she saw no darkness,
and, in reply to one who said, " The valley is not so
very dark, is it, darling?" she said, " Oh, if I could
only get into the valley!" and afterward, " Come,

Lord Jesus, come quickly;" and again, quite distinctly, "Jesus Christ came into the world to save sinners, of whom I am chief."

But a short time before her spirit took its flight she folded her hands, and with a sweet upward look, as though gazing upon "Him who is invisible," she said, in faintest whispers, "My Beloved is mine, and I am His."

The doctor came, and, after the usual greeting, she asked him how long he thought she would last. Upon his replying, "Not more than a few hours," she raised her eyes to heaven with a smile full of rejoicing. But she did not have even a few hours more of suffering. The doctor administered an opiate, which seemed to relieve her very much, and she said, gratefully, "I feel so much better." He then recommended moving her a little upon one side, to relieve the fatigue of having for many hours reclined in one position. Just before she was moved, her sister leaned over and said, "Jesus is very near thee still, is He not, darling?" She replied, "Yes, He is to be praised." Her position was changed, and almost in a moment, without a groan or struggle, she slept in Jesus. One sister was supporting her, the other knelt beside her holding her hand, and thought, as she nestled her head among the pillows, "how comfortable she is;" but in a moment, perceiving that she was passing away, exclaimed, "Almost home, darling, almost home!" and as she drew her last breath, said, "With the Lord—for ever with the Lord!"

Thus did this young disciple, in the twenty-ninth

year of her age, pass from earth to heaven, with songs of praise upon her lips, and was ushered into the presence of her Beloved, with words of faith and hope from those she loved best on earth. Her sister writes, "Praise was the most fitting language to express the feeling left in that chamber of death. We could but give thanks that our darling was safe at rest in the bosom of Jesus."

"Blessed are the dead which die in the Lord! Yea, saith the Spirit, that they may rest from their labours ; and their works do follow them."

Her "sister-cousin," on hearing of her death, expressed not only her own feelings, but those of most of the family, when she wrote :—

"I have just heard the sad and yet joyful news of our precious Alice's release from this world, and her entrance into everlasting rest. . . . It is almost hard as yet to think of the blank she has left, so vividly do I realise her overwhelming, transcendent joy in at last seeing Jesus face to face, and sitting down in His presence, never more to go out for a second, never more to feel a temptation, never more to lose sight of His loving smile, never to miss for an instant the touch of His hand. Oh, it is perfectly glorious to think of it! Darling, sweet Alice is satisfied at last! *Satisfied!* It fills my whole soul with joy to imagine it, and to try to realise a little of her rapture.

"I know well that for myself there is a very precious thing taken out of life, but it seems to me I could shout a song of thanksgiving as I think of the untold and unspeakable bliss upon which she has entered. Two days already she has been with Jesus! It thrills my soul to think of it, and to realise a little of what it must be!"

Her aunt M. W—— writes :—

" I feel so thankful to have been privileged to be present at her sweet, lovely death-scene. Her beaming countenance at moments when she looked round upon you all, the felt nearness of the dear Saviour, are among our precious memories to be cherished."

One of her cousins writes :—

" How sweet the remembrance of dear Alice is, even to those of us who saw but little of her, as she faded away ; that little revealing, as it did, the perfect support and consolation she found in her Saviour, greatly strengthens our faith in Him.

It seemed strange that she, the youngest of the cousins, should be called first to test the faithfulness of that Saviour whom we all learned to love together. But I don't believe any of the rest of us could have glorified Him so much in the furnace. By the longest and most painful life, she could not have borne a more faithful witness to the power and love of her Lord than she did in her short, happy life, and most triumphant death."

Another one of the five cousins writes :—

" Not only her life, but her death, has been blessed to us all. It seems as if she brought Jesus down to us. I have felt Him so much nearer and more real, since He was so manifestly with Alice. And it is so

strengthening to my faith to realise how He supported
her to the very end.   Sweet Alice !

> ' How many burdened hearts have prayed,
>   Their lives like thine might be,
>   But more shall pray henceforth for aid
>   To lay them down like thee.'

"The priceless memories of her pure and holy
life, and the hallowed recollections of her peaceful
death, are, indeed, a treasury of blessings."

The following extracts are from the letters of two
very dear friends :—

" I do not suppose any one not of your immediate
family could have loved sweet Alice more than I did.
She occupied a very warm corner of my heart, and I
feel as if one of the loveliest flowers of my heart's
garden had fallen—' the wind passeth over it, and it
is gone '—great was ' the grace of the fashion of it.'
Thanks for such a precious gift as that sweet child ! "

" In the midst of all the sorrow of to-day, I felt
how near Jesus was—the same Lord who wept not
for Lazarus, but for the bereaved sisters.   How real
this sorrow makes the sympathy of Christ, and how
the heart can rest upon Him through it all.

" You are rich in the memories of a life so truly
hid with Christ in God,—memories now beyond all
value, and pointing us to the source of all her joy
and hope and victory over the world.   May we
have grace to walk in her footsteps, in living faith,
and practical devotedness of heart to the Lord !

There is the same living fountain for us that so filled her soul, and overflowed to all around."

All through her illness dear Alice had a vivid realisation of the sadness to the surviving relatives, of all connected with the body after the spirit has departed. Once she said to her sister, "I should feel so differently about it if I could only take my body with me, but I cannot bear to leave it to be a care to you." In connection with this her sister writes, "She would not have said so if she could have known how all the distressing sadness was taken away. It was remarkable how sweet and almost beautiful everything connected with her death was. Entering the small hall chamber, where all that was left of our dear one lay, you could scarcely help the unexpressed wish that she could look down, and see how lovely and attractive her resting-place had been made. The soft light fell through the curtained window on the central object, draped, as was the room, in white. The choicest blooming plants from the conservatory had been brought to adorn the chamber, and on a little round table beside our dear one, just as her weary eyes had so often rested upon it, stood a beautiful tea-rose in full bloom, with her Bible beside it, and the easy-chairs drawn up close, as if we could read to her her favourite passages, as we had so lately done. It was a sacred place for reading and prayer, and several times we collected there and read together those words which were so precious to her. Even at the grave the sadness of death seemed swallowed up in resurrection, and almost more real than the lowered casket was the happy anticipation of her glorified body, radiant with life and beauty, rising joyfully to

"Hail Him triumphant descending the skies."

The following extract is from an account of her funeral, written by one of Alice's dear friends, to another at a distance who was unable to attend it :—

. . . "As I sat and gazed upon her sweet pale face, upon which was an expression of settled peace, I could not help saying to myself again and again, 'As a bride adorned for her husband!' And when I remembered her dying words, 'My Beloved is mine, and I am His,' it did really seem as if we had only given her to the arms of Him whom her soul loved. One bright ray of sunshine fell across the darkened room, and rested like a smile upon her lips, as if to lead our thoughts away from our grief to the joys which she had found. Such was the peace pervading the household, that it could not seem like a house of mourning. There we sat around dear Alice, knowing that she was with her Beloved, where she had so often longed to be ; and as the voices of the gospel messengers uttered one after another precious Scripture truths, I could almost hear her earnest voice assenting, and pressing home the subject upon our hearts, and see the still features warm into the old animation as the name of Jesus was exalted.

"I never felt so at a funeral. I have often felt the hush of *peace* at the Christian's burial, but never such a sense of joy. Death was indeed swallowed up! And when we gathered around the grave at Laurel Hill, nothing could exceed the beauty of that lovely spot. Under three beautiful trees it lay, with the hills sloping down to the river in front, and rising picturesquely across the water! As we gathered round, and stood beneath the trees, the birds singing down to us from above, a solemn hush was upon us. . . .

. . . "Presently the silence was broken by her brother-in-law repeating some of those lovely promises of resurrection in 1st Cor. xv. Then he gave Alice's messages. Oh, they were so sweet, so full of the love of Jesus! Tears fell fast, not from grief, but feeling. Then followed a prayer, and as we slowly turned to leave, our hearts were filled with thanksgiving.

"Whom He called, them He also justified; and whom He justified, them He also glorified," " that we might be *to the praise of His glory.*"

THE following hymns were very frequently quoted, and were particularly enjoyed by Alice; and, not being found in ordinary collections, are here inserted in order that her friends may have the satisfaction of referring to them.

HYMNS.

"The Lord will Provide."

THOUGH troubles assail, and dangers affright;
    Though friends should all fail, and foes all unite;
Yet one thing secures us—whatever betide,
The Scripture assures us, the Lord will provide.

The birds without barn or storehouse are fed,
From them let us learn to trust for our bread;
His saints what is fitting shall ne'er be denied,
So long as 'tis written, the Lord will provide.

We may, like the ships, by tempests be tossed
On perilous deeps, but cannot be lost;
Though Satan enrages the wind and the tide,
The promise engages, the Lord will provide.

His call we obey, like Abram of old,
Not knowing our way, but faith makes us bold;
For though we are strangers, we have a true Guide,
And trust, in all dangers, the Lord will provide.

When Satan appears to stop up our path,
And fill us with fears, we triumph by faith ;
He cannot take from us, though oft he has tried,
This heart-cheering promise, the Lord will provide.

He tells us we're weak, our hope is in vain,
The good that we seek we ne'er shall obtain ;
But when such suggestions our spirits have plied,
This answers all questions, the Lord will provide.

No strength of our own, or goodness, we claim ;
Yet, since we have known the Saviour's great name,
In this our strong tower for safety we hide,
The Lord is our power, the Lord will provide.

When life sinks apace, and death is in view,
This word of His grace will carry us through ;
No fearing or doubting with Christ on our side :
We hope to die trusting, the Lord will provide.

JOHN NEWTON.

The Quiet Mind.

I HAVE a treasure which I prize;
  Its like I cannot find,
There 's nothing like it on the earth;
  'Tis this—a quiet mind.

But 'tis not that I 'm stupefied,
  Or senseless, dull, or blind;
'Tis God's own peace within my heart,
  Which forms my quiet mind.

I found this treasure at the cross;
  And there to every kind
Of weary, heavy-laden souls,
  Christ gives a quiet mind.

My Saviour's death and risen life,
  To give it were designed;
His love 's the never-failing spring
  Of this my quiet mind.

The love of God within my breast
  My heart to Him doth bind;
This is the peace of heaven on earth,
  This is my quiet mind.

I 've many a cross to take up now,
  And many left behind;
But present troubles move me not,
  Nor shake my quiet mind.

And what may be to-morrow's cross
   I never seek to find;
My Saviour says, " Leave that to me,
   And keep a quiet mind."

And well I know the Lord hath said,
   To make my heart resigned,
That mercy still shall follow those
   Who have this quiet mind.

I meet with pride of wit and wealth,
   And scorn, and looks unkind;
It matters not—I envy none
   While I've a quiet mind.

I'm waiting now to see my Lord,
   Who's been to me so kind;
I want to thank Him face to face,
   For this my quiet mind.

"My Times are in Thy Hand."

FATHER, I know that all my life
    Is portioned out for me,
And the changes that are sure to come
    I do not fear to see ;
But I ask Thee for a present mind
    Intent on pleasing Thee.

I ask Thee for a thoughtful love,
    Through constant watching wise,
To meet the glad with joyful smiles,
    And to wipe the weeping eyes ;
And a heart at leisure from itself,
    To soothe and sympathise.

I would not have the restless will
    That hurries to and fro,
Seeking for some great thing to do,
    Or secret thing to know ;
I would be treated as a child,
    And guided where I go.

Wherever in the world I am,
    In whatsoe'er estate,
I have a fellowship with hearts
    To keep and cultivate ;
And a work of lowly love to do
    For the Lord on whom I wait.

So I ask Thee for the daily strength,
    To none that ask denied,
And a mind to blend with outward life
    While keeping at Thy side,
Content to fill a little space,
    If Thou be glorified.

And if some things I do not ask
    In my cup of blessing be,
I would have my spirit filled the more
    With grateful love to Thee—
More careful—not to serve Thee much,
    But to please Thee perfectly.

There are briers besetting every path,
    That call for patient care ;
There is a cross in every lot,
    And a need for earnest prayer ;
But a lowly heart that leans on Thee
    Is happy anywhere.

In a service which Thy will appoints,
    There are no bonds for me ;
For my inmost heart is taught " the truth "
    That makes Thy children free ;
And a life of self-renouncing love,
    Is a life of liberty.

A. L. WARING.

"Behold, the Bridegroom Cometh."

BEHOLD, a Royal Bridegroom
　　Hath called me for His bride !
I joyfully make ready
　　And hasten to His side.
He is a Royal Bridegroom,
　　But I am very poor !
Of low estate He chose me,
　　To show His love the more :
For He hath purchased for me
　　Such goodly rich array,
Oh, surely never bridegroom
　　Gave gifts like His away !

When first upon the mountains,
　　I, in the vale below,
Beheld Him waiting for me,
　　Heard His command to go ;
I, poorest in the valley,
　　Oh, how could I prepare
To meet His royal presence ?
　　How could I make me fair ?
Ah ! in His love He sent me
　　A garment clean and white :
And promised broidered raiment
　　All glorious in His sight.

And then He gave me glimpses
    Of the jewels for my hair,
And the ornament most precious
    For His chosen bride to wear.

First in my tears I washed me,
    They could not make me clean :
A fountain then He showed me,
    Strange until then unseen !
So close I 'd lived beside it,
    For many weary years,
Yet passing by the fountain,
    Had bathed me in my tears.
O love, O grace, that showed it !
    Revealed its cleansing power !—
How could I choose but hasten
    To meet Him from that hour ?

I said, I 'll wait no longer !
    He surely will provide
All for the toilsome journey,
    Up the steep mountain side.
He sought me in the valley,
    He knows my utmost need ;
But He 's a Royal Bridegroom,
    I shall be rich indeed.
Rich in His pardoning mercies,
    Bounties that never cease :
Rich in His loving-kindness,
    Rich in His joy and peace.
So then I took the raiment,
    And the jewels that He sent,
And gazing on His beauty,
    Up the hill-side I went.

And still with feeble footsteps,
　And turning oft astray,
I go to meet the Bridegroom,
　Though stumbling by the way.
I soil my royal garments
　With earth where'er I fall,
I break and mar my ornaments,
　But He will know them all.
For it was He who gave them;
　Will He forget His own?
Ah! for the love He bore me,
　He called! will He disown?
He sent His Guide to guide me:
　He knew how blind, how frail,
The children of the valley:
　He knew my love would fail.
He knew the mists above me
　Would hide Him from my sight,
And I in darkness groping,
　Would wander from the right.
I know that I must follow
　Slow when I fain would soar;
That step by step, thus upward,
　My Guide must go before.

Cleave close, dear Guide, and lead me!
　I cannot go aright!
Through all that doth beset me,
　Keep, keep me close in sight!
'Tis but a little longer,
　Methinks the end I see:
Oh! matchless love and mercy,
　The Bridegroom waits for me;

Waits to present me faultless,
　　Before His Father's throne;
His comeliness my beauty,
　　His righteousness my own.

　　　　　　　　　　A. S.

"All, all is Known to Thee."

"When my spirit was overwhelmed within me, then Thou
knewest my path."

MY God, whose gracious pity I may claim,
    Calling Thee Father—sweet, endearing
        name !
The sufferings of this weak and weary frame,
    All, all are known to Thee.

From human eye 'tis better to conceal
Much that I suffer, much I hourly feel ;
But oh ! the thought does tranquillise and heal—
    All, all is known to Thee.

Each secret conflict with indwelling sin,
Each sickening fear I ne'er the prize shall win,
Each pang from irritation, turmoil, din—
    All, all is known to Thee.

When in the morning unrefreshed I wake,
Or in the night but little sleep I take,
This brief appeal submissively I make—
    All, all is known to Thee.

Nay, all by Thee is ordered, chosen, planned—
Each drop that fills my daily cup ; Thy hand
Prescribes, for ills none else can understand ;
    All, all is known to Thee.

The effectual means to cure what I deplore ;
In me Thy longed-for likeness to restore ;
Self to dethrone, never to govern more—
      All, all is known to Thee.

And this continued feebleness, this state
Which seems to unnerve and incapacitate,
Will work the cure my hopes and prayer await—
      That can I leave to Thee.

Nor will the bitter draught distasteful prove,
When I recall the Son of Thy dear love ;
The cup Thou wouldst not for *our* sakes remove—
      That cup He drank for *me.*

He drank it to the dregs—no drop remained
Of wrath, for those whose cup of woe He drained ;
Man ne'er can know what that sad cup contained—
      All, all is known to Thee.

And welcome, *precious*, can His Spirit make,
My little drop of suffering for His sake.
Father, the cup I drink, the path I take,
      All, all is known to Thee.

ADELAIDE L. NEWTON.

Rest in Jesus.

WE rest in Christ, the Son of God,
　　Who took the servant's form ;
His love is our abiding-place,
　　And refuge from the storm.

At peace with God, no ills we dread
　　In Christ is our repose :
Our life is hid with Him in God ;
　　Secure from all our foes.

Not death, nor hell, nor Satan's power,
　　Can touch the life thus given ;
Its source and centre is enthroned
　　At God's right hand in heaven.

He lives in us—in Him we live ;
　　With life eternal blest :
And while by faith and hope we wait,
　　In Christ, *our life*, we rest.

The Will of God.

I WORSHIP thee, sweet Will of God!
  And all thy ways adore,
And every day I live, it seems
  I love thee more and more.

Thou wert the blessed end and rule
  Of Jesus' toils and tears;
Thou wert the passion of His heart
  Those three and thirty years.

And He hath breathed into my heart
  A special love of thee;
A love to lose *my* will in *His*,
  And by that loss be free.

I love to kiss the prints, where thou
  Hast set thine unseen feet,
I cannot fear thee—blessed will,
  Thine empire is *so sweet!*

When obstacles and trials seem
  Like prison walls to be,
I do the little I can do,
  And leave the rest to thee.

I know not what it is to doubt;
  My heart is always gay;
I run no risks, for come what will
  Thou always hast thy way.

I have no cares, O blessed Will !
  For all my cares are thine ;
I live in triumph, Lord, for Thou
  Hast made Thy triumphs mine.

And when it seems nor chance nor change
  From grief can set me free,
Hope finds its strength in helplessness,
  And gaily waits on thee.

Man's weakness waiting upon God
  Its end can never miss,
For man on earth no work can do
  More angel like than this.

Ride on, ride on triumphantly,
  Thou glorious Will, ride on !
Faith's pilgrim sons behind thee, take
  The road that thou hast gone.

He always wins who sides with God ;
  No chance to him is lost ;
God's will is sweetest to him, when
  It triumphs at his cost.

Ill that He blesses is our good,
  And unblest good is ill ;
And all is right that seems most wrong,
  If it be His sweet Will.

FABER.

U

The Border-Lands.

FATHER, into Thy loving hands
    My feeble spirit I commit,
While wandering in these Border-Lands,
    Until Thy voice shall summon it.

Father, I would not dare to choose
    A longer life, an earlier death;
I know not what my soul might lose
    By shortened or protracted breath.

These Border-Lands are calm and still,
    And solemn are their silent shades;
And my heart welcomes them, until
    The light of life's long evening fades.

I heard them spoken of with dread,
    As fearful and unquiet places;
Shades, where the living and the dead
    Look sadly in each other's faces.

But since Thy hand hath led me here,
    And I have seen the Border-Land;
Seen the dark river flowing near,
    Stood on its brink, as now I stand,

There has been nothing to alarm
    My trembling soul; how could I fear
While thus encircled with Thine arm?
    I never felt Thee half so near.

What should appal me in a place
   That brings me hourly nearer Thee?
When I may almost see Thy face—
   Surely 'tis here my soul would be.

They say the waves are dark and deep,
   That faith has perished in the river;
They speak of death with fear, and weep,
   Shall my soul perish? Never! Never!

I know that Thou wilt never leave
   The soul that trembles while it clings
To Thee: I know Thou wilt achieve
   Its passage on Thine outspread wings.

And since I first was brought so near
   The stream that flows to the Dead Sea,
I think that it has grown more clear
   And shallow than it used to be.

I cannot see the golden gate
   Unfolding yet, to welcome me;
I cannot yet anticipate
   The joy of heaven's jubilee;

But I will calmly watch and pray
   Until I hear my Saviour's voice
Calling my happy soul away,
   To see His glory, and rejoice.

Lean Hard.

CHILD of my love, " lean hard,"
      And let me feel the pressure of thy care ;
I know thy burden, child ; I shaped it,
Poised it in Mine own hand, made no proportion
In its weight to thine unaided strength ;
For even, as I laid it on, I said,
" I shall be near, and while she leans on Me,
This burden shall be Mine, not hers.
So shall I keep my child within the circling arms
Of Mine own love."   *Here* lay it down, nor fear
To impose it on a shoulder which upholds
The government of worlds.   Yet closer come—
Thou art not near enough, I would embrace thy
      care,
So I might feel my child reposing on my heart.
Thou lovest me? I know it.   Doubt not, then ;
But, loving me—lean hard.

Anywhere with Jesus.

Matt. viii. 19.

ANYWHERE with Jesus, says the Christian heart;
  Let Him take me where He will, so we do not
    part ;
Always sitting at His feet, there's no cause for fears ;
Anywhere with Jesus in this vale of tears.

Anywhere with Jesus, though He leadeth me
Where the path is rough and long, where the dangers
        be ;
Though He taketh from me all I love below,
Anywhere with Jesus will I gladly go.

Anywhere with Jesus, in the summer heat,
Anywhere with Jesus, through the winter sleet,
Anywhere with Jesus, where the bright sun shines ;
Anywhere with Jesus, when the day declines.

Anywhere with Jesus, though He please to bring
Into fires the fiercest, into suffering ;
Though He bid me work or wait, or only bear for
    Him,
Anywhere with Jesus still shall be my hymn.

Anywhere with Jesus, though it be the tomb,
With its frighting terror, with its dreaded gloom ;
Though it be the weariness of a long-drawn life,
Fainting with the constant toil, drooping in the strife.

Anywhere with Jesus, for it cannot be
Dreary, dark, or desolate, where He is with me ;
He will love me alway, every need supply,
Anywhere with Jesus, should I live or die.

Christ our Guide.

Isaiah xlii. 16.

I KNOW not the way I am going,
  But well do I know my Guide;
With a child-like trust I give my hand
  To the mighty Friend by my side.
The only thing that I say to Him,
  As He takes it, is, " Hold it fast,
Suffer me not to lose my way,
  And bring me home at last."

As when some helpless wanderer,
  Alone in an unknown land,
Tells the guide his destined place of rest,
  And leaves all else in his hand;
'Tis home, 'tis home, that we wish to reach;
  He who guides us may choose the way;
And little we heed what path we take,
  If nearer home each day.

A Little While.

Rev. xxi. 4.

BEYOND the smiling and the weeping,
    I shall be soon ;
Beyond the waking and the sleeping,
Beyond the sowing and the reaping,
    I shall be soon.
      Love, rest, and home !
      Sweet hope !
      Lord, tarry not, but come.

Beyond the parting and the meeting,
    I shall be soon ;
Beyond the farewell and the greeting,
Beyond the pulse's fever-beating,
    I shall be soon.
      Love, rest, and home !
      Sweet hope !
      Lord, tarry not, but come.

BONAR.

www.ingramcontent.com/pod-product-compliance
Lightning Source LLC
Chambersburg PA
CBHW021033030726
47496CB00006B/1515